CW01083481

GREEN INK

For Zephyr

PROLOGUE

The man lies sprawled on his back in the soaked muck of Palmerston Street. He coughs and he chokes. By his side his fingers flex. Curl and uncurl. Grip and release, trying to get some kind of purchase on the putrid city air.

A woman approaches him with a confident long-legged stride, athletic in her army breeches. She looks with fascination at the neat hole in his waistcoat. Her ears are ringing, a sudden and hellish tinnitus, a headful of breaking glass. She unbuttons the man's waistcoat and the shirt beneath it. The man trembles. Shivers... Seems to gather some strength from the bruised and frowning night, to borrow some energy from the density of it. Now he is writhing on the rutted and potholed ground, legs kicking in feeble agitation. He's a desperate beetle on its back. He whispers obscenities, gouges out a sob. She feels an intense relief. He's alive!

The man has been shot in the stomach, but looking at him now, all the woman can see is a prettily pink-frilled contusion on the surface of his belly. It looks almost innocuous. Almost artistic, in fact. Back in the war, an injury like this would have been taped up and he'd have been sent back into the crazed, star-shelled glow of no man's land within half an hour.

What she doesn't yet know is that the bullet has lodged near his spine. And that on the way there, it seared its way through his intestines, his pancreas, his spleen, shredded his diaphragm and drilled through his lungs. Tissue in every one of these organs is exenterated. Diced. The pressure wave caused by a bullet travelling at 850 feet per second has ripped flesh from his ribcage. Tendons have turned to pulp. Treacle-thick, treacle-black arterial blood is seeping into the cavity of his chest.

The woman may not know yet that there can be no good outcome, but the man does. As he lifts his head from amid the filth of Palmerston Street, the horse shit, the spilled vegetables, the slopped remains of hurried dinners, the congealing guck and the slimy rubbish, the man knows that you don't come back from this kind of wound.

No actual pain yet, but this man, this veteran of the Western Front, this former hero, knows that this too is not a good sign. When wounded, what you want is for Pain to arrive quickly, before the nurses, before the doctors, before the fussing with bandages, stretchers and ambulances. Pain first, first aid later, that's the rule of survival. Where Pain takes its time, where it dillies and dallies, it allows nastier things to get in. Shock, sepsis, gangrene and all the other microscopic jackals of fatal debilitation, if they can nip in ahead of Pain to begin their silent work, then you are taking the count. Everyone who has ever been in the forces knows this.

So, this is it, he thinks. This is how it ends. Doesn't seem right. Doesn't seem fair. Just as things were looking up.

He mutters something. The woman moves closer to him, that clanging in her head, it's still making her dizzy, making her slow.

'What?' she says. 'What did you say?'

'Bollocks. I said bollocks. Now just bloody well help me will you? Do summat!'

The flat and bolshy Northern vowels push hard against the folded arms of the London night, but there's no real power there. The man's voice collapses into a damp gurgle. No surprise that in this extremity his roots are showing. This happens to everyone. Like the poet almost says, in the end we show our beginning. Reveal ourselves for what we are, for what we have always been.

GREEN INK

Stephen May

Swift

SWIFT PRESS

First published in Great Britain by Swift, an imprint of Swift Press 2025

1 3 5 7 9 8 6 4 2

Text design and typesetting by Tetragon, London
Printed and bound in Great Britain by CPI Group (UK) Ltd, Croydon CRO 4YY

A CIP catalogue record for this book is available from the British Library

ISBN: 9781800754676
eISBN: 9781800754683

ONE

My Darling Pussy

1

FRANCES Stevenson watches as the prime minister removes his things in a hurry. The sturdy tweed jacket, the good walking trousers, the flannel shirt, the thick woollen socks. His vest. His underpants. A sudden hummock of clothing forming on the grubby carpet of this servant's bedroom. The room is lit by the marmalade glow of a single lamp by the bed, but it's enough for her to make out the curves and angles of his body and she smiles to herself. Skinny legs supporting a tummy as soft and as rounded as a new-risen loaf, long grey hair swept back from his forehead and ragged at the sides. A closely clipped moustache. Bright eyes in a rosy face. He looks, she thinks, like a hedgerow bird. An amorous sparrow. She feels especially fond of him at moments like this, when he shows his fleshy vulnerability. As he crosses the few feet from the door to the narrow bed, as he pulls back the thin blankets and slides in next to her, the fuzz on his legs tickles.

5

She doesn't mind. It's nice. She moves her hands through his sparse chest hair and over the vaguely feminine slopes of his torso, and David Lloyd George whispers in Welsh. Endearments, she supposes. My sweet pet, my thrilling girl, my only one, things like that.

She shivers. It's a draughty room. Chill intimations of autumn. Cold weather comes early for the servant class, she thinks. His own suite will be warm, the blankets soft, thick and plentiful, the remains of a fire in the grate, a cowboy novel on the table by the bed. A glass of whisky. Everything a prime minister could want. She wonders if she'll ever get to see it.

They kiss now and she moves her hand down to the junction of his thighs. Gentle as a nurse, she takes his shy pidyn in her hand. She feels him relax, hears him sigh. Like a man returning home from a long journey.

'My darling Puss,' he whispers, in English.

'My own sweet man,' she replies.

Bolder now, she strokes and squeezes. A few minutes of this and she'll roll on top of him, move up by inches and finally lower herself on his face, arms crossed and resting against the cool wall as she grinds her doodle, her gwain, against her lover's nose and mouth. She loves it when his head is trapped between her strong golfer's thighs. She loves his urgency then, his eagerness to please. Loves the way he works to find the secret places she's shown him over the seven years they've been together. Loves the way his lips and her hips synchronise movements. The way the liquid heat inside her builds.

The power is intoxicating. Here he is, David Lloyd George, triumphant wartime leader, the head of the world's greatest empire, in thrall to her. While David is beneath her he's not a politician planning or scheming, he's not a prime minister, he's just a man. No, not even that – in sex he's a beast, a hand-some animal, her Welsh bull.

She likes to get herself almost there and then climb off his face, to kiss her way back down his body, before rolling him on top of her. Once she's underneath, flattened against the bed by his comforting heft, she'll guide him in, will urge him on. She likes to touch her button while he heaves and pants above her.

The best thing, the very best thing, is to get there just before he does, to grasp him tight around the shoulders, nails digging deep. She loves the way orgasm is pulled from her, the way it makes her gasp against his neck. She loves to feel him twitch in sympathy inside her. That sudden flash of hot fluid, the way he grunts with relief. It's a sweet thing. A joy.

Tonight though, it seems his beloved pidyn is coy, reluc-tant, doesn't respond to her careful tenderness. Retreats from her. Hides.

'Well,' she says at last. 'This is disappointing.'

Her lover sighs. 'I know, cariad, I'm sorry.'

Don't you cariad me, she thinks. She can't help it, she's put out. Cross. They get little enough time for intimacy as it is and it's dispiriting to not be able to make it count. She's been looking forward to him arriving in her bedroom for days now, but he's not been able to get to her flat and now, at Chequers, the staff have insulted her – and, by extension, him – by sticking her in this garret away from the central buzz and bustle of the house, as if she were just another civil servant flunky, just another Liberal Party bag-carrier. She feels a stab of irritation. It's another of those nights when she realises how peripheral she is to his life. She went into this with her eyes wide open but still, it gets to her sometimes.

'Never mind. These things are to be expected at your age.'

This is cruel. David Lloyd George is fifty-seven and paranoid enough about losing his vitality, about his energy declining just as he reaches the pinnacle of his political life. He doesn't need Frances calling attention to it. He sighs again.

'It's not that, Puss.'

'What is it then?'

She waits, her head on his chest listening to the percussion of his heart. It seems unsteady to her, arrhythmic somehow. Dangerously agitated. She inhales the warm, biscuity smell of him. She feels mean now and she wants to make amends. She kisses a nipple, tries to reassure him that she's not really annoyed.

'Just politics,' he says. 'Just matters of state. The usual sewage. I don't feel like getting into it to be honest.'

Another sigh. A long exhalation, a kind of prayer. Now he's not a man coming home with relief in his heart. Now he is a man worn out, a man at the end of his rope.

2

Just politics. She's relieved. It could have been worse. So much worse. Could have been another woman. She knows he struggles to behave. Worse than that even would have been the news that he was unmanned by worries about his children or his wife. Things have been difficult since the summer, since his daughter discovered that Frances, her former tutor, the one-time schoolfriend of her sister, was rather more than simply her father's employee. The way she found out was unfortunate too. It makes her blush to recall it, and David must shudder to think of it too, although he is not the kind of man to dwell on past embarrassments.

'I wish you'd let me help,' she says. 'Things go better when I do. You know it.'

He does know it. This is why he took her with him to the peace conferences after the war. Her official role as private secretary isn't simply cover for a love affair. She takes it seriously and she's pretty good at it. Talking through the events of those tough first conferences with her had helped David clarify his thoughts. She likes to think that if it wasn't for her, Germany might have managed to wriggle out of some of its responsibilities, might have got too easy a ride. She takes some modest credit for helping to midwife the Versailles treaty.

She remembers the last French premier, Clemenceau, in Paris.

'I can see what David likes about you,' he had said, fierce eyes glowing, luxuriant eyebrows waggling. 'You are beautiful, yes, but you also have a fine mind. Very fine.'

Which was sweet of him, if not quite right.

She knows exactly what David Lloyd George finds appealing about her mind. He appreciates that she's bright and she's clear-thinking, but more than that he likes that she's not intimidatingly smart. For David, Frances's brain is like her body: nimble, athletic, flexible without being freakish. She won't disillusion him, so she keeps her intelligence artfully clothed, just as she keeps her wit innocently flirtatious.

Frances knows when to merge into the background. Yes, she'd like to be the next Mrs Lloyd George, yes, she'd like a child with him. She's always been explicit about that. She loves him and women in love want to be married, don't they? They want to have children with their lovers. That's normal. But for now, Frances accepts that a public life together is just not possible, and she'd never embarrass him by being too visible. She keeps herself a beautiful secret, her role in his life known by only the right kind of people in the right kind of places.

She has worked hard at becoming a perfect mistress and in return has a life she could never have dreamed of when she was a teacher. Good teachers are important, she knows that, but what she has now even the best teachers never have. Impact, influence, not just on a few bored children, but on millions of people. She helps shape the whole damn world. She has clout. How many women can say that?

Anyway, she's only thirty-one. She's got time.

'It's this political fund debacle,' he says now.

'Oh, that,' she says.

'Yes, that.'

'Have there been developments?'

'Maybe.'

She waits. She'll let him gather his thoughts. He hates being disrupted mid-contemplation, it can make him irritable, can even destroy his mood entirely. Thing with David is that a mistimed interruption can lead to him flouncing off back to his own room. David Lloyd George likes to express himself fully, likes to speak in proper paragraphs, ones with complete sentences that themselves contain multiple subordinate clauses. David Lloyd George is not a man to ration his words.

His talk now is a river, a subdued but steady flow. A plangent retelling of the incompetence of his friends and the skulduggery of his enemies. The bald fact is that They plan to ruin him. They plan to give details of exactly how much an honour costs. The precise amount you'll need to pay Lloyd George in order to gain an OBE or an MBE. How much it will set you back to become a lord and where the money goes and how it is spent. Which is embarrassing, as right now it mostly goes to Lloyd George directly and quite a lot of it has been spent on new houses, including one for Frances.

It's an outrage. So unfair. Everyone sensible knows that the sale of honours is one of the principal ways the whole party system is sustained. Done informally – a favour provided, followed by an apparently unprompted honour some time later – well, this is all right. More than all right. Expected. Done explicitly with price lists and negotiations over what is included in the sale, then it's scandalous, apparently.

People are bleating that this kind of trade should be criminalised, and those who participate in it disgraced, pilloried, obliterated. Especially those, like David, who have been honest and open – more or less – about how the system works.

When he finally comes to a halt, when that river has run its course, they lie wrapped around each other in the dark. She listens to the drumming of his heart again, and to other noises too. A house like this is never entirely quiet. Never dead silence even in the early hours. Always rustlings and creaks, always something moving. The purr of the wind finding gaps in old walls. Mysterious dripping sounds. Mice. Ghosts.

Time passes and the agitation of his breathing subsides, his pulse steadies. She feels safe enough to speak.

'Who are They?'

'Former friends, so-called allies, those who hate progress. The usual crew.'

'Yes, but who specifically?'

'I'm not sure. I think the plan is for the chief bastards to give the material to some plausible dupe who will write it all up for the papers, someone who will make a crusade out of it, someone who won't be bought off.'

'Surely everyone can be bought off for the right price?'

'Apparently not.'

'It's serious then.'

'It's serious.' Which is when he mumbles a name. She doesn't catch it at first.

'Who?'

'Victor Grayson. He's the dupe. You're too young to remember him, but he's always been a pain in the arse. A socialist. An infantile rabble-rouser. A discredited drunk.'

She does remember the name. He was in all the papers, all the time, for a while.

David Lloyd George's river of talk begins to flow again, this time rolling through the messy scrublands of Victor Grayson's sad history.

'Well, what's the problem?' she says, trying to keep impatience from her voice. 'Yesterday's man. Yesterday's *alcoholic* man. What damage can he do? Who will believe him?'

'People believe what they want to believe. And They – the bastards – are planning to give him receipts, letters, contracts. Everything he'll need to do maximum damage. And you don't know this man, he's not without charisma, he can make an impression when he wants to. And he's reckless. When he's desperate enough he'll do anything.' He sits up, seems full of energy suddenly.

Frances smooths the silvery squall of her lover's hair, murmurs to him as if he were a restless pony. Horses, men and dogs, they're not so different from each other.

How does he know all this, she asks. He is vague. 'Something someone said to me.'

'Who?'

'Just someone.'

She is instantly alert, on her guard. Vagueness like this means it was a female someone. Someone with designs.

'Come on, David.'

'Roberta.'

Oh, Roberta. David's daughter-in-law, the wife of his son, Dick.

'How would she know?'

'She's surprisingly well informed about things. More so than Dick, usually.'

This is true. Dick Lloyd George is an amiable lush, everyone likes him, no one is impressed by him. Roberta on the other hand, named after her father, the pugnacious self-made construction millionaire Robert McAlpine, is the opposite. Just twenty-one years old, she is nervily acerbic, energetically astringent. She is also someone who, in Frances's opinion, chooses her associates unwisely. Actors, musicians, headshrinkers. She is a proponent of faddy diets and quack health remedies. Always trying to get Dick and his father to try vegetarianism or some new juice. She needs keeping an eye on.

'He'll see a chance to get back in with his old comrades,' David continues. 'They despise him now, so he'll need something big to get back to where he was. Bringing down a government might do it.'

He lies back down, seems calm again.

It's amazing how he can do this, how he can put difficult things from his mind seemingly by an act of will. A real talent and a handy one for a man in his position.

'Maybe it'll all come to nothing. There have been plots against me before, plenty of them, and they've all failed. Your old man is tougher than anyone thinks.'

More relaxed now, David tells her that he's arranged a meeting tomorrow – well, today actually, he supposes – to discuss the problem. He's framed it as not really being about him personally, but about this fuss being a security risk to the whole system. Edward will be there, he says, and the police chap, Basil Thomson, and J.T. Davies of course.

'Of course.'

She feels his body ripple and shift and knows he's smiling at her dismissive tone. He knows better than anyone what she thinks of J.T. Davies.

'I'm not sure it'll do any good,' he says. 'I'm not sure the security people are ever entirely on our side, my love. It's frustrating because there's so much else I could be doing, so many more important things to deal with.'

This is true, she knows. There's Ireland for a start, people dying daily in street battles. There's the trouble with the trade unions, the threats of strikes at the docks, in the mines and on the railways, not to mention Europe and the ongoing tensions over the post-war settlement. There's Russia and there's Poland. There's the French delegation here at Chequers this weekend to discuss Mesopotamia. She's been worrying about that herself.

It's also true that this meeting to resolve David's own political problems might not go so well. He can be high-handed when dealing with civil servants, with his fellow cabinet ministers too, if truth be told. He is bored by them, looks past them, daydreams in their company, makes jokes at their expense, belittles them with his inattention, even when he's not belittling them with his actual words. She's better with officialdom than he is, she knows how to get the disappointed men in cheap suits to fall in line.

'I could chair the meeting,' she says. 'I should be there if J.T. is there. You should have invited me anyway. I could go in your place; let you get on with properly important work. It's not like I haven't chaired meetings before.'

There's a pause.

'I didn't like to ask you.'

She knows why not. This whole money-for-honours saga is an embarrassment to him, reflects badly on him, and he doesn't want his lover to see him in a negative light. Foolish man. She loves him because of his flaws not despite them. And as a beneficiary of the system she should be prepared to defend it. Anyway, she'll always take any chance to make herself useful to him, to resolve problems for him, and her record on getting her way – their way – at meetings is pretty good.

He sighs.

'Thank you, cariad.'

She smiles, kisses him.

'I haven't done anything yet.'

'But you will. If anyone can sort this out it's my own sweet girl.'

He turns towards her. They kiss.

'Cariad bach.'

'My own sweet man.'

'My darling Pussy, my thrilling girl.'

'My love.'

They kiss again. She moves her hand towards the centre of him, feels for his pidyn and yes, it's as she suspected, things are in progress there. He's back. Fifty-seven is nothing. David Lloyd George is a man in his prime.

'Hello,' she says.

'Hello,' he says.

Things are as they should be now. Not an old politician and his young mistress. Not that tired and tawdry story.

Instead, it's just two lovers alone in the dark. Two free people. A man and a woman without burdens, without worries. No children, no wife, no Europe, no Ireland, no trade unions, no French delegation. Just this. Just limbs touching in a narrow servant's bed in the velvet time before dawn.

Something occurs to her.

'Hey, dearest, what were you saying when you first came to my bed tonight, when you opened my door?'

'Did I say anything?'

'Yes, when you first arrived here – late – you spoke Welsh to me. I was wondering what you said.'

He chuckles, his moustache scratches her ear as he nibbles at the lobe. He puts a hand on her breast. How ridiculous this all is, she thinks. How daft, how lovely.

'Ah, I wasn't really talking to you, cariad. I was muttering threats to my Honourable Member. I was cajoling Mr Pidyn, the MP for my own girl. I was telling him to behave, to rise, to do the right thing.'

She laughs. 'He seems better disposed now.'

'Yes, yes, my darling. Mr Pidyn, MP, Minister of Love, he sulks sometimes but he can't ever resist my pet for long.'

3

Pity the poor secret serviceman placed in the hidden alcove behind the stud wall of this room. The man from C Division who has to use legible shorthand to record anything said or done, who has to type it all up using the approved departmental green ink. Who has to report the precise details back to his superiors. Who must leave nothing out. Every coo, every gasp, every half-formed whisper, they must all be pinned, fixed and interrogated for any meaning they might have beyond the obvious. You never know what might be part of a code. The sooner they get a machine for this work the better.

TWO

Kindness, Time and Money

1

THE wet dawn smears itself over the windows of the apartments and the shops, and Victor Grayson, self-proclaimed agitator, freelance scribbler, speechifier for hire and one-time firebrand MP, wakes up crying. This is happening more and more, nearly a daily occurrence now. As much part of his morning as the parched throat, the headache and the sense of generalised anxiety. It's the grog of course, he knows that. Just booze and going to bed too late and, perhaps, just possibly, the caravan of nameless – more or less faceless – lovers that pass through these borrowed rooms. And money of course. The lack of it. No one without money is ever free of night-time terror.

He notes in a foggy kind of way that he isn't in his bed but instead rising from under a pile of old coats on the couch in the sitting room. He moves naked through a chill grey light to the dirty sink. He stands on tiptoes and pisses in it. The urine is dark, toffee-coloured, and the smell that rises is sugary, like fermenting fruit.

Now he gets himself a glass of tepid, brownish London water. He rinses out his mouth and spits, once, twice, three times. No matter how dry and seedy he feels, he tries to avoid swallowing this stuff. London water is not like the clean Northern variety, it's acky, full of filth. Get a taste for it and it'll kill you faster than alcohol.

He moves away from the sink and heads to the broad window that overlooks the street. He goes slowly, carefully. His ribs are still sore from last week's kicking and there's rumours of cramp in his toes.

There's life outside in the murk. Already there is the beginning of the city's weekend clamour, the gossip and grumble of traffic, the trolleybuses nagging and whining, the market porters catcalling at the shop girls, those girls shouting back, police whistles. Dogs barking at nothing, the way that they do. Somewhere not too far off an outraged donkey makes its feelings known. The insistent rattle of the tube, like a beggar with a tin can wanting farthings and ha'pennies. London yawning, farting, getting itself going. All this activity muted by fog. It's like overhearing the distant rehearsal of some modernist orchestra, he thinks. Noises that were outlandish once but are increasingly accepted, welcome signs of progress. Reassuring even. All's well with the world because London is tuning up. If things aren't exactly shipshape now, these everyday stirrings suggest they might yet come right. London, like Victor himself, always has a hangover. Like him, the city wakes every day feeling as rough as a badger's arse, but, like him, just gets on with things anyway. Yes, there's life, so there must be hope. And this city, the place that can generate the most life, must also provide the most hope. There's logic for you.

Victor Grayson rubs his eyes, returns to the sink, splashes more water onto his face. He feels stronger now. Worries evaporating or, if not quite that, then retreating, definitely. Moving to the corners of the room, hiding under the furniture. It's daft to be weeping in his dreams, especially when he can never remember what they are. Except for these embarrassing tears, his dreams leave no traces.

He looks again at the restless street below. London. More precisely, St James's. More precisely still, Georgian House. *The epitome of modern metropolitan living in the very epicentre of the empire*, that's what it says in the agent's brochure. The truth is that the empire's capital, however squalid, however treacherous, however tainted the water, means more to him now than Liverpool, more to him than Manchester, more even than the mill towns of West Yorkshire, though these are places that have loved him fully in ways that London never has.

He looks again, peering hard. The threadbare plane trees choked by petrol fumes, the passageways between apartment buildings, the places where vans and carts unload. Nothing sinister there and he feels relief that the salaried yobs, the state-sponsored watchers, the publicly funded head-breakers, don't seem to be in position this morning. Maybe it's like his friend Hilda tells him, he's just paranoid and wouldn't be so melodramatic if he drank a little less and ate a little more. But last week's beating, that was real, and it had felt methodical, felt like the result of some kind of training, like the men dishing it out were recent graduates of a course. How to Hurt Without Inflicting Lasting Injury. Didn't feel random.

The room is cluttered. This flat is furnished with heavy, old-fashioned and mismatched objects. It is Victor's experience that landlords as a class lack taste as well as compassion. It's like an antique shop in here, one run by someone with no eye for value and no talent for presentation. As well as the fusty settee, there's a battered leather armchair, a sideboard, a variety of lamps that he resists lighting because when lit they seem to make the space more gloomy rather than less.

The epitome of modern metropolitan living? Balls.

There's a dining table which is too big for the room, and on which is piled a selection of yesterday's newspapers, half of them still unopened. Victor Grayson picks up *The Times* and squints at it. Just enough grimy light to read by. He begins, as ever, with the 'In Memoriam' columns. The war has been over nearly two years and yet these grim lists of dead boys still fill the front page. All of them seem to have lived nobly and died bravely and done it so others might live. Or they died for God. Or for England. Or for Peace. All claptrap. The truth is they died for sweet Fanny Adams. These children who would just be coming into their majority now, given a line or two of bad poetry to immortalise them. Lines paid for by mothers or sweethearts, lies commissioned to try and alleviate an ache that will never go away. It sickens him daily, the more so because he was once part of the industry that sent these children into the meat mincers of Flanders.

The thundering line of battle stands,
And in the air death moans and sings;
But Day shall clasp him with strong hands,
And Night shall fold him in soft wings.

This doggerel is dedicated to a Lieutenant Bruce Freeman, signed *Mother*, and what absolute, desperate, disgraceful blether it is. Victor was there. Victor knows that the only true line is the first one. As for the rest, Death never sang – it was silent or else it spat in your face before it ripped out your entrails. Whoever Lieutenant Freeman was, Day never clasped him in strong hands and Night didn't fold this child in soft wings. Instead it left him to rot in French mud, dumped him in the soil at Cambrai as so much manure for the growing of the wheat that England imports now.

He notes too that Lieutenant Freeman was folded into the mud just six weeks before the end of the slaughter.

Stupid sod. A typical Rupert. Six weeks of taking some basic care, of not leading patrols, of hanging back, of keeping his head down, and he might have returned from those pitiless foreign fields. Some judicious skiving through the final skirmishes of history's most pointless war and he might have had a life. Had children of his own. Might have saved his mother from despair.

It still makes Victor's blood boil, the memory of that officer class who fused incompetence with audacity. Public schoolboys who didn't yet shave, who could barely tie their own shoelaces, but who still felt they had to make a point of performing courage, of showing conspicuous leadership for the edification of the peasantry who made up the poor bloody infantry. The PBI, meanwhile, certainly despised cowardice but feared inexperience more, and, most of all, hated the rugger-field bravado of their supposed betters.

He needs a brightener now, but there is no whisky in the house. Why did he bring it out last night? Should have told his visitors that he had nothing in, but instead he'd acted like a big shot. Used up his emergency rations. Trying to impress is never worth it, it always costs you in the end. Then again, his guests should have brought more than bottled beer from the pub. What kind of chuff is it who, when invited round a new friend's place, only brings a couple of pints?

He moves on to the columns of personals. He much prefers the stories glimpsed in these short paragraphs. No one dying nobly here, instead you have Mrs Edith Hope possibly hearing something to her advantage if she contacts Messrs Andrew, Wood, Purves and Sutton, solicitors, in Bedford Row.

The men fallen on hard times wanting donated suits so they can begin new business lives. The once-in-a-lifetime chance to invest in the import and distribution of Egyptian cigarettes.

Or the more mysterious ads: *Pater, I feel my ignominious position acutely, will you not be generous and attribute it to a lack of years rather than wilful folly?* This is simply signed *N.T.* Or what about the message from a Fred to a Tootsie imploring her to wipe the old scores off the slate and let bygones be bygones. Why can't people communicate straightforwardly, rather than in code through the newspapers? Tootsie should tell Fred to stick it. He hopes she does.

But this won't do, he needs to find some real news. A story that will give him something to opine about in those periodicals still willing to give him a platform.

There's more in the *Daily Herald*. Plenty of raw material here. A paper you can rely on. Another night of reprisals by the Royal Irish Constabulary in Belfast, avenging the attacks on their officers by killing civilians. He reads the response from Sir Nevil Macready, the forces' commander-in-chief, saying that his men are only human. Three murders of civilians after the shooting of a policeman and the senior British officer is shrugging and saying, in effect, 'Oh well, what can you do? Boys will be boys. Police will be police. You can hardly expect them to simply turn the other cheek now, can you?'

There must be an article in that.

Or what about the prospect of peace between Soviet Russia and Poland? The Russians have made a lavish offer, the dropping of all territorial demands on Polish land. Well played, Comrade Lenin, well played, you really pulled the rug out from under the feet of the imperialists there. How can the warmongers of France and Britain claim they are defending Poland now? The military presence in Russia is revealed as what it is, an attempt to crush the revolution by force. Yes, definitely an opinion piece there, practically writes itself. The contrasting of the reasoned attitude of the new powers with the stubborn geriatric dogmatism of the old order.

He sighs. Runs his hand through his fine, dry hair. He needs to find something. He needs to start earning a proper living again.

'Anything in the fish-wrappers then, or is it just the usual garbage?'

He turns, startled. One of last night's guests – Hardit something? – is poised in his underwear in the doorway between sitting room and bedroom. In this melancholy light he is nowhere near as vivid as he had seemed in the Queen's Head and certainly not the giddy and muscular presence he had been in bed. His skin is a greyish bronze and he's thin, lilac rings beneath sardonic eyes, handsome in a smudged kind of way. A year or two ago he would have been beautiful, but now he's undefined somehow, a bit squishy around the edges. How old is he? Twenty-eight maybe? Certainly he's no older than thirty, but the longish hair is greasy and thinning at the temples. His short-legged union suit looks like it has seen better days too, but his smile is genuine and warm. It's also knowing. His strong-toothed grin is that of someone who has been in this situation many times and has decided shame, embarrassment even, are fripperies he can live without.

He comes closer, looks Victor straight in the eyes. 'Bit shickery are we mate?' Says it softly, kindly, but urgently too. His voice is deep, musical, the accent appealing in the way it blends with the English idiom. There's something he wants. The usual thing.

'You got out of bed,' the man says now.

'Yes,' says Victor. 'I was restless. Didn't want to disturb you.'

'It's all right, mate. We're pretty hard to offend. And it's a small bed for three.'

He puts his arms around Victor, pulls him into an embrace. Victor closes his eyes, feels his blood kindling. Victor rests his head on the man's shoulder and is humiliated to find his eyes are filling up again. His throat is constricted, it is suddenly hard to get a breath. The man strokes Victor's hair, murmurs wordlessly, soothingly. Victor relaxes, finds he can breathe again. He allows himself to exhale deeply, to ease into the hug. The man smells of sweat and tobacco. There's always this, Victor thinks: when nothing else is left, there is always this.

'Hey, steady on there.'

The men turn and face the new voice in the room. A bright, cheerful, female voice. Bubbles of laughter in it. Upper-class too. Upper-middle-class anyway. A voice trained to be charming, while giving orders that it expects to be obeyed. The woman with the voice is wrapped in a sheet, and she is skinny in the modern way. She is young, in her early twenties perhaps. Boyish face, but beautiful. Cheekbones you could ski down. Hair fashionably short. Mouth fashionably voracious. Long-fingered hands. She looks, it has to be said, like his wife. His dead wife. The fact that she's wearing a bedsheet as a robe just adds to the similarity with Ruth. She's fashioned it into a kind of toga, and he remembers his wife wearing something similar as Titania, as Viola, as Calpurnia, as Lady Macbeth. In her time on the stage Ruth Grayson played all the fiery temptresses, all the women with the quick wits. He should never have married her, but bloody hell, how he misses her.

The men move apart. Victor is conscious of his nakedness. How ridiculous is that? To be shy now? He drops a hand to hide himself from the woman's steady regard.

'Good morning, Babs,' says Hardit. 'Beautiful timing as usual.'

'Morning, H. Feeling OK?'

'Hip playing up a bit, but not too bad.'

Ordinary chit-chat, like neighbours meeting on the doorstep. He remembers that this Hardit Joshi was, like Victor himself, wounded at Passchendaele. It's coming back to him now, the conversation in the pub, the one about how they'd both been lucky, wounds bad enough to get them removed from the front and sent back to England for rehabilitation, but not bad enough to permanently maim or disfigure. Blighty wounds. The best kind. He remembers mentioning that Blighty was a corruption of the Urdu word *bilāyatī* and in return getting a spirited speech about how *all* the good words from the war were really Indian words. Cushy, pukka, dekko, chat – all of them from India. The fellow had begun to give painstaking proof of their deri-vation. In the end this girl here had given him money to shut up and get to the bar.

She breaks in again, that cool voice as sharp and as clean as a ceremonial bayonet.

'I have to say, boys, that was one of my more memorable Friday nights. Splendidly unexpected.' A twinkly pause. 'Give me a chance to have a piss, wash my bits, and we could try another go-round if you like.'

Hardit releases Victor.

'You sure you've got the time and the energy?' The tone is easy, light, teasing. It tells Victor that Hardit and this Babs are old friends, brave adventurers who trust each other implicitly. Pioneers of the great change in the ways of being that has happened since the war. Has happened for some people anyway. People with money. Or those without money but with things the monied want to possess. Like looks, like youth, like life.

It seems to Victor that every time there is a convulsion in society the rich find a way not just of keeping their old privileges, but of adding new ones. It is the leisured class, or their children, that get to dance in the fashionable nightclubs, who buy gramophone players, who listen to ragtime and jazz. Who get to take sexual pleasure whenever they like, with whoever catches their eye.

'It is disgustingly early, H. We have all the time in the world. As for energy, if it's anything like last night then I expect I'll be watching more than I'll be playing.'

How open these post-war women are. How bold. He licks cracked lips. Does he really not have any liquor in? How has that been allowed to happen? It must never happen again.

Hardit laughs, squeezes Victor's arm. 'I expect you might at that. It's fair enough, our friend here is pretty battered, you can't blame him for going a bit easy.'

'You noticed that,' Victor says.

'The bruising? Hard not to, my friend. Some truly startling colours there. Your chest is like a Turner sunset.'

'Didn't put you off though.'

'Quite the opposite, if I know Hardit,' says Babs, from across the room. 'He loves a contusion. The more vivid the better.'

Hardit smiles. A flash of those bright, strong teeth. 'Guilty as charged. And it's not like I don't have damage of my own.'

And this is true. Hardit Joshi has an impressive scar, a long, thick ridge curving under his ribs down towards his ball sack. At the top of this ridge is an indentation, a halfpenny-sized hollow in the skin, presumably where a drain had been put. Victor has a flash of memory from last night, his lips kissing that sweet depression. He catches Hardit's eye, who smiles again. Seems to know exactly what picture is in his mind.

'Anyhoo,' says Hardit now. 'Let's maybe have a cup of char first. Warm up a bit.'

Char. Another of those words the Indians have gifted to Cockney English.

There's something Victor needs to say. Something he needs to clarify.

'I can't pay for it. For the sex, I mean.'

Hardit and Babs exchange a look. Hardit says, 'We know that, matey. We've been through your cupboards. You never know, give it your all and we might leave *you* a few quid.'

Babs tells him that even if she was a professional, she wouldn't charge him.

'I was at some of those women's suffrage speeches you gave back in the days when we were smashing windows. Inspiring stuff, won a lot of people over I think. I was actually quite an ardent devotee of yours.'

'You're a socialist?'

'I'm a suffragist first, but yes, I suppose I am. Sort of. Somewhere between a socialist and an anarchist anyway.'

'I never know the difference,' says Hardit. 'Anyway, I thought we only believed in pleasure. We're radical hedonists, remember? Bohemians. Practitioners of ancient magic. Real magic. Magick with a K.'

His voice is offhand. Politics plainly bores him. He yawns. Babs ignores him. 'I also remember when you got chucked out of the House of Commons. Made you a hero in our house.'

Victor is embarrassed now. Those days are so long ago. Feels like they happened to another person.

'You must have been a child,' he says.

'I was ten, but always a lot of political talk at home.' She pauses, looks at him hard. Seems to Victor like she's looking at him seriously for the first time. 'I was militant for a while, you know, back then. I mean, I didn't just carry banners, I was a proper soldier for the cause. I threw stones at policemen's helmets, I pushed lighted rags into postboxes, rolled ball bearings under the hooves of police horses, all sorts. All great fun. Especially as I did it all with my mama. It was something we shared. Even my brother got involved. Revolution was a family hobby. We were champagne revolutionists. And when I'm thirty I'll finally be able to vote. Which is something.'

There's a silence, before Hardit says, 'But before that happens, before we all die of old age, maybe you can make two thirsty men some mugs of strong tea.'

'Chauvinist swine,' she says, but she's smiling.

31

So they have companionable tea without milk – Victor really needs to do some proper shopping – then they have companionable sex without real desire. It's only Hardit that puts any serious effort in. Sex plainly does not bore him. Victor lies back, eyes closed, trying not to think, to simply concentrate on the sensations, which is always harder to do sober, he finds. Babs meanwhile urges Hardit on with murmured encouragement. She also makes some telling interventions with those hands and that mouth. Brief, well-timed kisses and licks, the occasional smack on an arse –sometimes Victor's, sometimes Hardit's – but mostly she just sorts herself out. Deft hands as she does it too. Reminds him of the women and girls in the mills, the way their fingers flickered and danced, the blur of slender flesh amid the needles, the vicious whisper and clack of the looms.

Then it's cigarettes and small talk – the weather, the cost of living, shows they want to see, prospects of another war – cheeks are kissed, hands are shaken, oddly formal goodbyes considering what they've been up to this morning. They don't make plans to meet later.

4

The world turns. Tram and bus prices in London increase by a halfpenny today while in Pontypridd a twenty-year-old electrician called Joseph Ball shoots himself by the back door of his sweetheart's house. In Ashford, Kent, a monster cabbage twelve feet in circumference and weighing over half a hundredweight appears as part of the Harvest Festival celebrations.

And in Bury Place, Hardit Joshi sets about causing a small piece of mischief.

'Imagine you and your folks being Victor Grayson fanatics,' he says.

'My parents always felt guilty about what they had, were always fretting about not suffering enough,' she says.

This was true. This was why, despite their socialist politics, the war had suited them fine at first. Rationing! Knitting Socks! Generally Doing Your Bit! Her father joined up as soon as war was declared despite being too old. He lied about his age, taking ten years off, while her brother lied about his height, adding three inches on. No one was too fussy about details back then. Now her father's dead, her brother is damaged beyond repair, the family fortune is gone and her mother is a nervous wreck. She doesn't go to socialist meetings any more, she goes to seances instead. Doesn't even care about voting.

'Did they carry on supporting him when he got behind the war?'

Hardit tosses this little Mills bomb casually. It's his way. He likes to experiment with peoples' emotions. To cause a bit of trouble. Very much likes to pull pins, light fuses, then stand back and admire any fireworks. It's a thing he does.

He strongly suspects Babs has no idea that Victor became a major cheerleader for the war effort. After all, the man disappeared from the frontline of revolutionary politics for a while there after he lost his seat, and it was easy to imagine Babs developing other interests between Grayson leaving Parliament and the start of the war.

She laughs, 'Don't you try and bait me, H.'

'It's true. No bigger jingoist in 1914 than our Victor. Phrases like "sacred duty" came very easily to him. I heard him a few times. Very persuasive.'

This is not good news. Not what she wants to hear.

'Bloody hell, and I let that man… I…' She runs out of words, and it's Hardit's turn to laugh.

'Four hundred and ninety-six,' he says. It's a startling non sequitur.

'What?'

'The price of Mr Grayson's soul. Four hundred and ninety-six pounds. It's what he owed when he was declared bankrupt in August 1914. Now, can you think of anything else that happened in that month? Anything that might have provided a business opportunity to an unemployed and impecunious orator?'

There is a long pause while London's life leaps and flaps around them. Skinny, needy dogs, fat, lazy pigeons.

Another one for the list. The one she keeps in her head and constantly updates. The register of pernicious supporters of the war that is headed by the king. Lord Haig is on the list, the newspaper proprietors Lord Northcliffe and Lord Beaverbrook, the whole noble parade of lords in fact, including most bishops. Grayson is probably the first person on the list she's actually met, actually got close enough to give a piece of her mind to, and instead she gave him her—

Hardit derails her thoughts. 'It probably wasn't just for the money, of course. No one does anything just for the money, there'll have been a psychological impulse too. There always is. Anyway, think of it this way, chick: you didn't *let* him do anything. Everything was mutual. We had a good time, that's the main thing, always the main thing.' He pauses for a thoughtful beat. 'You know, I think the twenties are going to be terrific, don't you?'

Babs is frowning.

'"Chick", Hardit, "chick"? Did you just "chick" me?'

Hardit laughs, 'I fear I may have done, yes.'

Never any excuse for that.

5

From his living room window, Victor watches Hardit and Babs cross Bury Place arm in arm. They walk lightly, talking animatedly. They look happy, full of beans.

Modern love, Victor thinks. So casual. So easily given.

He has to acknowledge that he feels better now himself; calmer, the craving for a drink less intense. Some equilibrium established. No tristesse here, instead he feels the need to crack on. He needs to finish reading the paper, maybe begin an article, but if he can't find a subject he could simply carry on with his memoir. Tedious work, but it could be lucrative. Anyway, point is he has options, he feels optimistic about things. And maybe later the first post will bring a decent speaking opportunity.

Yes, there is a big day coming, he can feel it.

6

Once Victor is washed and dressed, he feels more alive than he has in weeks. He sits at the table and begins to rough out a new piece. In this story, written like something by Thomas Hardy perhaps, the ghost of young Lieutenant Freeman seeks out his mother and demands she stop moping and do something useful instead. Still dressed in the bloody rags of his uniform, the dead son urges the mother to go out and get redress for the wasted lives of a whole generation. Freeman's ghost will eloquently lambast a nation's parents for betraying their children, the bairns who fought in hope of progress but found they had been fooled into resisting it. No more bloody poetry, he will tell her. And if there must be verse then let it not be such utter shite.

No, wait, Victor has a better idea. Maybe it could be the story of an uprising of ghosts. The million dead on the march against the living mass murderers of the boss class. That really would be a war to end all wars. Yes, yes, that's it. That's the piece. He even has a title: 'The Army of Ghosts'.

Inspired, he works on it for an hour or two, so good to feel the words come alive under his pen. On a platform, extemporising at a rally, this often happens, words appearing just when he needs them. Making a speech, he can reach out and grab them, and then hurl them back into the air charged and resonant. All as easy as skimming stones. There's nothing more exhilarating than that.

It happens far less often when he's writing. Ideas still come easy but getting the words down, that's hard. As soon as he has a pen in his hand words become shy, evasive, well-camouflaged creatures, giving just a tantalising glimpse of themselves, before slipping back into his mind's tangled undergrowth. He has to search for them, plod after them, has to coax and entice them back out before he can pin them to the page.

Not today though, today the words are docile, they come easily and without him calling. There they are, corralled neatly into sentences, sweetly lining themselves up into metaphors. Today, now, he is a shepherd, and the words are his sheep. It is a precious time.

He works on until he's startled by a distinctive series of thwacks on his door. One. One-two. One. One-two. It's like a boxer hitting a heavy bag. Hilda Porter. Honestly, the manageress of the building has a future as a bailiff should she ever need a change of career. To be fair, the idiosyncratic rhythm of the knock is one they devised together, so that he would always know it was her rather than one of the other less welcome visitors he might have. The power of it, though, is all her own.

She'll be bringing the post and his instinct is to ignore her, but curiosity is a powerful force, often one that won't be denied, and besides, opening letters is a gesture of faith in the future. A modest investment of hope. Equally, to wave away the mail is to deny the future. Is to set your face against the possibility of change. Anyway, his wrist is starting to ache and even when writing is going well, the prospect of speaking to an actual human being is always preferable.

'Back in the land of the living then. Nothing like a night out with friends to revive the spirits.'

This makes him laugh. The land of the living, when he's been communing with the murdered children of the war. Revived spirits, when he's been creating whole brigades of ghost-soldiers in his notebook.

'Why are you smiling?'

'No reason, lovely. Come in.'

Victor likes Hilda. She is efficient and capable, often amused but rarely judgemental. She's good fun and talks sense. Sees the world in plain and uncomplicated ways. He admires the way she presents herself too. Her flat, open face. Her direct gaze from her wide-spaced eyes. The way she has dispensed with all the pre-war petticoats, crinolines and corsets, sporting the looser contemporary style while still looking coolly professional. It's not such an easy thing to manage. In London a lot of women try it and fail, but on Hilda it works. She has the long legs and broad shoulders of a tennis player and can show them off to advantage.

If he ever gets married again it will be to someone like Hilda. Even the fact that she's no socialist ('It's capitalism that keeps me in shoes, Vic') doesn't put him off. The older he gets the more he believes in socialism, but the more he finds the men and women who practise it tiresome. Too puritanical, prone to wagging fingers and pursing lips. Too suspicious of joy.

He thinks now that maybe Hilda will want details of his night with Hardit and Babs and maybe he will let her bully them out of him.

Hilda is not suspicious of joy exactly, but she is nervous of it for herself. She's from Suffolk, a country mouse still uneasy about participating in all the circus thrills of London. She prefers to live vicariously through the doings of her tenants. You'd never catch her having the kind of 'night out with friends' he had yesterday. It's a shame, really, because she's still young, just twenty-six, and this is surely the best time there has ever been for young women in the world's greatest city. Young women are the coming force, the world is theirs, if they could just see it. Particularly young women with clear eyes, broad shoulders and a powerful knock.

'I brought you some milk,' she says now, and he sees her wrinkle her nose as she takes in the state of the flat, the clothes and papers on the floor, the pots in the sink.

He appreciates the way she never says anything about the disorder in which he lives, though as ambassador of the landlords she'd be within her rights. He also admires the way she never offers to help him clean it up. So many women would, it's almost like they can't help themselves, are somehow programmed in childhood to save men from themselves – from their literal and their psychic messes.

That's another thing holding women back. If they ever want to take the power they deserve they're going to need to change that, going to need to lose the mentality of the conscientious student, the helpful slave. They'll need to start using that rage that burns somewhere in the hearts of all women. Smiling and willingly clearing up after your oppressor doesn't win too many revolutions. Hilda Porter hasn't yet learned to use her anger, but at least she sets clear boundaries – there are things she won't do for men, however much she likes them.

So it is Victor who makes the tea, while Hilda tells him what has grabbed *her* attention in the newspapers. Hilda likes the *Daily Express* and for her the big story is not Ireland, nor is it Poland: it is the plight of a six-year-old in Sheffield, a boy in a critical condition after having his face ripped apart by a Red Leghorn cockerel. It's the kind of story they often share, the sort of thing that tickles them both. Macabre definitely, but also comical somehow.

'Can you imagine it, Vic?' says Hilda. 'What if the kid goes and dies? How will anyone at the funeral be able to keep a straight face?'

And it's true. He can imagine it. Surely even the lips of the boy's parents will twitch with suppressed smiles. Such a gruesomely dumb way to go. Victor's own daughter, Elaine, is six. Should he contact his in-laws, her guardians, warn them to be on the lookout for savage chickens?

'How is little Elaine?' says Hilda.

'She's OK.'

He hopes this is right. As far as he knows she's happy enough up there in Bolton with her mother's parents, John and Georgina Nightingale. He gets letters. Routine requests that he sign the papers that would allow them to adopt her permanently, while passing on trivial news (how high she can jump, how much she can eat, the progress she's making with her reading and her counting).

'That's good.'

Victor thinks that maybe the real lesson of the boy almost killed by the cockerel is about the comic cruelty of everyday life. The world is full of random horror. Could he do a bit on the useless but unavoidable fears of parenthood? The black comedy of fatherhood. The humour in widowerhood even. Is he up to that? A bit out of his usual range.

Needs thinking about.

They drink tea. They smoke cigarettes. Below them the machine-animal of London turns, grinds, drills and – most of all – calculates profits with busy fingers. Up here on the fourth floor there is an oasis, a place of reprieve. A little canteen within the giant workshop of the city.

Eventually, Hilda sighs and says, 'You going to look at your mail?'

'No, I'll finish my article first. Reward myself by going through the post when it's done. Virtuous, see.'

'Impressive, particularly as one of your mysterious packages has arrived too. Usual thing, wasn't posted, was stuffed in the pigeonhole outside my office instead.'

'Ah yes, the most ill-gotten of my gains. The latest instalment of the advance for my memoir.'

'They must have high hopes of it.' She takes a sip of tea, winces. He always makes it too strong. A habit from his days as an apprentice making the mid-morning brew for the factory hands. 'When will you finish? You have at least one reader who is desperately keen to get her mitts on it.'

'Who's that then?'

'Me, you ratbag.'

'Oh, right,' he smiles. 'Anyway, who knows? You can't hurry the goddess Art, Hilda. Art is not a mule to be driven with sticks, kicks and curses. She needs kindness and time.'

Hilda raises an eyebrow. 'Kindness, time and money.'

'Yes. All of them equally important to the artistic process.'

THREE

Courtesan Murmurs

CHEQUERS, LUNCHTIME

1

D o you have a spare house? No, me neither. But some people do. People like Viscount Lee for example, and now he's given his surplus property to the nation. As a gift. No strings. What an absolute gent. It is the good Viscount's contention that with new prime ministers no longer selected solely from the landed gentry, they might need to borrow a stately home at weekends. Lee hopes that the gentle antiquity of Chequers might seduce even your most fervent revolutionary, enfold him in an embrace sensuous enough to discourage him from overturning the established order. The house will breathe honeyed words. *No need to tire yourself out guillotining the ruling class just yet*, she will say, *sit here in this beautiful armchair, put your feet up, have a sherry, have a cigar, let one of my liveried footmen bring you the papers.* Those courtesan murmurs will melt the flintiest Bolshevik heart.

In this way the new boss becomes the old boss. Better than the old boss, really, because the old boss did at least know about the traps being laid for him, while the new type of politician is desperate for guidance as he navigates a world he barely comprehends. A newborn lamb on uncertain legs in a field of smiling wolves. An easy mark.

This is the plan, though the house is not yet up to fluttering her eyelashes at the coming breed of prime minister. Chequers has stopped being one thing but has yet to become another. This room, for example, has the provisional, unfinished feel of a meeting room in an expensive but indifferently run chain hotel. Nothing on the walls as yet, no Renaissance paintings, no tapestries, just chipped coving awaiting repair and the heavy smell of new paint.

'I have seen more welcoming drawing rooms in a Tongan prison.'

This is Basil Thomson and he should know. Sir Basil Thomson, currently assistant commissioner C Division at the Metropolitan Police, head of the Home Office Directorate of Intelligence. The men taking notes on the prime minister's sweaty thrustings in dusty top-floor rooms? Well, they report to him. He doesn't enjoy reading these bulletins. Obviously not, he's not a degenerate. It's simply his duty, and Sir Basil always puts duty first. He is responsible for counter-revolutionist operations after all, and so, ultimately, it is Sir Basil who keeps the country safe from enemies both within and without. Before this he spent thirteen years as a prison governor, and that was just one of his former careers. Sir Basil Thomson has also been ruler, on behalf of the colonial office, of both Fiji and Tonga. He's also been a writer. A novelist no less. *The Indiscretions of Lady Asenath*, that was one of his. He doesn't do the fiction any more. He doesn't have time, but he hopes to get back to it one day.

Sir Basil joined the Met as CID chief in 1913, just in time to run the Secret Intelligence Service during the Great War. He had a pretty good war too. A lot of dangerous fellows ended up in front of firing squads thanks to him.

There are four others in the room: the Home Secretary, Edward Shortt, and the two private secretaries to Lloyd George, J.T. Davies and Frances Stevenson, who, as we know, will be chairing the meeting. Also present is the prime minister's latest protégé, Philip Baker. The thirty-year-old diplomat the prime minister has tasked with trying to wrestle the League of Nations into a shape that works for Great Britain.

Home Secretary Shortt is still new to the job, formerly minister for Ireland, where his big idea was to conscript Irish men into the French army. That way they could replenish the troops on the Western Front while not feeling they were sullying themselves by wearing British uniforms. An innovative plan, only slightly undermined by the fact that the French High Command had thought it was *une idée totalement merdique*. The experience of having his plan ridiculed has left Shortt with a distinct antipathy towards our Gallic allies.

He is also a regular contender for Monocle Wearer of the Year, as voted for by the readers of *John Bull* magazine.

And J.T. Davies, what can you say about him? Milky face, milky voice, milky hands. Eyes the colour of tap water. The twitchy, squirrelly face of a gossip. Frankly, the fact that he's

45

known as J.T. rather than John is the most interesting thing about him. That, and the fact that, like Frances, he is devoted to the prime minister, the man he gets to call L.G.

Frances Stevenson asks the men how they take their tea, fusses with milk and sugar, presses them to have some food – there are white and brown bread sandwiches, cheese and pickle or chicken, freshly made. There's ham. More exotic fare too. Olives. Stuffed vine leaves. In deference to the French guests here this weekend there are vol-au-vents. And they should make sure they take a biscuit as well. There are pinwheel cookies, and these are also freshly baked. A particular speciality of the new American cook.

Frances knows that until she's made the men feel a little cossetted, a little loved, she won't get much out of them. Her study of men of power has taught her the impact a little feminine deference can have. For many men, whether they know it or not, getting some attention from young women is exactly why they came into politics in the first place. Like they say, politics is just another kind of music hall, but one where the ugliest people are the stars.

When each man has tea the precise shade he likes it, when sugar is added, when they all have a sandwich, a vol-au-vent and a pinwheel cookie, when she has let them talk about golf, about rugby football, about cars, and when they have all spent some time agreeing that the *banderas* of the new Spanish Legion may well turn the tide against insurrection in Morocco, she can finally get round to the question they are here to discuss.

'So, Basil, what are we doing about the Grayson problem?'

She's made a mistake. She knows it at once. It's a strange thing, but not every powerful man is pleased to be treated with easy familiarity by an attractive younger woman. She sees him bristle. It's almost imperceptible – a casual observer might miss it – but Frances doesn't. That slight clenching of buttock, that tiny tightening of lip, that sudden blink. Still, too late now.

Sir Basil takes a deliberate, impressively silent, sip of dark tea from his cup. In matters of tea he has a navvy's taste. It started as an affectation at Oxford, but he has grown to like it this way.

He places the cup carefully down on the table between them. This care, this precision, this delay in answering the question are another sign that this is a Sir who likes his title to be deployed by everyone, but perhaps especially by a pretty private secretary who is known to be dancing the kibble with her boss. He wipes his smoky-grey moustache with a napkin held in big, pale hands. From the corner of her eye, Frances can see J.T. Davies smirking. On the surface Davies is mild and inoffensive, competent in a quiet, laborious sort of way. But nevertheless, several times a day Frances Stevenson finds herself wanting to slap him.

There is a short silence while the head of C Division looks pointedly towards the Home Secretary. The Minister sighs.

'Go on, Sir Basil, please.'

'Thank you, Home Secretary.'

How ridiculous, thinks Frances. Thomson has only been a Sir for a year so why is he getting all on his high white steed about it? And anyway isn't it all this flummery just another way to keep women down? Sure as eggs is eggs Edward Shortt will be a Sir as soon as his term as a Minister comes to an end. Frances, however, she can never be a Sir, no, best she can hope for is to become a Dame, and it's not an equivalent. Not really. Think Sir and you think of Camelot, Galahad, songs of heroes and brave deeds. You think a sword, a shield, a lance. Think Dame and you think drollery, comedy, pantomime.

Sir Basil takes a heavy, suitably Sir-like breath.

'Mr Davies. Miss Stevenson.' She is sure Sir Basil places a slight stress on their inferior titles. 'I don't think we need to do anything. I don't even think there is a Victor Grayson problem. I don't think there ever has been.'

And before she can stop herself, Miss Frances Stevenson has spoken out of turn again.

'Really, Sir Basil? It's my understanding that Grayson has been digging around looking for evidence of corruption by this government.'

At least she remembered to use his title this time.

Sir Basil Thomson turns dark eyes on her. Blinks.

'And, Miss Stevenson, if that is the case, is it possible that he might find some? Evidence of corruption I mean.'

He keeps his tone mild, but he knows a woman as sharp as Frances will hear the menace in it.

J.T.'s smirk is close to becoming a fully fledged grin. Frances flushes. God, how she wants to smash those insipid features. His big, bland goose egg of a head is an affront to her. Perhaps she could convince J.T.'s beloved L.G. that he makes her feel uncomfortable. She could get him sacked, demoted at least. Maybe she could say Davies put his smug

48

and milky hand on the arse of the prime minister's very own thrilling girl, his pet, his darling Pussy. That would do it.

Anyway, it is clear that Sir Basil feels he has sufficiently reprimanded Frances for her inappropriate show of equality with senior men. It is time to be magnanimous.

'Honestly, Miss Stevenson,' he says. 'I shouldn't worry yourself about it. Grayson hasn't got any compromising material on the government. My agent has been very clear about that, has persuaded me that the search of Mr Grayson's property was very thorough and there was no sign of anything incriminating. My agent – one of our very best I should say – also assures me that there has been nothing in Mr Grayson's recent conversation to suggest that he knows anything that could endanger national security or, indeed, cause any embarrassment to anyone close to the cabinet. We have had him under surveillance for some considerable time and, while he undoubtedly lives a dissolute lifestyle, one full of degradation, I don't think his activities are of real concern to us.'

He tells them that Grayson appears to spend most days in his flat writing and is only visited by three men regularly, all of them well known to the security service – Horatio Bottomley, Havelock Wilson and Maundy Gregory.

Edward Shortt laughs at this, a brief gruff bark.

'Well, there's three musketeers for you, a right trio of rascals.'

'Yes, all Liberal-supporting politicians – even Mr Bottomley, who claims to be an Independent – all with concerns about their finances and their reputations, all with a record of entanglements with the courts, all extremely pro-war. To pursue your analogy, Minister, I'd say that Grayson is perhaps their D'Artagnan, the innocent Northern lad the others have taken under their wing.'

No harm in making the Home Secretary aware that he too knows his classic literature. What serious writer doesn't know his Dumas?

Edward Shortt extracts his handkerchief from the pocket of his suit – the handkerchief brilliantly white and beautifully ironed, the sign of a man with a well-run household – and uses it to polish his monocle.

'No danger from them, I would say. I'd never lend them money, but they're all entertaining fellows in their way. And, as you say, very sound on the war.'

'And apart from these three,' continues Thomson, 'the only other people he sees are those – again mostly men – that he picks up in pubs and clubs and takes back home for late-night discussions on matters which we suspect may not be entirely political.'

The Minister barks again.

J.T. chips in now: 'I understand Mr Grayson is himself an employee of British intelligence.'

He says this with a mouthful of cheese and pickle sand-wich. Thomson's mouth twists. He's clearly one of those upper-middle-class men who abhor poor table manners, who will never listen to those who can't be trusted to eat politely in company.

'Is that correct, Sir Basil?' says Edward.

'Well, yes, and then again, no. Forgive my unpardonable lack of precision, but since the end of the war we have had no use for men like Grayson as propagandists, but rather than cut them off we have been using them to keep tabs on those of their acquaintance who might be conspiring to undermine the state. It would, I feel, be overstating the case to call these men employees. They are simply given a modest retainer to report anything they feel might be of interest to us.'

He takes another sandwich. 'But in any case,' he continues, 'we have decided to end our involvement with Mr Grayson. The information he has been giving has become increasingly low-grade, almost worthless in fact. He is, I feel, a busted flush so disdained by his former comrades that they tell him nothing. They may even give him falsehoods, hoping he'll pass them on to us. Whether that is the case or not, he is a man too despised by the revolutionists to be of much further use to us.'

There's a silence, the matter should be closed. The men all reach for more finger food. Ham. Olives. Those inviting little cubes of Greek cheese. So white, so sharp, so crumbly. It is clear that in a moment the subject will return to golf, motor cars or the weather.

Frances takes a noisy breath. 'With the greatest respect, Sir Basil, you have removed Grayson's source of income and I understand he is a reckless man at the best of times. A man who now has nothing to lose.' She frowns. 'If he does somehow, despite the advice of your agent, have information that would damage the government, will he not now have to try and use it?'

A sigh from someone, a rattle of teacup on saucer from someone else. She is becoming annoying. She must know it too.

'Miss Stevenson, I wonder about the reliability of your sources. Grayson is fast on his way to becoming a tragic figure, a man shouting drunken obscenities at the moon, the kind of person decent people will cross the street to avoid. He is not the compelling preacher of former times. He is done.'

Sir Basil Thomson tries to keep irritation from his voice, but he delivers this last sentence with heavy emphasis. Edward Shortt picks up another sandwich and snaps at it with ferocity.

'A poor bloody D'Artagnan then,' he says.

Frances Stevenson can't let it lie. She just can't.

'I'm not sure. My sources are impeccable. And it's not his contact with decent people I'm concerned about. I think we may have a loose cannon. An impulsive man with many links to the press and with those who would wish the PM harm. I know for an absolute fact that Mr Lloyd George would sleep easier if he didn't have to worry about the likes of Victor Grayson.'

There, she's said it. She can't be any more explicit than this. She has put the prime minister's wishes before them very plainly.

Somewhere outside a territorial bird announces its presence. From nearby Coombe Hill there is the exultant braying of a hunting horn, the tumult of hounds, all part of the stage set needed to make prime ministers feel that they have reached the very top of the greasy pole and so can stop worrying too much about actually Doing Things. Doing Things is hard work and usually ends in disappointment anyway.

Why not just relax? Indulge yourself in pastimes you never normally get the space for. You could do some sketching, play the piano, read a book. Take your nose out of that stuffy old red box, look around you. Smell the flowers.

Sir Basil Thomson clears his throat: 'Miss Stevenson, this is England, not Russia. Here, political opponents of the ruling party don't fall from high windows, they don't get mysteriously fatal illnesses after taking tea with our agents, they don't suffer sudden seizures while at the wheel of motor vehicles and they don't just disappear.'

He delivers this homily in his best prison governor voice, the same voice that has persuaded many villains that it's not in their interest to flout regulations. Sir Basil does well not to smile, actually. He has, after all, simply listed things that happen all the time, in jolly old England same as anywhere else. Communists do sometimes fall from heights, anarchists are prone to rare diseases, nationalists in automobiles do sometimes succumb to sudden swerves on dangerous corners, inconvenient agitators pop to the costermonger's or the haberdasher's never to return. All these things are happening somewhere in England right now. Doesn't mean that they will happen because of some mere prime-ministerial whim. It takes more than that.

Edward Shortt coughs.

'Miss Stevenson. If I understand you correctly, you feel it is the wish of the PM that Victor Grayson, a man who worked with us to raise armies for the recent war, should somehow be encouraged to vanish in order to spare the government some vague threat of embarrassment.' A sip of tea, the careful pushing of an olive into the wet space beneath the gunmetal hedge of his moustache. 'And, forgive me if I'm wrong, but didn't Grayson fight in the war himself?'

'Yes,' says J.T. Davies. 'Almost killed at Passchendaele.'

Edward Shortt lost his only son at Passchendaele. The information that Grayson shed blood in that battle settles things for him. He takes a pinwheel cookie, bites into it with ferocity. The conversation is now definitely closed.

He looks at Frances directly with his large, vaguely school-masterly eyes. His monocle sways gently on its chain.

'We must have a round of golf sometime.'

The way young Miss Stevenson looks on a golf course – her stance, her swing, her amusing competitiveness – this has been the subject of some entertaining conversation in Liberal party circles.

'Obviously, I wasn't suggesting – and the PM would never suggest – that we do anything illegal.'

'Of course not, the PM is a model of rectitude.' Everyone smiles at this. 'I'll have my secretary call you to make arrangements. For golf.'

2

A grey, reflective quiet falls upon the room. The meeting is over. The men reach for cigarettes or pipes. Philip Baker looks at his wristwatch. They're thinking of the variety of possible ways they can spend the afternoon. There are any number of agreeably gentle pursuits available. They could get out into the gardens. Smile at the antics of the new peacocks. If the

54

weather cheers up there might be croquet. Or maybe they can see how they're getting on with hanging the art in the Long Room. Or snooker with one of those Frenchies here to tweak the documents concerning the surrender of Ottoman territories in Mesopotamia. Maybe they could get a game with Premier Briand himself. See what he's like under pressure.

It is during this becalmed moment that a teenage girl explodes into the room.

'Jesus Christ, Frances! What are you playing at?'

Flushed, breathless, her voice stretched and tight, vibrating with hot musical fury, Megan Lloyd George is incandescent, a brilliant tornado of outrage. The prime minister's daughter is eighteen and equipped with flashing eyes, with slender but pugnacious shoulders. Militant teeth. And with her short dress, her flat suffragette's shoes, the passionate intensity of her voice, she lets you know at once that she is the kind of girl who just loves to be incensed. Lives for it. Even her hair is a proclamation. A wild halo of fierce and righteous disgust.

'I don't mind you screwing him but getting him to buy you a fucking farm! That's just pure bloody outrageous. That's theft is what that is.'

Her voice is ductile, bounces off the bare walls, reverberates back from the high ceiling. In her right hand she is waving a letter. It'll be from her father. The prime minister always shares too much with his daughter, Frances has told him off about this before. Always causes trouble.

The adults in the room are dazed. Edward Shortt, the Home Secretary, eyes wide, mouth open, is so startled his monocle has fallen from his eye. J.T. Davies quivers, his lips framing a perfect O, his hands twisting and writhing in his lap. Sir Basil Thomson is the calmest of the men – he's someone who has stood his ground in a Fijian knife fight – but even he looks discomfited.

'Megan,' Frances begins. She stops. What can she say? 'Megan, this is not the time.'

'You're telling me it's not the time. My mother is really bloody ill, and not content with taking her place in Downing Street you're playing the hostess here too. Acting like a bloody queen. So I agree, not the time.'

'Megan—'

'Queen bloody Frances the First. I can cope with that, I suppose. We're all grown-ups, but this, getting my father to buy you a house?'

'Megan—'

'No, not even buy, he's going to *build* you a bloody house, one with sixty acres of land too. So not even a house. A bloody *estate*. Christ, Frances. You've got some nerve.'

'Megan—'

'What are you going to do with all that land anyway. Grow potatoes? Breed rare pigs? Gloucester fucking old spots? Meanwhile my sick mother is banished. Hidden away in bloody Criccieth. It's an absolute disgrace.'

Frances closes her eyes, remembers again the moment when Megan had caught her and her father in flagrante. Arriving home early from her final term at school, racing up to her father's bedroom at the Churt house eager to surprise him, she'd burst in on them just as the prime minister had gulped his way to the moment of noisy climax. Definitely a surprise for all concerned.

Before that Megan and Frances had been close. Frances had been much more than a teacher, she'd been a kind of young aunt or big sister. They'd been best friends almost. Such a shame.

'Megan, your mother is very welcome to—'

'Don't you dare mention my mother, you fucking—' Megan has properly worked herself again up now. Her face is ferociously scarlet, her wide eyes an intense, blazing green. She looks around the room as she searches for the word, the perfectly weighted word, the one that will nail Frances's perfidy. 'You fucking *strumpet*!'

Frances laughs, she can't help it. Strumpet. Ridiculous. A word blown in on a breeze from the distant past. As if she were Nell Gwynn.

Megan stamps her foot. 'Funny, is it? Well, I'm going to talk to Tad, put a stop to this shit.'

Tad, Welsh for Daddy and a sly way of letting Frances know that she will never be part of the inner circle. This is ridiculous too. None of Lloyd George's children even speak Welsh, not properly.

Basil Thomson rises from his chair. Someone needs to take charge, and it seems it has to be him.

'Young lady,' he begins.

Megan rounds on him: 'What, *old man*? Come on, spit it out.'

She advances and Sir Basil Thomson, head of C Division, controller of the British empire's secret intelligence service, is dumbfounded. He feels his face grow hot. He sits down again abruptly. This is exactly why he has always been so opposed to votes for women. Flappers like this girl here having any say in the affairs of the nation? Disastrous. Might as well give the vote to parrots. Just because they can talk doesn't mean they can think, that's Sir Basil's considered opinion. Unfortunately for him it's an argument his kind have lost, and it seems there's no going back now. Women are everywhere and there's not much he can do about it.

It is at this moment that the hitherto silent Philip Baker intervenes. He's an ex-academic – formerly vice-principal of Ruskin College in Oxford and a fellow of King's College, Cambridge no less. Not only that, but he was a conscientious objector during the war who headed up the Friends' Ambulance Unit for the Quakers, and who, despite his pacifism, somehow won military honours. Not just British ones either. France and Italy had both honoured him. None of this is anything like as impressive as his other accomplishment: the fact that he won the silver medal in the 1500 metres at the recent Antwerp Olympics.

If anyone can calm the situation, well, maybe he can.

Baker gets between the enraged girl and the security chief.

'Come along now,' he says, his voice softly humorous, while also somehow being unequivocal, firm. 'No need for this. Let's go to a place, me and you. Talk about this. Sensibly. Like reasonable people.'

And to everyone's surprise, the girl subsides. She gives him a hard glare but allows her elbow to be taken by Baker's slender hand and led towards the door. If quietening truculent adolescents is ever a recognised sport, Philip Baker will be in with a shout in that event too.

Megan's last words are tossed over her shoulder as if she were flinging back a scarf.

'I'm not having it, Frances, none of us are.'

By 'us' she means the Lloyd George family, the other children and, especially, Margaret the steely matriarch, the person everyone loves for her quiet nobility and her unstinting support for her husband's career. It is Frances's view that Margaret is not all that noble, nowhere near quiet enough, and that her support has been quite stinting actually, if you think about it. Not that she can say this, though, certainly never to David Lloyd George.

Then they're gone, the Olympian and the harridan. A very smooth piece of diplomacy indeed.

Basil Thomson takes a noisy breath. Makes a visible effort to control his feelings. Frances apologises but the head of C Division is so rigid with rage that he finds he can't speak, and has to content himself with a stiff-necked nod. It's not that he hasn't heard profanity before – of course he has – but it is so much louder, so much more violent, when coming from a woman, especially a young one. His entire body vibrates with distaste. His hands are bunched into fists. But something else has happened. His antipathy to Miss Stevenson's manner has evaporated. He has sympathy for her now. She doesn't deserve to be treated like this.

Edward Shortt must feel something similar. His manner is considerate, almost avuncular. His monocle is back in place and his eye gleams behind its window.

'My dear, I have three daughters. I know what modern young women are like. These sudden storms die down as fast as they blow up.' A sly pause. 'But I'm serious about the golf. My doctor tells me I need more fresh air and exercise.'

The old dog. Thomson for one strongly suspects that the minister has more than golf on his mind. Would the Home Secretary risk his position in the cabinet for an intrigue with Frances Stevenson? Who knows? Reason doesn't play much part in these things. All of the men in the room know this from personal experience.

Edward Shortt bows gracefully, thanks Frances for the spread ('Those biscuit things, the American cookies. Delicious'), covers them all with the antiseptic wash of his smile and takes his leave.

3

Those left behind are an uneasy group. J.T. Davies, Frances Stevenson, Sir Basil Thomson and a few sad sandwiches, a few biscuits. Some lonely vol-au-vents. And embarrassment of course. Embarrassment is like mustard gas, squeezes fresh air from every inch of space, and it fills this room now. It has a smell too, barely detectable but there nonetheless, a staleness that speaks of generations of disappointing lunches and unopened windows.

'Frances,' Davies says suddenly. His voice firm for once. None of his usual milky giggle in it. 'Why do you put yourself through it?'

'What do you mean?'

'Well, you know I admire L.G., that I think he'll be remembered as one of the few truly great political figures of the twentieth century. But...' he pauses. Blinks.

'But what?'

'But he's a bit of a shit.'

'You can't say that to me.'

'Someone has to. Look, Frances, L.G. has another mistress, two actually.'

It acts like a slap. There is sudden heat on the woman's face. The blush seems to become her. Basil Thomson blinks. For the first time it seems to occur to him that Frances Stevenson really is an attractive girl. Those dark eyes. That pale skin, now going nicely pink. That softly curling hair. The full bosom. Proper hips. A real woman, and she has blossomed over these last few years. No doubt about that.

'I know about those,' Frances says, quickly. 'They don't mean anything. Here today, gone tomorrow dalliances.'

You can see her mind working. She has seen rivals off before, but she's wracking her brain to think who these latest challengers might be. The trouble is there are so many candidates. Party workers, maids, American heiresses, actresses, wives of fellow MPs. She's even suspected Roberta Lloyd George before now. David's eye is a tireless, indefatigable rover, and where his eyes go his hands often follow. But Frances is damn well not giving J.T. bloody Davies the satisfaction of knowing that this has come as news.

Davies's milky face is an elaborate fresco of concern and, yes, pity.

'Frances, the mistresses I am referring to are Politics and the Liberal Party. Who did you think I was talking about?'

There is a heartbreaking pause. This is the moment Thomson is completely won over to Frances Stevenson. No woman deserves to be humiliated like this. She needs help and it is clear that Basil Thomson feels his duty as a servant of the lawfully elected government – and as a man – is to give it to her.

FOUR

House of Murderers

1

WHEN Hilda has gone Victor Grayson tries to continue with 'The Army of Ghosts' – thinking now that maybe 'Ghost Army' will be better, simpler, more to the point – only it's not that easy to ignore the little stack of possibilities sitting there before him on the table like a precarious shrine. Especially now that he sees the package at the bottom, the foundation of this shrine, all the slender envelopes of his everyday post resting on its intriguing bulk. How much will he get this time? The amounts never seem to be consistent.

The packet seems to wink at him, beckons with a seductive finger. And the dawn headache seems to be creeping back. The truth is the writing mood was fatally wounded by Hilda's arrival, by tea and aimless chat. People and their prosaic concerns are always death to actual prose. The time, just a few minutes ago, when he could work with fluency is a lost Elysium, a vanished Eden. He tries to keep it going but after a few minutes' hard labour – much sighing, much sucking on his pencil – he abandons the task.

The idea that had once seemed so novel, so intriguing, so pertinent, now seems inert. Dead. Ironic that his piece about the ghosts of the Western Front coming back to fight with the complacent living should be so lifeless.

The problem is it's just too literary a conceit for him, too artsy an idea. Victor Grayson is, let's face it, no Thomas Hardy.

The mail is a disappointment of course. As predicted, there are the hair tonic ads, the ads for cruises, the ads for restaurants. There's a new Russian place – funny how so many of the émigrés fleeing the Bolsheviks seem to be expert cooks. He wonders for a moment about the effects of a revolution in England. Would all the dukes and the City moneymen run off to America to open fish and chip restaurants in Washington? Is there a feature in that? At the very least, it's the sort of idea he'd like to share with Hilda next time she calls around.

He always hopes there will be an invitation to speak and sometimes there is, but no luck today. Instead there is a letter telling him that he's a debaucher and a disgrace to socialism. There are more of these each week and it's disturbing that they know where to find him. This one is not scrawled semilegibly, as most are; the handwriting here is impressive actually, the obscene invective set down in the exquisite burlesque curves of Victorian copperplate.

Time to tear open the package and – hurrah! – it does contain cash. A substantial wad of it. It's not an advance for his memoir, however, though Victor never thought it was. This is his fee for providing regular feedback on the doings of his associates on the revolutionary left. It was a verbal contract entered into when the government no longer required his services as a recruiting sergeant during the war, and he needed another source of income.

He has never felt too guilty about this. Many of the leftists he reports on are fools to themselves and a danger to progress, and they need watching. Besides, he tries to make sure the information he gives is harmless, or misleading, or plain conjecture. He likes to stir just enough fact into his reports to provide some crunch, enough gritty morsels into what is otherwise thin soup to keep him on the payroll, but mostly it's time-wasting guff.

Now it seems something has gone wrong with his method, or maybe it's just that there's a round of public spending cuts affecting the security services, because this package – very unusually – comes with a note. No sensual Victorian copperplate here. This is a scribble in emphatic capitals and green ink, and everyone knows only the security services use green ink for their memoranda.

FINAL PAYMENT.
THERE WILL BE NO MORE. NONE.

Severance pay, is what this is. Victor leans back in his chair. Stretches. Takes a deep breath. What will he do now? He'll do what he always does. He'll duck and he'll dive. He'll bob and he'll weave. He'll survive. He always has. Something will come along, it always does. He'll Micawber it. Anyway, he has supporters, people he can turn to if he needs. He's still young too. Thirty-nine. No age. There's been talk recently of his returning to Parliament if they can find the right seat. But this dismissal does mean he really will have to complete the memoir. Not only that, he had better make it as racy as he can get away with.

He counts the money. Fifty pounds in a variety of denominations. The king staring into space empty-eyed in various muted colours. He fans it in front of his face. Closes his eyes and smells it. Breathes in deeply. New money, government money, money signed for in offices, has a funeral parlour smell. Smells of whispered prayers and embalming fluid. By contrast, real money, street money, pub money, smells of defiance and hope. Smells of beer and sweat and sperm. Today, though, he can't afford to rough it up, can't afford to give it life. Not really. Victor puts the thick wad of clean dead notes back on the solid table.

He hasn't seen this much money since the time when the comrades raised over a hundred pounds to send him on a much-needed holiday, and that was a long time ago. Should last a while, even with inflation at a disgraceful 15 per cent. Sometimes the thing Victor hates most about capitalists is how bad they are at capitalism. However, if this is likely to be the last lot of cash he has for a while, he needs to use it wisely. He'll get some essential supplies in and then he'll move his office from his apartment into the lounge bar of the Queen's Head. It must be 12.30 by now. Opening time. He deserves a drink.

Victor Grayson does the essential arithmetic: a bottle of whisky is twelve shillings, say, so half a case for three pounds twelve. Means his money will be gone after sixty bottles. Or in just two months at his current rate of consumption, even if he takes no other sustenance at all. Pays no other bills. Not a brilliant equation.

He does the same sum for beer: a pint is sixpence (was threepence in 1914!) so that's forty pints in a pound. Four hundred pints in ten pounds. Two thousand pints in fifty pounds. Not so terrible. Just need to switch from whisky to beer, he can do that. Is it sad to mentally turn his available cash into drink like this? Maybe, but it helps – makes him feel financially stable somehow. Makes him feel in control of his own destiny. Also makes his head hurt a little. Maths always has.

He gathers his things together, but before he leaves the flat he phones Scotland Yard. He asks for the usual contact but the policeman on the end of the line is baffled – or pretends to be – when he asks to speak to Detective Sergeant Schweitzer.

'No one of that name here, Sir. Never has been so far as I know, and I've been here fifteen years.'

In a way it's the answer he wanted. Very simple confirmation that he's been cut loose by the state. He's independent again, and there's a relief in that. Poor but free.

There is, of course, no Detective Sergeant Schweitzer, he has always known that. It was a name they chose for his contact because it sounded so foreign it was unlikely to be muddled with any real serving officer, and he didn't want to be put through to a traffic bobby simply because the spy handler and the plod had the same name. It's the sort of very British mistake he could imagine being made all the time. His opinion of covert operations people is not high. Q: What do they use in schools as an example of an oxymoron? A: Military intelligence.

He is moving away from the phone when it startles him by blaring back into life. But it's not the SIS phoning him back, as he had immediately assumed. Instead it is the soft hiss of the actor-manager Arthur Maundy Gregory reminding him about their drink tonight.

'It's Saturday, Arthur. Of course I'll be there.'

'Good, good. Because I have a new acquaintance I'd like you to meet. Could be entertaining for you.'

'Sounds mysterious.'

'No mystery, but with any luck will lead to fruitful collaborations.'

Victor knows better than to enquire further. Maundy Gregory likes his intrigues and his secrets, loves nothing better than making a drama out of the mundane, loves to make his confidants beg for information. He won't give him the satisfaction.

'OK, my cagey friend. I will see you there.'

And so, finally, dapper in his hard-wearing suit of dark Huddersfield wool, his cap-toe boots and his black fedora, with his dead money in a compartment in his faithful tan American satchel-bag – a souvenir from his honeymoon in the USA – and his old New Zealand army greatcoat folded over his arm, he is ready for the world. He takes a look around the confusion of his flat. Tonight, he'll have a clear-up. Tonight, he'll say goodbye to the old hit-and-miss shoddy Grayson, and be reborn as a steady grafter, devoted to the only things that matter: his writing, the development of his political thinking and the advancement of the working class. Oh, and his child of course. Mustn't forget Elaine.

This mood of cheerful determination takes him down the four flights of steps of his building, sustains him as he dodges between the cars and vans on busy Bury Place – Victor Grayson is not one to wait patiently on the kerb until there's a gap in the traffic – pushes him through the doors of the Queen's Head, escorts him to the bar, stays with him as he orders a prudent half of bitter (only thruppence ha'penny) and sees him over to a corner seat, where he can observe his fellow early drinkers and their dogs.

2

The Queen's Head is famous for being a public house where dog lovers gather, a legacy of its past as a ratpit. Until the 1880s it was a place where men came to see their carefully starved fighting canines catch and kill as many rats as possible. A place of threats, violence and savage urging to slaughter. A place where hard-earned shillings were gambled on how many animals would be torn apart. A place incarnadine with blood and guts. Hard to imagine now, when you see these quiet, defeated middle-aged sots sitting daydreaming in this soupy light, occasionally patting their solemn and dignified German shepherds.

It's a calm space these days, just enough background murmur to aid concentration. He pulls out his notebook and begins to write his long-delayed memoir. *My Search After God*. It's not a title his publisher likes and maybe he'll change it before it's in the shops, but Victor was going to be a preacher once and he sometimes thinks his whole life has been a quest for enlightenment, a search for something bigger than himself. In this conducive atmosphere, Victor makes good progress. He revises the early chapters – what he thinks of as the *Great Expectations* eyewash. The relentless poverty in the Liverpool slums, his work-shy father, his resourceful mother, his many siblings competing with him for scarce resources. The endless quest for food, for time, for love and what the struggle for these things does to you. The hardening of your heart, the attrition of your soul.

He's pleased with it. Reads pretty well. He has earned a whisky, but for once he has denied himself this, settled instead for another half of brackish London ale. Has enjoyed a conversation with a retired tram conductor about greyhounds. How they keep you fit, how they're a consolation in old age. See, he's still got it. That common touch that has served him so well, that was the making of him. The secret of his success. And when the old man and his beautiful dog leave, Victor cracks on.

He revises the passage where, inspired by the comic-book cowboy adventures of Deadwood Dick, he first ran away from home. Taking his father's old army revolver for protection against rustlers and marauding banditos, the seven-year-old Victor had got as far as the city limits before scurrying back home, arriving well after dark to find his parents hadn't even missed him.

He's also finished the chapter detailing his second, much more serious, attempt to run away. At fourteen he smuggled himself onto a ship bound for Australia, but was discovered two days out and locked in the fetid dark of the brig with the rats, before being put ashore in Wales, half-starved and without money. The captain made it clear Victor was lucky he hadn't been thrown overboard.

He had had to walk back to Liverpool, begging as he went. It took the young Victor seven days. Seven days of dealing with the reflexive hostility of strangers, talking wary shop-keepers into becoming benefactors, charming timid house-wives into welcoming him into neat kitchens for tea and toast. Aye, and sometimes he got further than the kitchens, he saw a few bedrooms too. At fourteen. These are the kind of adventures that make a man.

Similarly, he has sketched out all the key moments of his formative years: his apprenticeship in the Bankhall Engine Works in Bootle, his time training to be a preacher, his study at the Unitarian College in Manchester, how he made the acquaintance of Christabel Pankhurst, how he honed his public speaking skills on any and every platform – church halls, street corners, working men's clubs, trade union meet-ings, mechanics' institutes, temperance societies and socialist youth clubs. How he had accepted every invitation going. An example: he once spoke at a Labour Alliance bicycle club.

That was an entertaining day. No one more boisterous than a socialist cyclist with a thirst.

Back then Victor could make a speech about anything, anything at all. There was no subject he couldn't use to illustrate the need for socialism. Unemployment, evil of. Equality between the sexes, need for. Solidarity of the international working class, importance of. All of these, of course, but also Poetry and Socialism, Art and Socialism, Music and Socialism. Sport and Socialism. Cookery and Socialism. It was never put to the test, but he could have done Flower Arranging and Socialism were it ever requested.

Now – maybe twenty thousand words in – he is free to work on what he thinks of as the real beginning.

3

The Colne Valley by-election. That beautiful shining moment amid the hills and the mills. Victor Grayson, the Socialist candidate. (Not the official Labour Party candidate of course – that party had wanted some committee man, some grey-bearded timeserver. Keir Hardie himself tried to persuade the party to pick someone more experienced, by which he surely meant someone more pliable.)

But there are times when everything aligns, when forces arise that even the establishment can't resist. So Grayson writes easily now, a furious flow about the wave building, about the way the muse arrived dancing, bringing those beautifully wrapped bundles of words every day. About the way those words shaped themselves into perfectly balanced phrases, vivid images, how those phrases, those images, became suffused with golden mist, about how they took flight like perfectly weighted arrows, no, better than that, took flight like *eagles*. Swooping through the electric air. Yes sir, he were on fire then, conjuring lightning out of passion, ideas and a few jokes.

Helped that he were a very good-looking lad back then like. That always helps.

Helped too that his opponents didn't think he had a chance. The Liberals and the Conservatives, with their glib candidates, their neatly presented pamphlets, their motor cars. They didn't think they had to worry about the kid in the corduroy jacket who toured the villages in a farm cart.

That's another thing about capitalists, they have no imagination. They just couldn't picture it happening, so when Victor was declared the winner the country – outside of Yorkshire anyway – was stunned, outraged, hysterical.

And the most stunned? The most outraged? The most hysterical? The Labour Party. They hadn't endorsed him, few of their MPs had come up to support him, so how had he won? Wasn't right. The Liberals and the Conservatives hated losing, but it was only the Labour leadership that never forgave Victor for winning.

Ah, but the victory party, that were the stuff of legend.

4

Victor Grayson stops writing. His wrist aches, his head throbs, his stomach gurgles. Urgent messages from all the constituencies of his body suggesting that he take a break. The memory of it all makes him fretful. Besides, the pub has called last orders. The sad-eyed men and their long-suffering best friends have drifted from the safe, slow haven of the Queen's saloon into the fretful London streets and Victor follows.

Here there are so many men muttering to themselves or hopping through the damp fog on crutches. The blind, the crippled, the halt and the traumatised. Men chanting softly to themselves like so many confused monks. The legacy of war. In some sense it's also Victor's legacy. How many of these wounded souls joined up because of his oratory? More than a few. It's depressing to think of, especially coming after the exhilaration of writing about his greatest success.

What to do now that he's in the long beige corridor of the afternoon? Where to go? He has fifty pounds in his pocket and there is shopping to be done, supplies to get, but he doesn't seem to have the right kind of energy for that. He wants to keep writing, but he also doesn't want to return to the flat to do it. He runs through the options. The library? He likes working there but he also knows that the same sort of worn-out men he found in the pub will be in there now, listlessly turning the pages of newspapers, their dogs waiting patiently tied to the railings outside. The wrong kind of atmosphere for his current mood. There are always the most damaged war veterans in libraries too, the ones who can't stop twitching and gurning. The ones who jump every time someone shuts a book. You also find the destitute in libraries, the ones who never wash, who never change their over-ripe clothes, who go to the reading rooms to get warm and then torment themselves by reading cookbooks. As a good socialist he feels for their plight, but he also finds their company enervating. The way they hug themselves, the way they lick their lips as they read. The way they scratch at themselves. The way they stink.

It comes to him eventually. He's surprised he didn't think of it before. Dr Vaughan-Sawyer. Ethel. She's been one of the few to read early drafts of the first sections of his book and he values her opinion. She can read what he's written in the Queen's Head today, while he plans the next part. He's been meaning to visit anyway. Usually sees her every week or so, but things have got in the way. That's the thing with things, they trip you up, delay you, make you lose track of the thread of your life.

Even if Ethel's out, he is a familiar enough presence in her chambers to be allowed in by her daughter Petronella. She's a sweet child, she'll give him tea and cake and use of her mother's writing desk. He is greatly cheered by this notion.

Ethel Vaughan-Sawyer's sumptuous apartment is in Harley Street, a pleasant half an hour walk through Bloomsbury, which is perfect. In Victor's mind walking and writing are two parts of the same job. Whenever he gets stuck, he walks for a while and knotted thoughts untangle themselves. Walking is the proper pace for thinking.

So he sets out into Great Russell Street and past the British Museum, onto Bloomsbury Street, across Bedford Square with its oasis of green shade, and into Bayley Street before joining the throng of shoppers in the crowded thoroughfares that take you towards Marylebone – not that he notices them, so wrapped up is he in memories of his debut appearance in

75

Parliament and the problem of how best to convey the tumult of that moment.

5

Oh, those early days. The sheer bloody joy of them.

Victor's Grayson's first weeks in Parliament were spent learning the ropes. Not process or procedure – he never had time for that, what man of quality does? – but the real ropes, the important stuff. He discovered the appeal of double, treble whiskies in bars that never closed. Stumbled upon the doors that being an MP could open, the enticing invitations that a bright, good-looking young man with power could expect. The beds he could fall into after a long night, the warm bodies that appeared just when you needed them to. Yes, he began to find his way around Westminster pretty quickly.

When he was in the House itself, he sat quietly on the Labour benches – despite not being an official member of the party. He liked to sport a jauntily distinctive green Tyrolean hat while listening, apparently patiently, to endless debates about matters irrelevant to the majority of British people. What did the people care about the Marine Insurance Act? Did they give a stuff about the Crofters Common Grazings Regulation Act? Or two hoots about the Cinematograph Act? Did they care about even a tiny fraction of the bills crawling their way through the House?

Of course they bloody didn't. They didn't give a monkey's.

By October his patience was exhausted, the time for listening was over, the time for action had begun. On the 15th,

Grayson interrupted a debate about tweaking the licensing laws (to make them more restrictive) with a demand that Parliament adjourn to consider 'a matter of genuinely urgent public importance, the question of the unemployed'.

The Speaker informed him that such an adjournment was procedurally impossible, the rules were implacably against it, to which Grayson replied that he refused to be bound by such rules. All around ham-faced members bellowed at him to resume his seat.

'It is all very well for you well-fed men to shout "sit down", but I will not,' he said.

It took force to remove him.

He was escorted from Parliament by the serjeant-at-arms, but not before he had told the assembled right-honourables that he was only leaving the chamber because he felt degraded in a company that would not consider the unemployed.

'I refuse to be bullied into silence. I quit this house with pleasure,' and he then addressed his own side, the Labour men. 'You will not stand up for your own people. You are traitors. Traitors to your class.'

The same pattern the next day. Grayson, slipping quietly into the House, incongruous William Tell hat bobbing cheerfully as he made his way to the centre of a bench, choosing an opportune moment to spring to his feet and demand that MPs discuss the 'thousands of people dying in the streets while you are trifling with this bill'.

Once again, the other members remonstrated. Noisily, like farmyard animals. So much lowing, so much bleating. So much oinking and squawking, so many ruffled feathers. The

MP for Hackney South, and, incidentally, the founder of both the *Financial Times* and *John Bull*, a man as well fed as any in the House, Horatio Bottomley, stood up and crossed the floor to where a gesticulating Grayson attempted to make himself heard over the hubbub. Bottomley grasped Grayson by the shoulders, but the younger man shrugged him off.

'I shall not keep order. I am alone in this House, but I am going to fight!'

Eventually it was the Chancellor of the Exchequer, Herbert Asquith, who put forward the motion that Grayson be suspended, and this was passed.

Grayson was not cowed: 'I leave this house feeling I have gained in dignity,' and his final shot – 'This House is a house of murderers!'

And so ended any possibility of Grayson having a future as a Labour MP. He really was on his own now. For the second time in two days the burly but avuncular serjeant-at-arms led him from the chamber.

'Come along son, you've had your fun,' he said. 'Let the grown-ups get on with things now.'

But what had destroyed Grayson's career in Parliament made him a hero in the streets. The contempt Grayson had shown for the Mother of Parliaments – the way he had spat in her eye – had enhanced his reputation with the people he cared about most. Several young socialists made a pilgrimage from the North to London just to shake his hand, to buy him a drink. Young Yorkshire suffragettes sent him hand-knitted socks and scarves. One or two sent him their underwear.

*

This section of the memoir, the part he is still constructing mentally as he stands outside his friend's flat on the third floor of the Harley Street apartment block, will concentrate on the idea of the solitary hero standing up against the complacent ranks of the establishment. The alternative is to recall the reality of a glassy-eyed drunk shouting and waving his arms around like a hoodlum at an Association football game. Just a Northern yobbo in a silly holiday hat being led away by a wearily tolerant usher. A man who has seen it all and has found it all ridiculous.

Someone should write a history of England from the point of view of these patient men. Someone. But not Victor Grayson.

FIVE

Joyless Arseholes

PALMERS GREEN, AFTERNOON

1

HER brother has lost his face again and there is much noise and commotion and general upset. As Babs lets herself into the house, she is confronted with tears and yelling. There is also laughing, although of a disconcertingly manic kind. The tears and yelling come from their mother, while the mad laughing comes from Maurice himself, whose forgetfulness has caused the whole situation. He doesn't care about whether he has his face on or not, it's his mother who can't bear the thought of the reaction he'll get out in the streets. It doesn't matter how many times he tells her that most people are unfazed by disfigurement these days – that everyone knows someone who looks like him – she gets hysterical at the idea that there are people shuddering at the sight of her boy, the boy who was so beautiful once. Only, sometimes he forgets where he left it. The way you and I might be with our keys, that's how Maurice is with his face.

You know, don't you, that we're not talking about his real face? We're talking about the metal mask that he wears to protect onlookers from the gruesome reality of the place where a face once was.

These days, where other people have cheeks and lips, Maurice has only a ragged circle of peeled and raw flesh surrounding the dank cave that was once a mouth. It should be noted that his eyes remain lovely, a peculiarly fine pearlescent blue.

The mask is a rudimentary metal simulacrum of the face of Erich von Stroheim. This is an unusual choice. Other similarly wounded veterans have gone for masks intended to give them something of the look of a robot Valentino but, while he can see the joke of that, Maurice is more discerning, his cinematic tastes more mature. He was also tickled by the idea of giving himself the face of an Austrian. Not just any Austrian either, but a man famed for playing wartime enemies of the Allies such as the sinister Von Bickel in *The Hun Within* and the bestial Prussian Von Eberhard in *The Heart of Humanity*. It's in that latter film that Stroheim's character, maddened by lust, tears the buttons off a nurse's uniform with his teeth. Later, annoyed by a crying baby, he simply throws it out of a window.

This is how Maurice sometimes chooses to disguise the damage done by a fifty-two pound Albrecht mortar shell, one that, in order to guarantee maximum damage, was loaded with metal fragments, with washers, nails and screws. With any old iron.

'You never know,' he told his sister soon after the mask was first fitted. 'One day I too might get to throw a baby from a window.'

He knows he is unlikely ever to tear the uniform off a nurse. And definitely not with his teeth. His surgeon in Sidcup has worked wonders, but some miracles are beyond even the most talented wielders of scalpels.

Clearly relieved by Babs's appearance in his attritional struggle with their mother, Maurice scurries into the hallway. His body is as well proportioned as it was when he first joined up, and he moves as well as he ever did. Lithe. Catlike. It was only his face that was obliterated. The very smallest of mercies.

'Hey sis, want to come to the flicks?'

Babs marvels, as she often does, that his voice, like his eyes, like his body, was also left more or less intact by that German shell. There's a rasp and whistle as the words emerge from the fissure where a mouth should be, and he also pauses at odd places in his sentences, like a man hopping across a stream using unevenly spaced stepping stones, but mostly – and surely it's been achieved by an effort of will – he still has the urbane, mischievous, softly seductive intonation of the undergraduate he was in 1914.

'What's on?'

'I don't know. Who cares? It's the flicks! All films are worth seeing. Everything gives you something. And actually, you know, I think I prefer it when the films are terrible. They're funnier then. Gives you more to talk about over supper.'

It is, perhaps, obvious why Maurice likes to retreat to the shadowed bunker of the cinema for hours at a time, why he likes to remain for the credits, why he'll sometimes watch a programme several times over. He might be used to the reactions he gets in the streets, and most people he meets are thoughtful enough to not mention his blasted features, but still, in the cinema you're just another indistinct lump, and you don't have to worry what people are thinking.

It's true what he says, that everyone these days knows a man with a shattered face, but it is also true that a lot of people think that the damaged and the disabled should stay in, not go around reminding people of all the horrors in the world.

Even when your fellow citizens don't think like this, it's sometimes good to be in a place where no one has to be kind or considerate. Where no one has to suppress their initial shock or feel the need to tell you about their own similarly wounded family members.

Babs can see that it must be irritating to be reminded of your difference, even when people are nice. Not that Maurice himself says this. He just says being wounded is no biggie, lots of chaps like him around, people are wonderful, always friendly. He just likes the flicks is all.

'I've found it!'

Their mother, the honourable Lady Wolsey, descends the staircase with Maurice's metal face in her hand. She is flushed with triumph. 'It was in the kitchen. In the cupboard with the tea caddy.'

'Ah, yes,' Maurice says. 'I was making a pot of tea for the man from the ministry.'

'You had the pension people round again?'

'Yes, they're assessing me again, and on a Saturday too.

83

They don't rest, these chaps. They were seeing if I'm still worth all of my two pound ten shillings a week, or whether, face or no face, I should start earning my own money like a real man.'

'Real men are terrible,' Babs says. 'You don't ever want to become one of them.'

'You're right, sis. Tried it once. Didn't like it.'

2

And so, minutes after she returns home, Babs is outside again, out among the weekend throng. There is the standard-issue piss-yellow London fog forming now and through it go the factory men with their chalky faces – the men who came back safe from the war, or maybe didn't go at all – men making the most of the fleeting weekend hours, already anticipating some lovely shouting at the footer match, some beers after. A sing-song. A bit of a do.

Then there's all the anxious women in their thin coats, many of them pushing scowling husbands in wheelchairs. These are the men with parched eyes, the men who can't work, the men who suspect their loved ones wish they'd stayed back in France, that they were underneath the green fields, pushing up the poppies.

And the children. The coughing children with their twitching, translucent, ratlike faces blotched from cold, their hand-me-down clothes, their unfathomable cheerfulness. And the cats. So many thin cats in London, all out padding through the streets on their important secret missions.

Babs and Maurice mooch past the cafés and the grocers' shops. He sings as they go – it's a thing he does, snatches of music hall tunes or hymns. Not loud but constantly. He sings as they move past the coffee stands, past the ABC cafés and the Lyons Corner Houses, past the brown pubs with their sad promises. The smell of the city a melange of smoke and town gas, tripe and onions. Fried fish, reheated soup. Noxious leftovers. Dog shit. Horse shit. All manner of shit.

Past the buskers and the beggars they go, past the newspaper-sellers, past the advocates for the niche churches. The Evangelists, the Adventists, the Jehovah's Witnesses. They're all doing well right now, though not as well as the spiritualists. They are really having a moment.

And always the fog, moving around them sluggishly but deliberately. Wrapping itself around their ankles, rubbing its scent against their shins. This country is a disgrace, she thinks. The architecture is a disgrace, the weather is a disgrace, the bloody people are a disgrace. Bombs, she thinks, we need bombs. Death and destruction, not on distant battlefields, not in Russia or Manchuria or Ireland, but right here in Palmers Green. Something to clear the streets. Let's replace this feral fog with honest fire. A whizz-bang up the jacksie of the nation. Something that might make these people wake up. Something – anything! – to stop Maurice humming away behind that mask in that mindless way he has. Did he do that before the war? Maybe he did.

It annoys her that she can't remember. The condition doesn't seem to be mitigated by the pills he takes. The ones for the tremors, and the ones for the pain, they do nothing for the verbal tics and the musical logorrhoea. These spasms of not-quite-songs. Maybe they even make this habit worse. Anyway, she decides it's another thing that she'll blame on the men on the list, the war hawks, the deathmongers, the jingoists, the fat politicians, all the traitors – the Victor Graysons and their kind – everyone who sent her brother and his friends to France.

It comes to her that it's not true what Hardit said to Victor this morning. She does believe in something besides pleasure, and she can name it now. She believes in vengeance.

3

In truth, if she were being honest, Babs's war had started off in a jolly fashion. The 4th of August 1914 had been her seventeenth birthday. Do you remember being seventeen? The exultant early summer of life when promise collides with possibility; the age when change, upheaval, revolution is something to be embraced with wild ferocity. The gleeful age when those twin pirates Desire and Imagination take control of your emotions, seize the cargo of your soul. Seventeen is the age when, without your realising it, you are seeking mistakes, the more catastrophic the better. And war, well, war depends on a craving by the eager innocent for calamitous experience. If the children can't be persuaded war is fun as well as glorious, well, it just wouldn't happen.

Babs – although she was still Barbara then – knew instinctively that this war would provide countless opportunities for monumental mishaps and extreme scrapes. Would give her the biggest holes for her to fall into and then have to dig herself out of. There were those spoilsports who said it was all going to be over by Christmas, but Babs hadn't believed that bullshit for a minute.

Within a week she had joined the Voluntary Aid Detachment, and a little while later was in a big house in Hertfordshire learning the basics of nursing. The inestimable value of hot water and soap.

But that wasn't all she learned.

Her fellow volunteers were mostly of a similar background to her, middle class or above, but more worldly-wise. They were funny and sharp and Christ they could drink. Her own parents had been disapproving of alcohol, whereas some of these girls came from homes where drinking was seen as an essential accomplishment of a well-brought-up young lady. This was doubly true of those who had been to boarding schools, which was a surprising number.

Taught at home by a series of sighing governesses, Babs had never known the camaraderie of school. And it was during her VAD training that she realised how poor her education had been. Yes, she'd learned the piano, yes, she'd learned some French, yes, she'd read some classic literature – those Brontë girls, that Austen lass – and yes, her parents had seen to it that she knew all about Karl Marx, and yes, they had been among the first to get a subscription to the *New Statesman*, and yes, of course, they had taken her to hear the likes of Victor Grayson speak – but oh, there are so many things you can only learn from the company of a bunch of wise-cracking mates.

The thrill of learning how to smoke for example. How to ride a bicycle. How to kiss properly. The French way, with tongues and everything.

Because, yes, these girls, her new friends, seemed so casually knowledgeable about sex. None of them owned up to having actually done it, but several had felt a penis stiffen against them at a ball. One or two had even seen one. Claimed to, at any rate. Not that they called them penises. They demystified these appendages by giving them names. Cheerful working-class names as a rule too. Dicks or Mickeys. Johnsons or Jocks. One girl (a particularly well-educated sort, a girl who had been destined for Oxford) had departed from the norm by calling them muttoniums. From the Latin apparently. It was all very intriguing and had intensified Babs's natural desire to see and feel one for herself.

It was all the greatest fun, and then she was in London on an actual hospital ward with the casualties coming in, and she was suddenly seeing way too many penises and in ways that weren't fun at all.

Looking back, it was probably while she was bathing the ruined private parts of weeping soldiers, that flayed flesh where cock or balls (pebbles! plums! whirligigs!) should have been, that she first decided she was going to bring as much sexual pleasure into the world as she could. That it was in those first weeks on the wards, surrounded by the damaged and destroyed, some of them weeks or days away from death, others facing a lifetime groping in impotent darkness, that she would serve no god but Pleasure.

4

Now the liverish yellow fog waits for Babs and Maurice out-side the ramshackle glitter of the Queen's Cinema, where they sit eating ice cream from a cardboard tub, listening to an almost-in-tune piano and half-heartedly watching the newsreels. Four killed in Dublin. Mysterious deaths of children in New York. Aeroplanes crashing. Ships sinking. People starving. People dying of everyday diseases that we should surely have cured by now. It's all so bloody grim. The only really interesting story concerns a strike by blind workers in London.

There's fog in here too, of course. Blue-grey this time rather than yellow, the result of all the cigarettes the people here suck on. Cinema and fags. Two cheap consolations of modern life.

'Fleapits like this are on the way out,' her brother whispers.

'Is that so?'

'Palmers Green is going to get its own new *palais de kino*. The Palmadium.'

'The Palmadium?'

'That's right. A super-cinema. A veritable picture palace. Two thousand seats. Restaurants, bars. Will be like a luxury cruise ship on Green Lanes. String quartets in the foyer, com-missionaires in the crapper to hand you your towel. Will you bloody well quit that?'

Maurice has twisted around in his seat to confront an urchin in the row behind, one of a group of such kids gig-gling and munching and, in the case of this particular child, kicking the seats in front of them. The urchin, his face an indistinct blob under a discharge of dirty-yellow hair, stares back blandly and then, with an insolent little smirk, kicks the seat again.

'Right,' says Maurice.

'Leave it,' says Babs. 'He's just a kid.'

'No, sis. Tyranny must never be allowed to go unpunished. We're gallant little Belgium, and this sod is a miniature kaiser,' and with that he removes his mask, leans over the back of his chair, right into the urchin's space, all the while contorting his own ruined features into a gargoyle rictus. He snarls in a theatrically blood-chilling manner. From deep inside Maurice pulls out a sound somewhere between the crump of a shell and the squawk of a tortured goose. Some of the kids around them shriek, some are genuinely terrified, others simply delighted at all the additional entertainment being laid on in front of them.

The child in question is ostentatiously unbothered.

'I'm not scared. My dad's face is worse than yours. Can shout louder too.'

Maurice is interested now. 'Really?'

'And he's only got one leg.' The kid's voice is full of pride.

'And is he here?'

'He's picking us up at the end of the main film.'

'And what will he say about your annoying other audience members?'

'He won't care. He lets us do what we want. He says' – the kid screws up his face, trying to get the impression of his dad just right. He sits up, his shoulders back, his whole demeanour suddenly more adult and when he speaks again his voice has a preacherly depth. He's a decent actor – 'Do what thou wilt shall be the whole of the law.' He drops back into his natural speech. 'He says that means the world has been stolen from us, so we should do whatever we want, whenever we can.'

'Sounds like an interesting chap, your dad.'

'And what about your mother?' says Babs.

'Ain't got no mother.'

'She died.' This is the girl next to the boy. 'Day Daddy came out of hospital she was hit by a tram.' The child is matter-of-fact.

'Main film's about to start,' says the boy.

'Just quit kicking my chair,' says Maurice.

'What's it worth?' says the boy.

'Bloody hell, kid's incorrigible,' says Maurice, but there's a grin in his voice. 'Here, I'll give you a penny.'

As he rummages for the coin, Babs says, 'What was all that about tyranny not being allowed to go unpunished? You've just taught the miniature kaiser how protection rackets work.'

'A useful life skill. Besides, I like him. Has something about him.'

'For Chrissake give it a rest!' A shout from somewhere in the dark, plainly aimed at them.

'So many joyless arseholes in the world,' says Maurice. He says it quietly, as if to himself, but the boy must have heard because he chuckles and repeats Maurice's words. 'Joyless arseholes.' It's a phrase he clearly likes the sound of.

*

The film is called *Helen of Four Gates*. It stars Alma Taylor and tells a story of madness, cruelty and endemic domestic violence in poverty-stricken rural West Yorkshire. It is rather beautifully shot, the scenery is stunning and the intertitles are written in a version of Yorkshire dialect, something which Babs has never seen at the flicks before and which she finds sort of charming. *Yah're a nowt and yah muss mend o'yer ill ways.* The ending is hopeful too, with a young woman making a life for herself away from those who would hold her back. The film reminds Babs of Victor Grayson. So these were his people, she thinks, the ones he came to London to represent and ended up enticing into the murderous latrine of the Western Front.

It's a restful way to spend an hour and when, as the lights come back up, Maurice asks her what she thought, she doesn't really know what to say.

'I liked it,' she says, finally. 'Could have done with some jokes. And I still think the theatre is better. It's plain weird not hearing people talk, and the music to films is always annoying. That plinky-plonk piano. What did you think?'

'I thought… I thought it looked superb, but the story was a bit melodramatic, all that waving of arms. Felt old-fashioned too. The scenes were quite long. Of course, whisper it, but the best films now are European. The very best of all are German.' He raises his voice:

'Hear that everyone? *Die besten Filme sind deutsche Filme!*'

The extra effort involved in raising his voice, of fashioning ruined vocal cords around the German language, means he descends into a series of rasping coughs. Maybe he should have taken his own advice and whispered it.

Babs laughs, is half-afraid her brother's bold statement will cause a ruckus, but the people of London in 1920 are very used to damaged young men saying odd things at inappropriate volume and, just as they no longer point at missing limbs, they don't question strange remarks, even ones made in German.

Now Maurice fixes his eye on the urchin in the row behind. 'What did you think, young man?'

The urchin just stares for a while. Now that the lights are fully up Babs can see he has a pretty face – delicate features, honeyed skin, long eyelashes, light dusting of freckles over his nose. In the end the kid shrugs. 'I thought the lady was hot. Nice gams.'

Maurice laughs. 'I agree,' he says.

Babs frowns and says, 'How old are you?'

'Twelve.' Just one word, but he packs a lot of expression into it. The boy's voice is very London, very I-know-what-you-are-going-to-say-and-it's-not-worth-saying. His voice is old, is what it is. Much older than his face.

'Twelve!' she yelps, and sees by the way his eyes flicker that, yes, that was exactly the reaction he was expecting. What he was hoping for, anyway.

Next to her, Maurice chuckles. 'Oh come on, sis. I know you were thinking about all sorts of naughtiness when you were twelve.'

'I don't think so.'

'You were, I read the diaries.'

'You read my diaries!'

'Of course I read your diaries. As your brother it was my duty. And I must say some of your pashes were most eccentric. The milkman's boy? I mean, come on.'

Babs makes a decision not to be embarrassed. 'Alfie Carter was a good-looking young chap. Lovely hair. Cheeky smile. Good whistler.'

'Yes, and dead now. The Dardanelles.'

'Really? That's sad.'

'Sad,' repeats Maurice, and he laughs, the sound vinegary and thin.

The kid, unsurprisingly, has quickly grown bored of all this incomprehensible ancient history and taken his grubbily angelic face away, dragging his sister with him by her skinny arm.

Babs and Maurice catch up with them in the foyer and see him greeting his father and it's not true that the father's face is worse than Maurice's. At least he has a definite good side along with an equally emphatic bad side. Looking at him straight on, you can see that the left of his face is plumply healthy. The other side, well, not so much. In fact, in the same way that Maurice's face resembles the crater left in the earth after the shell that did for him exploded, so the right side of the urchin's father is like an aerial photo of the trench systems of the Western Front. It's criss-crossed by vivid lines where mutilated skin has been stretched, patched together and stitched. Like a particularly detailed Ordnance Survey map. His right eye is missing, and the empty socket is a dark foxhole. The ear is gone, replaced by a blancmangy mass of flesh. A lopsided standing stone of jellied cartilage. His head is shaven and, while the left side is as shiny and smooth as a worn linoleum floor, the right side is a no man's land of lumps, bumps and dents joined together by animal tracks of scars.

He has, as the urchin had promised, just the one leg. One and a half, really, if you wanted to be generous. His left leg is missing below the knee. He supports himself on battered wooden crutches. Babs notes the neat sewing of the hem of the shortened trouser leg which clothes the missing limb. A man with at least one steadfast and helpful woman in his life, she thinks. A mother? A sister?

Maurice introduces himself with breezy good humour. 'I win I think, old boy.'

He's always been like this. It is one of Maurice's great skills, that he can speak to people he's just met as if they have been friends for years.

The urchin's father, who has introduced himself as one Robert Clark, knows immediately what Maurice is referring to.

'I'm not sure about that, mate. I think it's probably a score draw. Where did you get yours?'

'Ginchy. Rum Jar from a Flying Pig. Nipped out for a wazz at the wrong moment.'

'A what from a what?' The urchin is interested now. His eyes gleam.

'Particularly fiendish German bomb, and the mortar that fires it. Looks like a giant pig.'

'Oh.' The urchin looks oddly disappointed.

'Got mine thanks to an ill-advised picnic in Argonne Forest,' says Clark, 'and it wasn't even the Huns. Doughboy patrols getting twitchy every time a twig snapped.'

There's a moment of smiling quiet, a shared remembrance of the gung-ho jumpiness of their American allies when they first arrived in the trenches. How their arrival scared the

Boche all right, but also unnerved those who had to serve alongside them.

'You get tidied up at Sidcup?'

'Yeah, good old Harry Gillies.'

Babs knows all about Harry Gillies. His practice is where all the family money went. It's why they live in a terrace in Palmers Green rather than their grand old detached place in Hampstead. He's the star of the reconstructive surgery business. And yes, yes, yes, a genius obviously, a saint obviously, but even geniuses have to live. Even saints need nice houses, with gardens and servants.

'I say,' Maurice says, 'I don't suppose you'd like a toot later would you?'

'A drink? With you and your wife?'

'Oh, this young harlot isn't my wife. She's my sister.'

'What's a harlot?' the two kids say in unison. Which makes the grown-ups laugh.

'A harlot is a girl who's no better than she ought to be,' says their father.

'No one is better than they ought to be,' says the girl, clearly puzzled.

'A harlot is a nasty name for a woman who reminds men of what they're most scared of,' says Babs.

'What's that then?' says Robert Clark. His good eye twinkles, the good side of his mouth curves mischievously.

'You know what it is. It's themselves. Or rather, it's their own desires.'

'I'm not scared of anything,' says the boy.

'My sister's a feminist I'm afraid,' says Maurice.

His flippant tone annoys her, makes her say more than she should.

'More than that, I'm Babalon.'

'Who?'

'Come on, you know your Crowley. Babalon. The Scarlet Woman, the lover of the Beast, I sit astride him arrayed in jewels and holding a golden cup in which I keep a record of all the filthiness of my fornications. Using sex to bring about the end of the world. At least that's what I'm working up to.'

The good side of Clark's face blushes.

Next to her, Maurice laughs. 'Who's this Crowley then?'

'He's the guy that said "Do what thou wilt shall be the whole of the law." You know, it's the line Mr Clark here taught his son. It's from Crowley's *The Book of the Law*. I thought he'd know that.'

'I'm sorry,' says Clark.

'A feminist and an intellectual,' says Maurice to Clark apologetically. To his sister he says, 'You should have gone to university instead of me, Babs.'

'I know,' says Babs.

'Can I be a femnist?' says the urchin's sister.

'Kids, eh,' says Robert Clark. 'Hear everything. Take it all in. They'd make great spies, don't you think?'

Babs squats so that she is eye level with the girl. 'I think you're already a feminist,' she says. She bites out all the syllables. *Fem.In.Ist.*

'Am I?' the girl says.

'Course you are. You don't let yourself get bossed around by your dad and your brother, do you? You stick up for yourself.'

97

'I try to. Sometimes.'

'Well, then. You're an apprentice feminist at the very least.'

'I'm afraid you've got trouble now,' says Maurice to Robert.

'I don't mind. Kids of the working class have to learn to speak up, whichever sex they are. April here knows she can be whatever she wants to be.'

'Is Alma Taylor a *fem.in.ist*?' says the girl.

'I don't know, I hope so,' says Babs. 'Why?'

'Because I think I want to be her.'

'Alma Taylor is a harlot,' says the urchin firmly.

The two men spend some time deciding on which pub to meet at in the evening. There's some chat about how together they might frighten the customers, so the venue needs choosing with care.

'Of course, I have got my special face.'

Maurice produces the metallic visage of Erich von Stroheim from his knapsack, passes it to Clark who turns it over in his hands.

'Nice.'

'Obviously, I really wanted one in the form of Mary Pickford, but they wouldn't do that for me.'

Clark laughs.

Good God, thinks Babs, they're flirting. They're arranging a date.

'Let me see.' The urchin snatches it from his father's hands, holds it against his face. This mask has never looked so monstrous, thinks Babs. On Maurice it's OK, almost amusing, but on the urchin it's chilling. The aggressive flesh-toned paint, the tragic way the makers have tried to suggest a contoured cheekbone. This twelve-year-old will be an adult in time for the next war. Could be fully grown just in time to have his pretty, perky face blown off and to be measured for a mask of his own. If he's lucky. Babs feels like crying.

'Maybe leave it behind tonight,' says Maurice. 'We should wear our real faces with pride.'

'Like medals.'

'Like medals, exactly.'

5

As they make their way home to Conway Road, Babs ignores the constant giddy jibber-jabber from her brother. He's in a semi-hysterical mood, breaking out into choruses of the most ribald trench songs, saying hello to the majority of the passers-by, shaking the hands of bewildered policemen, thanking them for their service.

These days Maurice is only ever quiet amid the flicker and shadow of the cinema, it's the one place he takes a break. Maybe it's a response to the trauma he experienced in the war – not just being blown up, but things like the time he saw a tank drive over three wounded Huns manning a machine gun nest. Things like that. Maybe it's a fragment of washer left lodged in his brain somewhere, a rusty Teutonic nail buried deep in his hippocampus. Babs doesn't bother trying to understand any more, and she's grown used to blocking out his noise when she needs to. Maurice himself says it's his natural personality and so he shouldn't have to repress it.

*

As they skirt the many kinds of shit, as they flap away the obese late-summer flies, as they pass again those pubs, those grocers, those chop-houses, those cafés, those ABCs, those Corner Houses, those bakeries and those confectioners – all the many varied places where you can purchase momentary and artificial comfort, all of them perpetually busy because of the lack of real sweetness in the lives of the people – Babs muses about how irrelevant it is to think things. How useless it is to read things and discuss things. None of that matters. Doing things, that's the way. Doing things is the only way. Action not talk. Immediate action, all the time. Getting things done.

SIX

Every Eden Is Temporary

HARLEY STREET, AFTERNOON

1

THROUGHOUT his life Victor Grayson has been lucky enough to be befriended by a number of mature women. They seem to respond particularly well to his special mix of good looks and cynical vulnerability. Sometimes these ladies are interested in the giving and receiving of physical comfort, but often they simply want to be a mother to someone they see as a lost boy. Even at thirty-nine, Victor can seem impish, in need of a firm hand, a sympathetic ear and a soft bosom. Dr Ethel Vaughan-Sawyer has all these attributes and is good at deploying whichever seems most necessary at the appropriate time.

As one of the few female doctors with her own practice, her specialism is women's conditions: everything gynaecological obviously – including hysteria – but also neurosis and mental exhaustion. Fury too. Everyone is talking about the epidemic of fury among women. Sometimes repressed, sometimes not. Whatever the cause, desperate husbands, concerned fathers, they'd like it treated. Fury stalks this post-war land and generally it wears a dress.

Dr Vaughan-Sawyer is an actual surgeon by training, still works at the Royal Free Hospital, though less than she used to (her eyesight is not as good as it was), but she is also much influenced by the theories and practices of Dr Freud. She often finds talking cures are better than surgery, especially for her more bourgeois patients. They certainly provide her with a decent living. Which is good, because since her husband's death early in the war she's had to rely on earning her own money in order to keep herself and her daughter.

Dr Vaughan-Sawyer offers women the opportunity to be heard, which is always popular. A good therapist is harder to find than you think, but she is one of the best. Virginia Woolf is a client. So is Millicent Fawcett. So is Roberta Lloyd George.

Her apartment, which also contains her surgery, is well appointed. There are thick Afghan rugs on the floor, soothing prints on the wall – portraits of ladies reading or sorrowful Pre-Raphaelite maidens dying beautifully in wooded glades. There is bespoke furniture with the clean lines and lurid coverings that the well-off favour these days. Good quality work, though. Nothing faddy, nothing just knocked up or bought off the peg at Heal's. There are large windows, so the place is filled with light during the day, and as darkness falls with the expensively subdued glow from perfectly placed lamps. Her Danish maid, the unobtrusive and expressionless Kristiana, keeps the place immaculate. The flat is scented with Fiddes Supreme Wax Polish and feminine empathy.

Dr Vaughan-Sawyer also employs a regular team of dress-makers, beauticians, hairdressers and personal fitness technicians to ensure that her body and face rival the subtly luxurious presentation of her flat. She is fifty-two this year, but you wouldn't know it. She could be any age. She has the skin and hair of a younger woman, but the wise eyes of a much older one. She also has the curiosity and sexual appetite of a student. She's political too. Subscribes to all the important progressive European journals. Was arrested twice on marches for women's suffrage. No wonder that she and Victor were drawn to each other.

When he visits Ethel Vaughan-Sawyer, Victor is occasionally invited to experience the solace of her large bed, but what Victor looks forward to most is what he considers to be his friend's most efficacious medicine, regular glasses of Martinez. This cocktail – equal parts gin and sweet vermouth, plus maraschino liqueur and bitters – is the original – the ur-cocktail that led to the much inferior American dry Martini.

Not all evolution is progress.

Grayson considers Dr Vaughan-Sawyer's skill in making a Martinez another example of her good taste and discernment. Sometimes, if there has been a run of especially irksome patients, the tired doctor will eschew the effort of making the Martinez and will get Petronella to mix it, or she'll even begin her evening with a glass or two of absinthe, what she calls 'surrendering to the embrace of the Green Fairy'. Victor has learned to make sure his visits are short if the Green Fairy is in the house. Things can get just too strange.

As today is a Saturday there's a chance that Dr Vaughan-Sawyer will be out, enjoying what London has to offer an independent woman of means – the shops, the cafés, the theatres – but no, she's at home and it is very much a relaxed Martinez day. She is pleased to see him, purrs in that subtly perfumed way she has as she mixes the drinks. Tells him that she'd been hoping he'd call round. That there is a package for him actually, left by one of her more political clients. This happens sometimes: requests for interviews, fan mail, enquiries about speaking engagements. Ethel Vaughan-Sawyer acted as a kind of unpaid unofficial agent when he first fell from grace with his comrades, and still fulfils this role occasionally.

The package is intriguing, heavy too.

'It's a two-parcel day!' says Victor, theatrically, deliberately emphasising his accent for comic effect (always makes posh Londoners laugh). 'I knew summat good were round corner.'

'Don't open it here,' says Ethel. 'Someone's gone to real trouble to make sure it's properly secure. Really belt-and-braced it.' And it's true, this is an exceptionally well-wrapped parcel, about twelve inches square with a lot of adhesive tape used, in addition to all the string and brown paper.

'Who brought it?'

'Chap I've not seen before. Petronella let him in, I probably wouldn't have done. A bit of a dandy. Those new wide, straight-legged trousers. Fancy jacket, self-important air. A lot of big political talk in a loud voice. And I caught him trying to chat my clients. I got rid of him as soon as I could.'

'Still, a parcel. That's always exciting.'

'Is it though?' And what does Ethel Vaughan-Sawyer, headshrinker to traumatised women, mean by this? Is she remembering the day her husband's blood-soaked uniform came back to her? Rusty brown stains everywhere. Even on his socks. No, like millions of women who lived through the war while their husbands and sons didn't, Ethel Vaughan-Sawyer no longer thinks that the arrival of a parcel is unadulterated good news.

If Victor were to review how his day has progressed so far, he might consider it to be a satisfactory one. Any day that begins with sexual congress is unlikely to be a complete waste, and while, yes, he received the news that his services were no longer required by the government, he has chosen to decide that rejection is simply motivation to change his life. A liberation as much as it is a problem. Plus, since he got that brutal note in green ink, he has written a lot and hardly drunk anything. He thoroughly warrants this Martinez. He twirls his cocktail, delighting in the way the light through the big windows causes the deep red of the drink to glow and spark. A welcoming fire in the hearth of the glass.

It will take an hour or so – three drinks anyway – for the mood to sour.

Today is not one of the days where they tumble into bed. Petronella's here, but even if she wasn't, it is clear that the mood for today's visit is friendly but businesslike, uncharged by desire.

He's meant to be getting on with the bloody memoir, moving forward with it while Dr Vaughan-Sawyer reads what he's done so far, but he can't concentrate. He finds he is keeping too beady an eye on his friend's smooth, well-tended face.

He wonders what she thinks of that Victory Party scene?

Victor making his first speech as MP from the back of a flatbed truck in front of the Dartmouth Arms. His voice attractively hoarse from campaigning, but his words punchy, finding their mark.

'This is a victory for pure revolutionary socialism... I have been returned through the work, the devotion, the love, the idealism of the people of the Colne Valley, and being returned I feel my duty is to be the old men and women's MP, the starving child's MP...' Victor Grayson's arms stretched wide, as if to embrace the entire constituency. 'You have voted, you have worked for socialism. You have worked for the means of life to be the property of all classes. We stand for equality, human equality, sexual equality...'

The valley exulting. Dancing and singing on the cobbles. Proper cavorting. Impromptu parties, pubs full and the hum of revolutionary talk so loud that there were policemen on the streets to protect the houses of nervous mill owners. Policemen who were seen shaking hands with – drinking with – exuberant workers. Some of those police had been sent up from London and even they caught the joyous mood, waltzing with mill girls, carousing with fustian-makers, roistering with weavers.

There were babies conceived that night, some by new lovers and some by long-standing couples who hadn't felt amorously inclined towards each other since the end of the war against the Boers. Nine months on in West Yorkshire there was a definite spike in the number of baby boys registered with the name Victor, and quite a few Victorias from parents that were emphatically not royalists, that had demonstrated no love for the last queen until then.

Has he managed to capture the sheer bloody joy of that day? The way the people did what Shelley had asked of them in that poem, the one he'd quoted so many times during the campaign. The Yorkshire people had risen like lions from slumber and they had bloody roared!

Could Ethel feel it? Did he take her there? Could she see it? Could she climb aboard, use his words as a magic carpet to cross space and time back to the Colne Valley of 1910? Maybe she just considers it so much sentimental tosh. He takes a swallow of Martinez, feels the sweet thick burn of it as it travels down his gullet.

A writer should never really be in the same room as someone reading their work. In the presence of an active reader of his latest draft, the writer becomes too much the body language expert. Every flicker of an eyelid, every scratch, every restless movement in the reader's chair, every cough or sigh is monitored, forensically analysed for what it might mean, and the worst interpretation placed on the evidence. Every few moments the reader will be interrupted by the writer asking where they've got up to. It's a strain no relationship should be subjected to.

Unfortunately for Victor his friend the doctor seems to be grimacing, frowning and blinking rather a lot, and he regards this as damning. She must hate it! She protests that no, no, no, she doesn't hate it. She can see it's good. But Victor, impetuous fool that he is, has to press her. Come on, be honest, he says. Just admit that you don't like it.

He is so persistent that eventually she cracks. She makes the friendship-ruining mistake of giving her true opinion of a writer's work.

She is carefully circumspect at first, but he knows the final verdict will be difficult to hear because she drains her Martinez before she begins and pours herself another drink. This one a neat absinthe.

'I don't hate it, Victor. I really don't. I like it.'

'But?'

'But I just wonder if—' She stops, she's treading on thin ice and she knows it. Dare she go further?

'You wonder if what?'

'I just wonder if people will, you know, actually care?'

His face is a picture, and not a restful one. The way his eyes bulge, the way his mouth twists. It is melodramatically, comically, horrifying. Much more a Munch than a Millais. She almost laughs.

'No, I don't mean that exactly. Of course they will care, your early life, your election, it's all interesting and all very well written, but I just wonder if the casual reader – not a committed socialist but an ordinary citizen – will want to know more about the humanity of the narrator.'

'How much more? What kind of humanity exactly?'

His voice is detached, he is performing disinterest, but he's just not that adept at such dissembling. Few writers are. Who can really feign indifference to how their work is received?

'Well, your romantic life for one thing. Your courtship of Ruth, your marriage, how you coped with her death. What it's like being a solo parent to a motherless child.' She stops, takes a breath. 'And, perhaps even more than this, your affair with Harry. You don't have to be explicit. A hint will be enough.'

Victor Grayson stands, so suddenly that he is dizzy. He sways. Strange shapes pirouette across his vision. He reaches for his hat and coat. His face has reddened, his fists are clenched, he actually snarls. Like a dog. This visual, audible, theatrical fury is shocking. Once again, Dr Vaughan-Sawyer has the urge to laugh. But, you know, men; so touchy, so sensitive to mockery. They are also at their most dangerous when they feel ridiculed. A sensible woman goes carefully in the presence of a man who feels he has been belittled. She kills her laugh, shakes her head.

'Oh, Victor, come on. We're not going to fall out about this are we?'

'No, it's fine.' The flash of red fury is over, but his voice is so stiff, so cold, that this time she does laugh. She can't help it. As predicted, it does not help.

'I'll see you soon, Ethel.'

'Oh, Victor. Finish your drink at least.'

'No, I don't think so. Places to go, people to see.'

'You're a caution, you are. I'm just trying to help you sell books. These days readers expect honesty, authenticity. They don't simply want your opinions; they want your life. They want to hold your heart in their hands.'

'If you say so.'

An awkward hug and he is out in the smoggy streets, quietly seething. What does Ethel Vaughan-Sawyer know about writing? What gives her the right to criticise? The anger is a physical pain. Readers, who cares about them? Why should they get his heart? Why should he dissect himself for them? Vampires is what they are. Bloodsuckers. Tears form. Actual tears.

And he's only gone and forgotten the bloody parcel! Well, he's not going back up there. Humiliating to return to her apartment moments after leaving it. Especially if it looks like he's been crying. He'll fetch it another day, or he'll make her send it on to him. She's had it a while so a bit longer won't hurt. Probably won't be important anyway.

In an hour or two he will simmer down and it will occur to him that criticising is exactly what he asked Ethel to do, but until then his eyes will itch, his guts will flare and flame.

Most writers go through several phases when dealing with editors and critics. In many ways they replicate the well-known stages of grief. They begin with Anger and Denial, move through Bargaining and end with Acceptance. Sometimes Acceptance goes too far and the writer takes the critique on board wholesale and damages his own work as a result. Somewhere between thinking *this critic is an absolute ignoramus, an utter Philistine* and *this critic is an insightful genius and actually quite kind considering* there is a sweet spot where an outside evaluation can be given its correct weight. Knowing where that sweet spot is, well that's a conundrum. Getting the response to expert outside analysis right is largely a matter of being in the right frame of mind. Making sure you've had a good breakfast before receiving it always helps.

But Harry Dawson? Really?

And Ethel? What of her feelings? Well, as a good, empathetic therapist she feels sorry that she's bruised her old friend's ego, but she's been honest and that's important for the long-term health of a friendship. And, also, she's still got this sodding parcel. Well, she's damned if she's going to act as a post office for her touchy friend. She looks in the top drawer of her writing desk – Ethel Vaughan-Sawyer always knows where everything is, no sweary hunting for forgotten bits of paper for her – finds the card of the man who brought the package round, picks up her telephone. If he wants it given to Victor, he can jolly well do it himself.

2

Harry Dawson. Harry effing Dawson. Back in the insipid Marylebone air, Victor is free to think about beautiful, hopeless Harry Dawson. He may not be in the memoirs, but he is often in his thoughts. Too often really.

An extraordinary thing about human beings is how they can, if the moment is right, if the stars align, reach an understanding in an instant. Sometimes people can bond before they're introduced, before they even meet. So it was with Victor and Harry.

You have to imagine Victor on a platform talking about –
well, who knows, who cares? The likelihood of revolution in
Russia. The oppression of native peoples in the colonies. The
price of cod. Really, could have been anything – and he was
not yet the gifted orator he would become. He stumbled, found
himself scrabbling for words, and he couldn't quite pitch his
voice right. Sometimes he sounded panicky, squeaky, an animal
whimpering in a trap, his throat squeezed and tight. At other
times his voice dropped into an almost-basso profundo, and
a Scouse one at that. It was like being an adolescent again, the
time when you can't trust your body and your voice least of all.

At this point in his speaking career, Victor still needed the
help of a scrap of paper with scribbled prompts to which his
eyes would flicker nervously. Hard to connect with people
when you need notes. No surprise then that his audience was
sparse, restless, more interested in discussing the price of fish
than listening to the skinny youth trying to rouse them to
overthrow capitalism.

He was on the point of giving up, of rushing to the end of
his speech, chalking this defeat up to experience and vowing
to do better next time, when he locked eyes with a tall fellow
around his own age, possibly two or three years younger. It
was like a thump to the chest. Victor actually stopped speaking for a moment, had to swallow hard. Had to lick his lips.
God, the kid was beautiful. Sad eyes, rhyming with a wide
mouth. His thin moustache a tattered bridal veil. Skin like
newly fallen snow and, my God, the smile. Sudden sunshine
through clouds. A rainbow. A song only Victor can hear. A
whole opera in his head.

There was a moment where Victor felt like a man on a high wire above rocks. He could fall now and everything would be over.

But he didn't fall. Instead, he found himself. Came back to himself. Suddenly he was turning somersaults on that string above the chasm. He was making his audience laugh, making them murmur with approval, making them sigh, bringing them nicely to the boil. He had them.

He didn't look again at the tall fellow, but he could feel the hunger of his gaze upon him. He was performing just for him now, exciting the crowd just for him, had created this whole magic trick just for him. The crowd that moments ago were indifferent, borderline hostile, were now committed socialists and supporters of Victor personally. He had turned the dirty water of vague interest into the strong wine of activism and offered it up for some nameless youth in the crowd.

He looked for the boy – his muse! – during the prolonged applause, but couldn't see him and again felt that blow to the heart. Maybe he hadn't been watching Victor after all, maybe he'd lost interest, wandered off. Maybe the trick had been in vain.

But no, there he was, giving a sad little wave as Victor descended from the back of the cart from which he'd been speaking. They exchanged a handshake, a few words, a cup of tea with the organisers of the talk, a vegetarian meal. Victor seems to remember the organisers were Quakers. Very worthy, nodded a lot.

*

113

And then they were alone in Harry's room, straining against each other on sweaty sheets. Writhing wordlessly on top of rough blankets. Victor had known sex before – of course he had – but not like this. Not with this desperation, this hard heat.

Harry was thin but tough, broad-shouldered, muscular from work in the dyeing factory. He spent every day hauling bolts of heavy cloth from warehouse to dyeing room and back again. It was work that made you strong. For a while. Before it began to kill you.

At the end of that first hour, they vowed to be together always.

Always, it turned out, was out of reach, impossible, but Quite Often, well, that was easier to get to, that was very possible.

Every new couple believes they have reinvented sexual intercourse, redesigned it, made the oldest rituals new again. Harry and Victor felt they were bending love into fantastic new shapes, doing things few others had done. Had anyone been as creative as they? Hard to imagine it. Their meagre rooms were transformed by their movements. Their writhing exudations. Their glorious noise.

Their love was pure, which meant their sex could be beautifully filthy.

No need for shame.

For Victor, the joy of physical love between men was another thing the elites had tried to keep to themselves: 'Throughout history, from the days of Greece and Rome onwards, rich and powerful men have loved each other like this,' he said. 'It's only poor men who are meant to keep their hands off one another.'

In the intervals where they did manage to keep their mitts away from each other, Victor talked and Harry listened, nodded, agreed. He was always a receptive audience, the first to get an inkling of what Victor might say to galvanise his audience. Quite often too, Harry was there in that audience. Part of it, applauding, stamping his feet, all the time dreaming of the moment when he could get Victor out of his clothes and get him into bed or onto the floor of a room somewhere. Sometimes, very daring, they found a dark corner in the streets, to grope and rummage, to bite and suck. The risk of discovery heightened the pleasure. Victor in particular was fond of a shadowed alleyway. A park, a graveyard.

Every Eden is temporary. Always lent, never given outright. Adam and Eve got notice to quit and so does everyone else, in the end. Victor and Harry's idyll began to turn cold in September 1904 with Victor's move to Manchester to study. Harry caught as many of Victor's speaking engagements as he could, but his lover was stretching himself thin, moving from one overflowing meeting to another, keeping himself going with coffee and whisky. Often he collapsed exhausted onto the couches of supporters and, once there, Harry feared, he might do more than simply sleep.

When he suggested this, Victor laughed and said, what did it matter? They were free. Not for them the chains of the hearth and children. They were revolutionists not bound by the petty morals other people live by.

Harry did not find this reassuring.

When he couldn't see Victor, Harry sent letters. Anguished, passionate letters, lines written in a fever. Letters that worried that Victor's new life would take him away, that Harry would be forgotten. He reminded Victor that they had sworn to face the world together always.

Victor's letters in reply were cheerily placatory. *Don't fret. I still love you*, they said. They contained descriptions of what he liked about Harry's body (everything), what he wanted to do with Harry next time they met (everything).

Inevitably, however, they met less, talked less, fucked less. After a while it was clear Victor had become too much the star. Too visible. Too in demand to be tied down to one lover. A short time after that Victor was an actual MP! Unbelievable. Little chance to meet at all then.

All of this young Harry Dawson said he could understand. He swore that he could take it. He would live on what crumbs he could get. He was proud of the work Victor was doing, after all, knew how necessary it was. He just didn't want to be completely forgotten.

Don't worry, wrote Victor. *When we next meet we'll burn a Player's Weights to old Therapina the wizened goddess of reconciliation and lick one another's epidermis on the first convenient occasion. To blazes with miawling and grump. I love you as ever, with the same devouring passion and intensity and thickness. It is the droop of your moustache that takes me... Your handwriting that always pulls the stopper out of my heart.*

And then Victor found himself committing a betrayal his lover couldn't take. He fell in love with Ruth Nightingale.

Married Ruth Nightingale. Had a child with Ruth Nightingale and stopped replying to the increasingly distressed letters of Harry Dawson. Eventually, eventually, Harry got the message: the droop of his moustache was no longer doing its thing, no longer taking Victor anywhere. No matter how hard the handwriting pulled, the stopper stayed fixed in his heart.

3

Victor finds he has a headache that only whisky will soothe. He seeks sanctuary in the Prince Regent on Marylebone High Street, a pub with a famously casual approach to the licensing laws and which is already busy with noisy workers – young clerks mostly, men in cheap suits with stiff hair and pallid faces, who make up for the enforced orderliness of their weekdays with rowdy weekends. Their shoulders are always tight, and their fists are always clenched.

Established in a corner towards the back of the place, he can reflect on his last and most painful meeting with Harry Dawson. The one that took place two years ago, when Victor's share price had seemed to be on the rise again and requests from socialist societies to speak had been coming often enough to make him think that the good times might be returning. The Big Days might be on their way back. He'd lost a lot of his radical friends forever, but with the war almost over, he could imagine sitting with the mainstream Labour men, keeping them honest while his war service neutralised accusations of anti-Britishness.

Yes, two years ago in a gloomy corner of a pub very like this one. A conversation that began awkwardly and deteriorated from there.

'Why are you doing this, Harry?'

'Surely that's obvious?'

'If you needed money, I'd have given you money.'

'Would you, though, Victor? I don't even get a Christmas card off you, so why should I think I'd get any brass?'

'If I had money and if you'd approached me properly, I'd have given it to you, you know that.'

'I know no such thing.'

Harry had looked terrible. Ill. No muscle on him, his once beautiful hair less thick than it used to be and lustreless. His beard already speckled with grey. The untrimmed moustache inadequately hiding bitter lips and brownish teeth. He smelled slightly faecal too. The scent of the workhouse hovering around him. Poor wages, plus hard work, plus time, plus depression. A corrosive sum.

Harry Dawson was only thirty-three and already he looked defeated. If he hadn't been attempting a crass shakedown, Victor might have felt sorry for him. As it was he felt only an extreme kind of irritation. If they'd been out in the streets Victor might have taken hold of his former lover by the threadbare lapels of his jacket and slapped him.

'Anyway, Harry, mate. I have no money.'

'Victor, mate,' heavy sarcastic emphasis here, 'I'm not certain I believe you. But maybe you also know where to get some. Happen you have rich friends, some titled noblemen – or ladies – who can lend you some scratch if you're desperate. And I think you will be desperate to see these letters safe.'

Because that was why Harry had tracked him down. He wanted to return Victor's letters. For a price. And if Victor couldn't meet that price, well, he would have to offer them to other potential purchasers and that might be a shame because those buyers might not have Victor's best interests at heart. They might use these letters to shame and discredit Victor if he ever wanted to return to the bigger stages.

'And that's what you want, isn't it, Victor? Really, if you're honest. Another taste of power, another shot at sitting in Parliament. Another helping of that pie.'

'Well, I couldn't do a worse job than those who sit there now.'

'Happen. But you won't get near that shithouse if the world sees what you wrote to me.'

'No one will be interested, Harry. Not any more.'

'We'll see.'

A silence. An observer would say – did say, later, when reporting back – that it was Victor whose nerves seemed steadier. He was the calm soldier making rapid decisions under fire, while his one-time paramour and current black-mailer looked jittery, squirrelly, scared. This observer said that at that moment she had assumed that Grayson would send Dawson packing.

It hadn't gone that way.

Grayson had stood, had pulled his battered wallet from his pocket, had extracted a substantial number of notes, which he handed to Harry with no more than a curt nod. In return

Dawson handed over a large envelope. Grayson opened it, took out the bundle of letters – secured with a pink ribbon, as the observer recalled. He flicked through them, looked down at Dawson and nodded again.

Then he did an astonishing thing. He placed the envelope on the stool next to him, and, right there in that busy pub, he kissed Dawson hard on the mouth. The embrace lasted long enough for others in the pub to notice, for the thrum of conversation to quieten, and when the kiss was over Grayson held Dawson by both shoulders and said – calmly, quietly, reasonably – 'OK, lad, well done, you've got through it. It's over now. It'll be reyt.' A pause. A smile, then: 'Now then, off you jolly well fuck, you daft prick.'

It's not Victor's way to check the details of things. If it were he would have noticed that at least one letter, one of the most explicit, was missing. Was already sold to another party.

Here, now, in the Prince Regent on the 25th of September 1920, Victor Grayson takes a slow pull at his warm pint. It's sour, soapy. Hardly anyone knows how to keep beer these days, he thinks. Especially not in the South of England. Why is that? Why do Southerners know so little about what matters? Why do they not seem to care about their ignorance? Why do they refuse to be educated? And his next thought is, No, Ethel, thanks for the advice but no, Harry Dawson will not be a character in my memoir. He never earned the right. Besides, even a hint of the truth of things between Victor and Harry would be enough to terminate Victor's relationship with his publisher. And that's a relationship he just can't afford to fuck up.

Ruth, though, Ruth is different. She should be written about, should be honoured in that way, but is he up to it? That's the question.

SEVEN

Wet Bob

CHEQUERS, AFTERNOON

1

O NE of the frustrations Sir Basil Thomson has with the institution of government is how suspicious it is of new technology. How grudging it is, how late to appreciate any benefits it might bring. The telephone, for instance. He can remember how excited everyone had been when offices started installing them. Changed everything. Thoughts communicated instantly across hundreds of miles. Read something in your office in London, something that demands instant action in, say, Barlinnie, and you could get the relevant operative on the machine, discuss the question, issue your order and then, later, check it had been carried out.

We've been able to do this for nearly fifty years – there are telephones in ordinary private residences now – and yet how many are there in Chequers? One. One, as if the government's new mansion was simply some averagely pricey apartment in Sloane Square. There are more telephones in the average church than there are in Chequers.

That one phone is in the lobby too, the building's most public space, where there's always comings and goings, and usually a couple of bored coppers stationed within earshot. And when you try to access it for vital government business it is likely to be, as it is now, monopolised by some junior clerk billing and cooing with his moll back in the city.

Sir Basil taps Loverboy firmly on the shoulder with a stern forefinger. It is not a tap you can ignore, though the young advisor tries. Sir Basil speaks:

'OK, chap, hop off now. There's a good fellow.'

Loverboy swivels to face him. He is in his twenties, acned skin, lubricious reddish hair, thin neck adorned by a two-clip, two-shilling bow tie in a painfully vivid lilac, pale eyes that blink too rapidly and too often. He seems briefly belligerent, prepared to argue, but Sir Basil meets his eyes with bland good humour. He wears authority easily, has done ever since he was a doyen of Pop back at Eton and that brutally Darwinian body of senior prefects knew a leader when they saw one. The ability to impose his personality on others has only grown during his time running colonial authorities and jails. Famously, he once put down a prison riot with an arched eyebrow and a jocular exchange with the ringleaders. He's always said that the skills learned at Eton will stand you in good stead in any company.

For form's sake, Loverboy takes the time to murmur a couple more fondnesses to his True Love, and then huffs his way out of the lobby.

'Good for you,' says a middle-aged plod to Basil Thomson. 'He's been on that thing for an hour, what if someone important is trying to get through? That's the thing with young people, though, isn't it? Selfish. And we all heard all his business. Some things should be kept private if you ask me.'

No one did ask you, is what Basil wants to say. The average rank-and-file flatfoot annoys him. Plebs, most of them, but he keeps quiet. One thing he's learned in his time at the Met is that you don't ever want to slight the peelers. They can make your life difficult in a thousand small but irritating ways. He nods and picks up the telephone. It is unpleasantly warm against his ear. Clammy too.

His conversation with his leading field agent, the one tasked to keep an eye on Victor Grayson, is complicated by the need to talk in code. And by code he means Tongan.

There was a time, not that long ago, when Basil Thomson could confidently assert that he was the only white man alive who could speak Tongan, and it's a rare skill even now. So rare that soon after becoming head of C Division Basil Thomson taught the basics to a hand-picked study group of agents. The alphabet, numbers, key words and phrases, all that. If they're overheard discussing sensitive arrangements in that language it won't matter. Some of his fellow senior secret service officers – nearly all of them Oxford graduates – use classical Greek or Latin to do the same job, but Basil is of the opinion that this is foolish. There are far too many educated people around these days to make this safe. What if they'd used Latin to hide their plans when taking on the suffragettes? The leaders of that movement – fully certified bluestockings, most of them – would have known what was up in no time. One problem the SIS has now is that so many enemies of the state are overeducated. They read too many damn books.

Sir Basil Thomson believes that many of the world's problems are caused by the spread of ideas so ridiculous that only very educated people will believe in them. These brainy types, with their love of committee work in dusty back rooms, gain control of the political agenda and then cause institutions to rot from the inside. So many of society's difficulties start with university bods being given license to act on their mad ideas in places where they can do real harm.

Takes a while, and he has to raise his voice to do it, but eventually Sir Basil manages to make his agent aware of exactly what he wants and how he wants it done.

'Just to be clear, we're using the Dawson letter?' crackles the agent down the line, his Tongan nimble, fluent. *Ke mahino, 'oku tau faka'aonga'i 'a e tohi Dawsoni?*

'Yes.'

'And this has to be tonight?'

'Always best to do these things straightaway.'

This last sentence is delivered in English and with some noticeable irritation. Basil Thomson is not really the kind of manager who appreciates his wishes being questioned.

As he replaces the receiver, something occurs to him. Best to be sure. He makes his way over to where the constable stands and asks him, apparently casually, if he ever spent time in the South Seas?

'Sir?' replies the copper, plainly baffled.

'You've never been to Tonga?'

'I'm afraid not, sir.'

'You're certain?'

'I'm sure I'd remember if I had, sir.'

'Well, that's splendid news. Carry on, my good man.'

2

Thirty-five miles away, in the musty cellar in Scotland Yard allocated to C Division, Hardit Joshi also replaces the receiver of a telephone on its hook and sighs.

He spends a long moment sitting, thinking. His day – a Saturday! – is now full of errands. Full of administration. Just getting the letter from the file – that in itself will mean signatures and permission slips from various sniffy and suspicious managers. Then he'll have to set up a meeting with Grayson – one that won't be anything like as much fun as their last one was – and getting him there on a Saturday evening when he'll almost certainly be drunk won't be easy either.

It'll also mean revealing himself to Grayson as something more than a casual bed-partner. And that in turn will mean he has to frighten him sufficiently that he never steps out of line, never speaks about what he knows, always keeps properly mum about being blackmailed by the government, and is Grayson the kind of character that you can pressurise like that?

It is Hardit's experience that everyone steps out of line eventually. In the end, everyone talks. This sort of messy operation always ends the same way, and, given that, you might as well do what you're going to have to do right at the start.

Also, he can't really do this on his own. He's going to need help.

No wonder that Hardit Joshi sighs again as he picks up the telephone once more.

It is answered promptly, and Hardit is equally quick in getting to the point. No need for small talk in this call.

'Hilda? I need a favour I'm afraid.'

3

Sir Basil Thomson wanders the passageways and staircases of Chequers. The half-light of the narrow corridors, the cheap wooden panelling on the walls, the institutional smell. Gravy. Soap. It's all so dingy and dispiriting. Not so much like a hotel now, more like being back at school. Back in a prison even. And not one of the important ones. A Wakefield rather than a Parkhurst. A Chelmsford rather than a Scrubs.

He feels grouchy and aimless until he bumps into Frances Stevenson hovering outside the games room and realises that this is what he has been hoping would happen. A chance meeting with this vexing but intriguing example of the modern woman.

Initially lost for something to say, he wonders if she'd like a game.

'The rules are a bit complicated, but the best way to learn is through actually playing. I can talk you through the scoring as we go.'

'I'm not sure that will be entirely necessary, Sir Basil. I've been known to pot a ball or two. I'll rack them up, shall I?'

A cigar, the comforting rumble of the snooker balls, the simple physics the game demands, some inconsequential chat with a pretty girl. The enlivening tension in the muscles as you stretch to make a difficult shot. The way the phosphorescence of the lamp above the table reduces everything to this – the flat expanse of the baize, lush as a well-maintained lawn. A man with a cue in his hand and a game to play is, at least for a while, a man without serious worries. Just simple solvable problems in a refuge from the intractable world.

Occasionally the sleek young head of a clerk pops round the door to the games room. A glance from Sir Basil and that sleek head vanishes. Halfway through the game an older, more distinguished head appears. Basil Thomson, who is paid to know these things, recognises him as Philippe Berthelot, principal diplomatic advisor to the French premier, Aristide Briand. On this occasion it is Miss Stevenson who sends him on his way.

'Not a good time, monsieur.'

The distinguished head nods gravely and departs.

As they play, they talk. Frances is full of questions. She asks him what it was like growing up as a bishop's son.

'An archbishop's son, if you please, Miss Stevenson.'

'I beg your pardon, I'm sure.'

'Not to worry. Being an archbishop's son is like being the son of God Himself. Your father is distant, remote, capricious and his word is Law. He also expects you to make sacrifices in order to glorify his name. Luckily, I was sent off to school very young.'

And what, she asks, were his school days like?

'Averagely brutal, full of casual atrocities. I was a wet bob though, and I found succour in that.'

'A what?'

'A wet bob. A rower. Won medals for it. I was always happiest on the water. Still am. A place where all the ordinary humiliations of a life disappear. Oh, good shot.'

He bangs his cue on the floor in appreciation. Frances smiles shyly. Her teeth flash. She frowns. Her tongue peeps out, glosses her lips, disappears again.

Sir Basil does win the game, but it takes him longer than he had expected, and he has had to concentrate hard, and, worryingly, he half suspects that Frances let him win so as not to damage his ego. This suspicion would itself normally knock his self-esteem, but today he finds he doesn't mind. To be absolutely honest he prefers billiards anyway. There's something a little uncouth about snooker. Something unsubtle and brash about it.

Needless to say, Frances had required no lessons on the rules or the scoring system. She was adept at putting a little dab of side on the white, just enough to get it to spin back to where she wanted it.

It is only now, after the game has finished, that he becomes aware that he has asked no questions about her life. Bad manners, which he deplores. Determined to rectify this he asks her where she learned snooker.

She takes her time replying. And when she does her voice is brisk, schoolmarmish.

'Well, look, for you it's just a game. You learned it at school, played it against older boys, and so you gradually got better. Your improvement was organic, natural. And then there was the whole "winner stays on" thing.'

'What?'

'"Winner stays on" means that the best players get better because they get most practice and the worst get comparatively worse still, until they just give up. Which is a shame for them, because snooker is more than a game, you know this. It is around the snooker table that bonds are formed, lasting friendships built.' She's smiling, leaning on her cue, looking very much at home.

'This is why I paid a boy to teach me, just as later I got another boy to teach me golf, because if you want to get on, golf is another skill you need to have. The fairway and the clubhouse are where deals are done.'

She explains that she realised early on that being good at games was an important competence, enjoyable not just for its own sake but because it helped develop the relationships necessary for a career. Any career. Army, banking, medicine, the law, politics, the civil service, even your precious secret service. All of them games, really, and organised as if they were school sports.

'If you ask me,' she continues, still smiling, but with her eyes cool and serious, 'women need special games rooms of their own. Places away from men, where we can learn all the real necessities for progress in the professions. Places where we can smoke and swear. Tell risqué stories. Places with card schools as well as billiard tables.'

'And Association football pitches too, no doubt,' he says. He makes a strange noise in his throat, a sort of snort, a sort of chuckle. Somehow both. Somehow neither. 'Maybe places where women can wrestle or box?'

'Why not?'

'Isn't it obvious why not?'

'I don't think it is, no.'

She fixes him with a shrewd look. He's unsettled by it. That face, he thinks. That corona of golden hair. The way it helter-skelters around her neck and shoulders. That refulgent gaze. It skewers him.

Sir Basil Thomson knows the threat women pose to men of standing. Adam and Eve, Samson and Delilah, the Queen of Sheba and Solomon. Jezebel. The sirens. His upbringing and education have furnished him with many examples of dangerous women, and, God knows, there were temptresses aplenty in Fiji and Tonga. Sir Basil Thomson likes to think of himself as someone who has been tested but has come through unscathed in that department. Immune to the charm of the ladies. Nevertheless, he is in danger of becoming thoroughly unmoored by Frances Stevenson. Needs to get a grip on himself.

'I don't deny it, Miss Stevenson. Friendships forged on a playing field or around a card table are helpful to an ambitious man. For good reason. Playing games with a man allows you to evaluate his character. And character is everything. Besides, people who are good at games tend to be leadership material. Cool heads. Good in a crisis – so I'm not actually sure what your point is?'

'My point, Sir Basil, is that some people don't get to play. Never get to demonstrate their own cool heads. Never get to show their own leadership material. Never even get to learn the rules. Women, for example, women are excluded from all these games. They're often played where we're forbidden to go, for a start. Even if they're not taking place in spaces explicitly off-limits, then there's such a prickly jungle of male-ness to get through, such a poisonous fog of dislike and disapproval that a lot of sensible women just won't bother. If we do ever break into the games room, then we have to be tough enough to submit to scorn and ridicule. And do it with a smile. We have to ostentatiously ignore the grotesque words tossed in our direction. Worse, we're often expected to join in, to abase ourselves. To pretend we like it. It's degrading and its exhausting. And let's not forget the games themselves are designed for the male physique.'

This is undeniable. After all, hasn't Sir Basil Thomson just spent forty minutes watching his small opponent contort her-self – delightfully, it has to be said – across the table in order to reach some of her shots?

'You don't sound very fond of the male sex, Miss Stevenson.'

She gives this some thought. Frowns very prettily.

'I shouldn't be. But still, somehow, I find I love men. Some of them anyway. Peculiar, I know.'

She is smiling again, and Sir Basil finds he's smiling in return. There's a sudden constriction in his throat but an equal lightness in his heart. Something shifting. Oh my word, he thinks. He is like a man who has been sitting all day in a dark room and now someone has come in and pulled back the curtains, has shown him that the world outside has been bathed in sunshine all this time.

He takes a breath, shuts his eyes, recomposes his features. It's always important to him to be able to control his face.

'But I ask again, how come you have got so good at games?' he says, at last. 'How come you triumphed over all these barriers to accomplishment when so many others haven't?'

'Because I may have the body of a weak and feeble woman, but I have the hide of a rhino. And I picked good teachers. If you think I'm good at snooker, you should see me play poker. What you need to know about me, Sir Basil, is that I'm a stubborn bitch.'

Sir Basil flinches at the use of the word "bitch" and Frances laughs. 'Come and walk with me in the gardens, Sir Basil. You can tell me if you think I'm good leadership material.'

He feels suddenly embarrassed. 'No need to call me Sir,' he says, his voice sharper than he had meant it to be.

Frances laughs again, her golden curls bounce.

'I think we might be becoming friends,' she says, and links her arm through his.

They saunter through the walled gardens, they admire the *Sorbus torminalis* – the chequer trees – that give the house its name.

'This tree has other names, of course,' Frances says. 'It's also called the wild service tree.'

'Really? Intriguing.'

'I thought it might appeal to you. Your being the head of our own wild service and everything.'

It seems a good moment to tell her that he thinks he has solved the Victor Grayson problem.

She blushes slightly. Looks at him with wide eyes. His heart jumps, there's a sudden warmth in his belly, his skin prickles.

'Good news, thank you,' she says. She bites her lip. 'You haven't, you won't, I mean, he's not going to be…' Her voice trails away.

If pushed, he'd have to admit that he is quite enjoying her discomfiture, the way she is momentarily wrong-footed. The way she clearly doesn't know how to feel. She has, he knows, the justified trepidation of someone who has got what they want.

'I don't think we're going to have to do anything too drastic,' he says. 'I am confident that if Mr Grayson were thinking of causing trouble, we'd be able to persuade him otherwise.'

'The PM will be pleased.'

He says nothing. Damn the PM, he thinks. Where is he anyway, and why is he letting his woman sort out his problems for him?

'He's off hiking at the moment. David always likes to get a good long walk in after lunch.'

He is startled. This telepathy that so many women seem to have, the way they can answer questions that you haven't got around to asking yet. There's something uncanny about it. Another reason to go carefully when around them. Maybe all women have secret knowledge. Maybe all women have the potential for witchery. He keeps his eyes on the trees, the deep lustrous jade of the broad leaves just beginning to turn golden at the edges.

'Wild service, eh?' he says, for want of anything better. The silence was getting just a bit too prolonged, just a bit too pregnant with possible meanings. He was feeling the weight of it.

Frances laughs again. A delighted, exuberant, almost mannish laugh. She takes his hand.

'So, Basil. Tell me about some of your most famous cases.'

4

The famous cases. He knows the ones she means, the ones everyone wants to hear about. The capture of the dangerous Irish nationalist Roger Casement. The arrest of Carl Hans Lody, the first spy to be apprehended in the war and almost certainly the bravest man Sir Basil has ever had to have executed.

Then there's Harish Chandra, who was persuaded to turn from would-be assassin of Lord Kitchener to becoming a British agent, and a man very helpful in rounding up those Indian nationalists who might have caused trouble for the British administration while their attention was fixed upon Europe. Who might have demanded greater responsibilities for their Indian people as a reward for sending soldiers to the frontlines. The recruitment of people like Chandra kept the price paid for Indian support affordably low.

But the case people are most fascinated by is the arrest of Margaretha MacLeod. Mata Hari. That was an investigation he'd taken a very close interest in, one where he had to insist on doing all those difficult interrogations himself. If you want to ensure something is done properly, always best to do it yourself.

It wasn't easy either.

The stress of being locked in a room with the famously sultry exotic dancer, persuading her to open up to him, making her feel grateful to him, getting her to think that there might be something he could do to save her. And then ensuring she was convicted and shot.

People don't understand the strain involved in that sort of work. That was another story of a man having to be strong to guard against female wiles.

Sir Basil Thomson finds he doesn't want to go into all that again, not right now.

He clears his throat. 'I can't really talk about these things. Still classified.'

'I understand,' she says.

A sly smile. It's like she can see into his heart. He blushes, she laughs. 'Let's see if I can get my revenge,' she says.

'I beg your pardon?'

'I mean, let's see if we can get a game of croquet. That is, if you're not worried by the thought of a woman hitting your balls with a mallet.'

She wins at croquet, and he finds he doesn't much care about this either. She accepts his congratulations with a smile and orders tea for them both, which they drink in the indifferent shade of a wild service tree. It is surprisingly intimate. Leaves and branches create the sense of a private room. He's not really an al fresco kind of man, doesn't like the idea of flying insects in his tea, but this is all right somehow. She smiles at him.

'Imagine for a moment,' she says, 'an army that can harness the power and potential of its women. You'd double the strength of your fighting force. More than that, actually, because with the way the world is now women are practically invisible. Snipers, assassins, spies. Women can get closer to vital targets because they are suspected less, because they are invisible.'

'Women are hardly invisible.'

'Most of them are. In this society anyway. For every Mata Hari sleeping with generals, getting secrets from them in the bedchamber, there's a thousand mousy, anonymous girls serving tea, cutting cake, dusting mantelpieces, generally hanging around picking up unguarded talk between strategists who don't even see them. Right now, in a thousand apartments across London, there are charladies getting close enough to do away with enemies of the state. If we don't do it, you can be sure the Russians will. Or the Germans.'

'Or the French,' he says.

She smiles. 'Definitely the French. It's something to think about, anyway.'

In fact, it is something he has already thought about. Not that Frances Stevenson needs to know this, but he has been wondering for a while now if it is not such a big step from employing Indians and other citizens of the empire to employing women. The problem is how to keep them properly controlled. How to use their special powers without risk. Using women in the service, like giving them the vote, is to mess with some new type of powerful explosive: you have to make sure the benefits outweigh the risks. You need proper protocols in place. You have to know what you're doing.

EIGHT

Humanity's Best Friend

ST JAMES'S, EARLY EVENING

1

His first thought is that his wife's death doesn't seem to have changed her much. Twenty months on and her look is still that mixture of suffragette bold and Girls' Friendly Society timorous. That straight dancer's back. That frank, defiant way of looking at the world. That actress's poise. Those whisky-dark eyes set within a white-poppy face. Her hair, cut short but somehow still unruly. A strange, dynamic stillness in the shoulders. The sense of an explosion contained. Yes, she's still his little howitzer. His little pocket rocket. Yet all of that bravado diluted by the nervous way she has of twisting her gloved hands together. The way she flinches if a passer-by comes too close.

Is he surprised to see his wife's ghost materialise two hundred yards away on the other side of Piccadilly, outside the door of the famed Criterion and holding the hand of their daughter, Elaine? Not really. This sort of thing happens all the time in London. He has long held that humans don't vary all that much in their looks and so at any time you'll find your-self convinced you've just seen a relative, an old schoolfriend, a former lover or a one-time comrade-in-arms. In a big city, ghosts of old lives are everywhere. You cross paths in a fleeting way with so many other souls that the living and the dead, friends and strangers – they're almost bound to get mixed up in your mind. And the more alone you are, the more your memory will play these kinds of tricks. An ordinary person in modern London, even one unfuddled by drink or untrauma-tised by warfare, is often startled by sudden glimpses of faces he knows. Memories like little landmines waiting to explode beneath your feet.

That roast chestnut seller, isn't that Mick Kelly, who you went to college with? That tired-looking lady with half-closed eyes in the underground station, isn't that Betty Greene who works in the office of the *Clarion*? The man ahead of you in the queue at the butcher's, the one in the corduroy newsboy cap? You're sure you've seen him somewhere before. Didn't he try and sell you a Bible tract once? Didn't you maybe share a foxhole for a terrifying hour under shellfire near Mons?

And that woman in the bus shelter? Isn't that your ex-wife? Or that woman in that shop? Or that woman on the top deck of the omnibus? Or that woman in the park? Aren't any of them Ruth?

So this woman, familiar to him in so many particulars, is just another one who can break his heart by the simple act of not being the one woman he really loved.

*

Once Victor is over the road and one hundred, fifty, twenty yards away, he can see this girl is too young anyway. She can't be more than eighteen. She actually looks less like Ruth than the girl from last night (and this morning) did. The child whose hand she holds, though, well, that is definitely Elaine. Which is something of a turn-up. A bit of a kicker.

'Daddy!'

It's distressing how pleased she is to see him. 'Daddy! Daddy! Daddy!' She runs to him, dancing around the feet of tutting shoppers like a puppy. She clings to him, arms gripping like barbed wire around his waist.

'Mr Grayson?'

'Daddy, I'm hungry.'

'Stuff and nonsense, duck,' says the girl with her. 'You had a teacake not a half hour back.'

A short sentence but it's enough to hear the thick Bolton of her voice. The millstone grit in it. Not like Ruth's at all. His wife's vowels were honeyed – Southerned – by money, by elocution lessons, by the need to catch the ear of West End theatre producers. Because obviously – obviously – women with unfiltered Northern voices could only expect comic parts at best.

'And who are you?' says Victor, mildly.

'Virginia Harris.' She says it with downcast eyes, as though she was giving her name to a policeman.

'We call her Ginny,' says Elaine. 'Granny said Virginia was too grand a name for a maid. And Ginny is much more easier to say. You know, I really am hungry.'

Her voice has become so tragically forlorn that Victor laughs.

'Come on,' Victor says. 'We can get a bun somewhere.' He selects a smile for the maid. Tries to make it a properly re-assuring one. 'She's a growing lass. Growing so fast too. And so strong. Yes you are, chuck, you're squeezing the life out of me. In fact, I think I might faint in a minute. Yes, yes. I'm going. I'm dizzy, blacking out. Quick! Call an ambulance!' He adds movements too. A hand to his heart, a slight stagger. A wobble. A simple little piece of panto, but it works. Elaine is delighted. Giggles. Even this Ginny flashes a wan smile.

'Oh, Daddy.'

'Come on, let's find a caff and you can both tell me exactly what you're doing hanging about the doors of the Criterion.'

His daughter gazes up at him. Adoring, lit from within by love. It's like a punch to the face.

'I don't know, Mr Nightingale told us to stay here.'

'And where is old John now?'

'Grandad said he had Business.' Elaine makes it sound like it's the most important thing in the world.

'Aye, the old devil always has business. What kind of busi-ness, that's the question. Look, if we go and sit in that café over there, we can see the spot where you were standing. We'll see grumpy Grampy John whenever he appears.'

Elaine titters – grumpy Grampy! – and her nanny is re-assured and minutes later they are in a small Italian place, the Café Roma, with lemonade for the girls and strong tea for him. What he really wants is a carafe of rough Tuscan wine, but it is one of the outrages of post-war life that, even in a self-conscious recreation of Italy like this, a man can't get a glass of red.

'So,' he says at last, 'you've wandered a long way from Bolton today. Assuming you did come down today?'

'Yes. Midday train.'

Ginny tells her story in quick, jumpy sentences. She is nearly twenty. A maid-of-all-work for Mr Nightingale and his wife. They're so nice, so kind. She loves working for them and living with them. She has her own room and it's right nice, at the top of the house. It's quiet and climbing all them stairs every day keeps her fit ha ha. And so does running after this little mite of course. It's important to keep fit, the Spanish flu taught us that.

At this point Elaine chimes in. 'Ginny played football in the war, Daddy.'

'Is that right? Munitions factory, were it?' The gun factories were famous for the prowess of their female soccer teams. He smiles to himself, not at girls playing footer, but at how his manner of speaking has reverted back to Scotland Street, Liverpool. The girl Ginny smiles too. Maybe she's guessed that his idiom is normally more standard these days, his accent softer. Elaine is beaming. She's with her Ginny and her Daddy, two people she loves, and they seem to like each other. And she's in London! With ice cream! And she's been on a train! Life, just this minute, is as good as it can be. All this Victor can read in a quick glance at his daughter's face.

'Aye,' Ginny says. 'Place had all sorts of teams for girls.'

'She played in front of, like, a million people once, Daddy. Scored two goals.'

'A million?'

'Twenty thousand,' says Ginny. 'Played cricket at Old Trafford too. Spin bowler. A shame it all had to stop when the men came back.'

She sips her lemonade. No, not so like Ruth, he thinks. Ruth would have knocked her drink back in a couple of hearty swigs. Ruth was never one to savour her pleasures. Drink, sex, work, politics, soon as she got the chance she hurled herself at everything.

And now Victor asks why Ginny's here with Elaine.

The girl shrugs. 'I don't know. Seemed like it were kind of a sudden thing. We must be staying for a day or two, though. We had to bring cases.'

'We left them at the station,' says Elaine.

'Well, I guess Grumpy John will tell us his reasons when he gets here.'

'Daddy! It's *Grampy* John!'

'That's what I said.'

'You said "Grumpy".'

'Really?'

'Yes!' Elaine's eyes narrow. There's a sly look now. An I-know-your-game look. 'You're joking with me, aren't you, Daddy?'

'Me? I never joke. I tell you what though, kiddo, if you keep talking your ice cream will melt. Look, it's happening already.' He picks up the teaspoon from his saucer, dips it into Elaine's bowl. 'Look, some of your ice cream has already melted onto my spoon and – oh no! – it's melting all the way to my mouth.' He swallows it down, so sweet, so cold, and he remembers that he hasn't eaten today.

Elaine squeals, 'Daddy!' but turns her attention to her bowl with serious intent, which gives Victor the opening to ask Ginny about the atmosphere in the house. The girl takes an uneasy glance at Elaine.

'It's all right,' he says. 'She's otherwise occupied now.'

The girl takes another dainty sip of lemonade. And another. Yes, here's someone who knows how to make an audience wait when she needs to. She's already proved she can communicate a lot of information in a few words, now she's showing she knows the value of a well-judged pause. Bravo. Victor admires this sort of thing. Girl has an instinctive grasp of the tricks of the storytelling trade.

'It's what you'd expect,' she says. 'They're still grieving for Ruth and for the little one.'

'Elise?'

'Yes, of course.'

Yes, stupid of him. His second daughter had lived for less than an hour and her only act in this world had been to kill Ruth, who had only lived for four days after her birth. 'It's a gloomy house, Mr Grayson. Oppressive.'

Yes, he thinks. This is true. He knows it from personal experience. Doesn't matter how bright the day or how wide open the curtains, it always feels dark somehow in that house. It had felt like that when he first visited with Ruth back in 1912. It was that gloom she was running away from. It was like Ruth was the only real source of light in that house and had to get away lest it be extinguished by her parents' need for it. To protect herself she took her brightness, her dazzle, from her parents and ran away with it. First towards the theatre, then towards Victor.

Even when they were first married and literally starving, when they were on the bare bones of their arses out in New York, she didn't want to go back. Didn't ever want to take refuge with her mam and dad, despite knowing how lavishly they would treat her, how much they always wanted the prodigal daughter home. Took a pregnancy to force her to return.

'I get her out of the house as much as I can. Try to make sure she has fresh air and that,' says the girl.

'Good, good. Thank you for that.'

John and Georgina had loved Ruth. No question about that, but they had loved her too much, nearly drove her mad with their suffocating devotion. Thing is, they want to crush Elaine in the same way. They may be implanting a similar need to escape in her too. Or maybe she'll just become a hothouse orchid unable to live anywhere else or do anything for herself. Maybe they will succeed with Elaine where they failed with Ruth. And Elise? Well, the death of any child, even one that hasn't started to live yet, that's the death of Hope, isn't it?

'Daddy, I'm bored.'

He laughs. Yes, she's his child too, he thinks. Fears boredom the way others fear injury or death. Even in the trenches, even wounded, it was the boredom of war – all that waiting around – that made him suffer the most. It's boredom that drives a man towards sex, towards drink, towards performing, towards writing, towards anything that can transcend or defeat ordinary consciousness. For most people, most of the time, to be conscious is to be thoroughly bored and most people put up with that. Boredom is the price you pay for security. But boredom can be a dangerous drug. Some people just can't take it. Some people aren't strong enough for that.

2

And so for the next little while he plays some games with his daughter in Café Roma. He does the classic hide your face behind your hands and then, when you take your hands away, you're pulling a stupid face, gurning away like crazy. Always a good one. He does the equally classic pretending to steal her nose and making it seem like it's reappearing between two fingers game. These are games that never fail.

Sure enough, she yelps, she chuckles and she chortles, but he suspects there's something dutiful in the way she laughs.

'I think she's maybe a bit old for these sort of games, Mr Grayson,' says Ginny.

'Yes, I'm a big girl now, Daddy,' Elaine says. 'I am six, you know. I like dominoes.'

He's embarrassed, and a little put out – she'd been humouring him! – and Christ he needs a drink, and it's now that the door to the café jangles and John Nightingale walks in.

'Grumpy!' shouts Elaine.

'What?' says John Nightingale.

'I mean Grampy. Grumpy is what Daddy called you.'

'Did he now?'

Great.

'Just a joke, John. To amuse the kid.'

Victor rises, extends his hand, braces himself for the strength of Nightingale's grip. Man of business that he is, his father-in-law likes to establish physical dominance early in any encounter. John Nightingale is a bank manager but built like a rugby player, and has developed a muscular manner designed to intimidate savers and borrowers alike. He's in his sixties now but shows no signs of ageing beyond his frosted hair and a deep crease between extravagant eyebrows.

Nightingale was no fan of the theatre – it was always a source of worry to him once his daughter became involved – but there's an irony here because he actually looks more like a stage version of a successful man of business than he does a real one. He is the very image of Manly Propriety, looks like the very model of a Patriarch of the Manufacturing Class, whereas in Victor's experience most actual moneylenders are nervous, cramped and spiteful men.

'Well, from now on you'll have plenty of time for jokes with your father, girl.'

There's a silence. One that Nightingale is plainly enjoying. 'Aye, I thought that would make you stop and think.'

In gruff phrases he explains that, since Victor hasn't signed the adoption papers sent to him, since he hasn't even replied to the many letters he's been sent proposing that he and Mrs Nightingale become Elaine's legal guardians, then maybe Victor should become properly responsible for his daughter, maybe the girl should live down here with him. He can bring her up as a strident suffragette if he likes. The Nightingales will wash their hands of all responsibility for her. Will just move on with their lives, maybe get ready to enjoy a proper retirement like other prosperous couples their age. Foreign travel, the seaside, all that. Europe is opening up again now, would be nice to see some of it before they're too old.

'I'm giving you one last opportunity, Victor. I have the necessary papers right here.' He taps his briefcase. 'All properly drawn up and notarised. You can sign right now and we'll assume full legal guardianship of Elaine – you can still come and visit of course – or you can refuse and that's it. We'll leave the girl and you won't hear from us again.'

Victor knows how this is meant to end. He's meant to squirm and give in. He's meant to be shocked into submission. Meant to be so wrong-footed, so horrified by the idea of becoming the full-time carer for his own child, that he just signs over the only good thing he has left in his life.

Never going to happen.

'Fuck off, John,' Victor says, quietly. Man looks like he's been slapped. Victor almost feels sorry for him. Almost laughs. 'Just leave the girl and fuck off back to Bolton.'

He has, as far as he can recall, never said "fuck" to his father-in-law before. Feels good. He should have done it long ago. He should have done it often.

'All right then, lad. You've made your bed. I'll send on her things. Come on then, Ginny.'

It's a blur after that.

A bewildered maid getting slowly to her feet and struggling into her coat.

An agitated Italian waitress plucking at Nightingale's sleeve.

A weeping child.

All so bloody noisy.

'One tea, two lemonades, *due gelati*,' the waitress says.

Elaine is beyond tears already, she is screaming now, deafening shrieks, and all the while she's trying to entwine herself with Ginny.

'Mr Nightingale… Mr N-night—' Ginny is stammering, on the verge of tears herself.

'Victor? Anything else to say?' says Nightingale. He sounds triumphant. Victor knows that even now his father-in-law expects him to crumble.

'I'll pay for the drinks and the ice cream,' Victor says.

The waitress makes a decision. 'Is OK, is on the house.' And she scampers away back behind the counter, keeps watch on proceedings from a place next to the till.

3

Victor shuts his eyes and gradually the hubbub around him fades. The screaming stops eventually – how long does it take? A minute? An hour? – then there's just murmurs and muttering. Victor mentally barricades himself against any actual words, finds he can reduce it to formless syllables. A cold music. The café door jangles. Once. Twice. Now there's silence, blessed silence. At last.

Victor feels like he could sleep now. Just rest his head on this cheap wooden table and sleep for a year.

He could sleep and dream of Ruth. Ruth appearing at the British Socialist Party meetings to recite Elizabeth

Barrett Browning's poem 'The Cry of the Children'. Her voice cracking most affectingly when she came to the final lines –

> ... the child's sob curseth deeper in the silence
>   Than the strong man in his wrath.

Ruth and he being applauded at Walthamstow on the evening of their wedding. Victor had a speaking engagement and there must have been two thousand Socialists shouting hurrah when he introduced her from the stage. She had blushed very prettily then.

Ruth shocking that London journalist when she told him that not only did she share her husband's militancy but she sometimes wished he'd go further, that she believed that the British state had murdered Mrs Pankhurst by starvation, that the women of England were justified in burning down houses...

Ruth gorgeously, sensationally, explosively drunk in that rancid New York apartment the day they discovered she was pregnant...

'Daddy?'

She's still here. Elaine is still here. Some part of him had assumed that John Nightingale had taken the kid. That this whole visit had all been a performance, an intervention designed to shake Victor up. His so-called superiors have been trying that sort of thing on Victor all his life. At home, at college, in the union movement, in the Labour Party, in Parliament, in the army. People staging events to shock him into obedience. Events that usually end in frustration for the tinpot Gauleiters behind them. Now it seems that this one wasn't bluff. That his new life is one of bedtime stories and laundry and clearing up dominoes. It'll be finding a proper house. One with a garden. Finding schools. It'll be times tables and staying in to check homework. Then, later, it'll be catastrophic rows in friendship groups. It'll be boys and dances and important chats about menstruation. About sex. It'll be adolescent arguments and worry. It'll be responsibility. Maybe he'll have to get a job. His world will shrink to a grim routine of work and childcare. It'll be a long prison sentence until his daughter gets married to some idiot. Ten or fifteen years of a slow death. Then grandchildren, and the whole thing starts again.

Elaine already seems like she's recovered. She's started telling some story about girls at school. Somebody said something to somebody else and it was terrible because a third somebody found out what was said and told everybody and so for a whole day, more than that maybe, no one spoke to anyone. It was awful.

'Sounds like paradise,' says Victor.

'Daddy!' Her voice has the dark whine of an incoming mortar shell. Victor had forgotten just how dull children are. How little they have to say that's of any interest at all. Thing about children is, they know fuck all about anything, and yet still they just babble on. They might fear being bored, but they are relaxed about generating boredom in others. Megalomaniacs all of them. Despots. If children were countries, they'd be absolute monarchies ruled by the unhinged.

Where is her suitcase? At the station, she'd said. Well, that means Euston. Has to. If they're smartish they can catch Nightingale and Ginny. Maybe they can get a cab. And didn't that Ginny girl say she thought they were staying a few days?

'Come on love, we need to hurry.'

'Where are we going?'

He deflects. 'How would you like to ride in a real London taxi?'

As it happens, they don't need a cab. John Nightingale and Ginny haven't got far. There they are just a hundred yards or so down, amid the litter of Vine Street. With them are two beefy policemen, from the nearby station no doubt. Typical of John to stop and pass the time of day with random coppers.

'Hey, hey!' Victor is gasping. It may have been only a couple of hundred yards, but the jog has left him winded already. Small consolation that his daughter is wheezing worse than him.

'Hay is for horses, Victor lad,' says John Nightingale. God, the insufferable smugness of the man.

Victor takes a moment to recover his breath, to try and salvage some dignity. He needs to take himself in hand. This can't go on. He's only thirty-nine but it seems he has the lungs of a pensioner.

'All right, John. You win. I'll sign. You can adopt the poor little beggar. You'd better treat her right.'

'Or what?' says his father-in-law. A man incapable of being magnanimous in victory. A man who can't take yes for an answer.

153

What can Victor say in response? He's powerless and Nightingale knows it. Maybe if the memoir does well. Maybe if he gets back into Parliament. Maybe he can get some kind of revenge then, but right now there's nothing.

And so, bizarrely, right there amid the bustle of St James's, to the sound of a crying child – the Nightingales are really going to have to toughen her up somehow – one of the policemen agrees to have his broad back used as a desk, while John Nightingale gets out the documents and points to the various places for Victor to scrawl his signature.

When it's done, when the policeman has straightened up with a vaguely comical groan, Victor nods towards where Ginny is attempting to comfort Elaine.

'Good choice, by the way, John. She's a very presentable piece of skirt. Bravo. A man of your age and accomplishments deserves some comforts.'

John Nightingale grows pale, then flushes. 'What the hell do you mean?'

'You know what I mean. You're schtupping her. No need to be ashamed. It's perfectly natural. I'd mebbe do same in your shoes.'

This is a guess and probably a wrong one, but Victor knows it will needle John, will upset him, and God knows the man deserves needling, deserves upset. No one has ever deserved these things more.

John takes a deep breath. A visible effort to control himself. His moustache waggles like an infuriated caterpillar on the cakewalk of his upper lip.

'All right boys,' he says now. 'You know what to do.' To

Victor he says, 'I was going to let you off this part, but I can't now, I mean how can I, after you've made that disgusting insinuation.'

The way things are dawns on Victor. The penny finally drops.

'Oh, I see.'

'Good,' says John Nightingale. 'I wondered when you would.'

Victor looks intently at those bland public service faces.

One of the policemen nods gravely, the other grins.

'Do it professionally, like you did before,' says John. 'Don't go mad, however strong the temptation. Don't break any bones. Not too much blood.'

'Some though, eh,' says Grinning Cop. His smile shows the ugliest teeth Victor has ever seen. A rocky protrusion of misshapen greenish nubbins.

'You can rely on us, sir,' says Nodding Cop.

'You know I'll complain. I'll take your numbers,' says Victor.

'What numbers?' says Grinning Cop.

And it's true. A quick glance shows him they've unstitched their identifying numbers from their shoulders. Professional, see.

The last image Victor Grayson ever has of his daughter is her curious stare as he is led towards an alleyway off the main drag, Man in Moon Passage. At least she's stopped snivelling, he thinks.

It is, of course, also the last ever sighting Elaine Grayson has of her father, and we don't know what she thought.

She's been asked, many times. But she doesn't remember. Forgetfulness: so often humanity's best friend.

Just like the one last week, this beating is efficient rather than brutal. The filth mainly use their weapons to whack his shoulders, his thighs, his buttocks and his upper arms. The fleshiest places. They want to hurt, but not permanently. A couple of times their clubs connect with his face, but later Victor will reflect that these blows were accidental. A momentary loss of control. The chief purpose is to scare and to humiliate.

He doesn't resist. It's clear from the moment they get into the alley that struggle is hopeless, a waste of energy, that it will give at least one of the policemen pleasure. In any case there is a big part of Victor Grayson that actually welcomes the assault.

As the first blows knock him to the ground, he feels a strange exhilaration. *I deserve this.* He doesn't want it – who actually wants to be kicked in the kidneys or whacked on the collarbone with a baton? – but this is definitely what he deserves. *This will make me feel better. In the end.*

Absolution of a kind.

The attack lasts a matter of minutes. Just enough time for a couple of market porters to pass by, ostentatiously not intervening. Their whole body language is *Don't mind us lads, we haven't seen anything.* Instead, it is Ginny flying in yelling and kicking at the shins of his assailants that stops them, that football talent coming in handy.

They aren't violent with her, they seem more amused than anything, but it means they leave off Victor. Grinning Cop winks at her, Nodding Cop touches his helmet in salute and tells them to mind how they go.

Victor picks himself up – it takes a little while – and takes a further minute to check that nothing is broken, that he can still hear, see, smell, speak. It is just after he has conducted all the basic checks that Ginny Harris slaps him hard across the face. The force of it sends him rocking back on his heels, it makes his teeth shiver. It is much more shocking than any blow delivered by the coppers.

'What's that for?' Victor is distressed by how childish he sounds, his voice high-pitched and petulant. A handful of whining notes, feeble bubbles, rising into the air without force.

'You know what it's for.'

He does know. It is because he'd said she was being tiffed by John Nightingale. He laughs. Winces. His ribs hurt.

'Fair enough, lass. I apologise. And if you accompany me to the Criterion I will make it up to you.'

The sounds of the busy street at the end of the alley roll in. Cars, vans, lorries. Distant drilling. The whole machine of the city grinding on. Her eyes widen. Then she frowns, takes a breath.

'Might as well. I have nothing else to do now.' To his questioning look, she says, 'I have left Mr Nightingale's employ.' She pulls herself to her full haughty five foot two. 'Will I be all right dressed like this?'

A hot flash of memory. The first time he'd gone dancing with Ruth she had looked just like this. Both excited and shy.

'He said I won't get a reference, but I don't care,' she says. She pauses for a second, looks Victor up and down. 'It will take quite a bit of brass to make things right, tha knows.'

He laughs again. Winces again. So good to hear that Lancashire voice.

'I have brass,' he says.

NINE

A Gift Nobody Wants

1

S HE is in her bedroom. It's a cramped, bare space. Cell-like. In the old Hampstead house she was used to a degree of opulence. Aubusson rugs, heavy drapes, big soft bed, walls painted every couple of years. Bespoke furniture. A chaise longue even. She was used to it, but she never really liked it. She prefers this spartan cube. The utilitarian wardrobe, the solitary chair, the single bed with its yellowing mattress. The one decoration in here a handwritten poem in green ink on beautiful handmade paper and tacked to the otherwise bare wall. It's much like her room in the hospital dormitory when she was a VAD nurse. When she first began to discover who she was and what she wanted.

She stands in front of the mirror. She looks good. She doesn't believe in false modesty. Some would say this olive-green jacket fits her a little snugly, but she likes that tightness over her chest. The trousers are loose, but the combination of braces and Sam Browne belt holds everything in place.

The knee-high boots meanwhile are the best she's ever had. Comfortable, durable, stylish. The leather beautifully supple, like another skin. Wearing them, she can appreciate what her brother told her about the importance of good footwear in the trenches. A boot that rubs or allows ingress of water will incapacitate a soldier in no time. 'Shoddy boots are as dangerous as snipers,' he'd said, which is why he'd bought his own rather than relying on those produced by the War Office.

She completes the outfit by putting on the peaked cap. She pouts, does the head-tilt. Perfect.

A sudden waft of millefleurs.

'Oh, Barbara, not this again! Why? Why?'

It's her mother, materialising in the room the way she does. It's like she can move instantly from place to place, her physical arrival only announced a few seconds beforehand by the scent she's been using for Babs's entire life. She is invisible and silent as she travels around the house. Her own kind of magick. Everyone has some kind of special power and this stealthy – miraculous – arriving and leaving a room is her mother's.

Whatever has brought her here is driven from her head by the sight of her daughter all dressed up in her son's uniform. She sounds instantly on the verge of tears. It's hard to know why, given that she finds Babs dressed like this probably once a week. Then again, Babs herself is uncertain about why she likes to dress up in Maurice's old gear. It just makes her feel good, is all. The thick socks, the coarse military flannel of the trousers against her thighs. The thrilling bulk of the revolver in the holster. And the two of them, they're the same height, same slender build, why not wear the same clothes once in a while?

'Why can't my children just be normal!'

It's the despairing prayer of all parents throughout the ages. She turns on her slippered foot and vanishes. The scent remains.

With a sigh Babs stands, adjusts her britches and follows her mother out onto the landing, follows the millefleur trail down the stairs. How does her mother look so frail but move so fast? A mystery. Something freakish about it definitely.

Babs herself walks steadily, her stride long. That's another thing she likes about the uniform. Just wearing it seems to give her a masculine lope. A hint of wolf. She just seems to become more purposeful dressed like this, more balanced, a hint of predatory swagger in her every movement.

As she seeks her mother out Babs wonders what she means by 'normal'. She assumes it's to do with acting as everyone else does, but has her mother noticed what people are doing out there? How they're living? The world's gone insane since the war and the sickness that followed it. An entire generation is shell-shocked, even the ones who went nowhere near the battlefields, and no one is agreed on how we should behave now. The new normal is really a 'no normal'. A free-for-all where all kinds of quirks can flourish.

2

Babs had hated the war, but she had to admit that it freed her too. War, Sickness, Sex and Poetry. There's an unholy quartet of rescuers for you. Three bona fide Horsemen of the Apocalypse and one of their hangers-on riding a donkey behind them.

'There's another one just come in.' This was her friend Marion Bradshaw. Wonderfully unshockable, beautifully Northern.

'Another what?'

'Another bloody poet.'

It was true there had been rather a rush. This was back in early 1916 and it seemed like every second patient was writing verse. Not just the officers either. Poetry was like TB in that way, highly infectious and didn't seem to discriminate by class. It was a disease anyone could catch (though officers were much more likely to get published).

'This one does seem a bit different from the others mind.'

'In what way?'

'Go and see for yersen.'

This one was indeed a bit different from most of the others. He wasn't self-consciously melancholy for a start, nor did he cry for his mother. He was witty, well read and handsome. And he was Indian, a Sikh.

He was also pretty good at poetry and that really was an exceptional thing, especially among those who self-diagnosed as poets. Confident too. No modesty, false or otherwise. Self-assured enough to recite his work for her from his bed on the first day she tended to him. A full five minutes, eyes half-closed. Hypnotic. Pulled her in, even if she couldn't understand a word. He had a compelling voice for one thing. Musical. Humorous. Somehow contriving to be most soothing and arousing at the same moment. You could lose yourself in it. He also had that face. The kind of sympathetic, fine-boned visage you could rest your eyes on quite happily.

That always helps.

'My "Jangnamah France",' he had said at last.

'Your what?'

'Jangnamah is an ancient form of Sikh war poetry. I've adapted it to this time of immense European stupidity, to tell the story of this ludicrous conflict from the point of view of a humble ambulance driver.'

'Well, I thought it sounded good. Really. Mesmerising.'

'It is maybe not a work of genius. But it is, I can assure you, better than almost everything else people are writing today.'

He really thought he was up there with the best. On a par with the likes of William North and Robert Bridges. Better than Rudyard Kipling, that was for sure. Far, far better than Mr Sassoon. She liked this confidence.

'I'm impressed by how you've memorised it all.'

'Only amateurs have to read their work from a book,' he said. 'If it's a struggle for the writer to remember his own lines, then they probably weren't worth composing in the first place.'

They smiled at each other and she was sorry that he probably wouldn't be staying too long in the hospital.

Trouble was, he wasn't even wounded, not really. He was recovering from an appendix operation. That's the thing about ordinary illnesses, they don't have the decency to take a break just because the number of war injuries are piling up. Like poetry, they increase. More limbs shredded by German 08/15 rounds doesn't mean fewer microbes burrowing into vulnerable cavities in hazardous ways: for one thing, war can make people forget to wash their hands. Can put the basics right out of their heads.

'Anything you need?'

'Some books would be good.'

'Anything in particular?'

Which is how she found herself handing a little list to an anaemic young bookseller in Hatchards of Piccadilly.

'Um, *Psychic Wedlock*, *The Mysteries of Eulis*, *The Book of Lies*, *The Book of the Law*, *Over the Brazier*, *Joy and the Year*, *Why Men Fight* and *The Voyage Out*?'

'If that's what it says there.'

'So they're not for you?'

'No, for a sick friend.'

'Yes, I can see he's sick all right.' He smiled thinly at her puzzled frown. 'These are works by perverts, inverts and cowards. In a better-ordered world they'd be banned. The people, I mean, not just their work.'

'Why?'

At this point the anaemic bookseller had looked around carefully before putting his pale, long-fingered hand up to his mouth to hide it as he spelled out a word in a hurried whisper: 'S.E.X.'

'What?'

'Sex. Sex!' He was practically shouting the word now. He needed, thought Babs, to get a hold of himself. She felt as if every eye and every ear in the shop were angled towards her. Judging her. Condemning her.

'Oh.'

'A couple are just books of very bad verse, one is a defence of conscientious objectors, one is merely a pretentious novel, but the others, the others, are manuals for immorality. Dangerous handbooks about how to use certain sexual practices to gain access to dark primeval forces.'

'How thrilling. Have you got them or not?'

The anaemic bookseller sniffed. 'We've got some of them, but on your own head be it.'

Turned out Hatchards had the bad verse and the pretentious novel, but the handbooks for immorality she had to track down by trawling through the second-hand bookshops of Charing Cross Road, by chatting to booksellers a lot less anaemic and more accepting than the Hatchards man. Some of those booksellers were women, and some of them even seemed excited as they rifled through their stock looking for this incendiary material.

When she had next visited the patient he seemed pretty robust. He was walking about making himself very at home on the wards, doing flirtation with the nurses and banter with the men. Although it was hard to tell the difference between these modes, to be honest. He was pretty limber already. She felt a little stab in her heart at the thought that he'd be gone from this place soon.

'I got you your books.'

'They're not my books.'

'What?'

'They're *your* books.'

*

So started the next phase of her education. Hardit Joshi was, it seemed, a follower of Bertrand Russell, a believer in free love, in desire unfettered by societal bonds and by the traps of custom and creed. More than this, he was a believer in sex magick, as propagated by the likes of Ida Craddock and Aleister Crowley – the belief that ritual and incantation plus some serious fooling around could lead to the harnessing of powerful forces. As Hardit explained it, orgasm, suitably dressed up with the correct ceremonies, was the equivalent of the Christian communion or ecumenical prayer, only more so because, unlike communion or prayer, it actually worked. Got you what you wanted.

And when he had completely recovered from his illness, he took her dancing, then to a hotel to show her all the ways in which a Free Lover and a Sex Magician was an improvement on her most recent partners, the men she'd taken pity on. Those sad soldiers who were not only physically broken and mentally shattered, but who were also too often ensnared by convention, who thought the process of seduction was 1) making extravagant promises of marriage, 2) buying her a port and lemon before, 3) popping their muttonium in and out of her for a minute or so. This happened so often that she had begun to think a six-stroke coitus must be prescribed in British army regulations. She imagined a page where it was set out in prim army prose that five strokes was termed a 'quickie', while seven was an obscenely languorous and luxurious session. Six strokes. Six emphatic thrusts. That was the way of the standard British male.

Hardit was the opposite of those hidebound boys. He was inventive, creative, attentive and faithless. He also knew the London clubs where the deviants gathered. Where boys looked like girls, girls looked like boys, where Jamaican jazz musicians could frolic with debutantes and, more often actually, their mothers. Places like Dalton's, Brett's and the Bedford Club, places where no one so much as raised an eyebrow at the English nurse and the Indian ambulanceman.

He also got invites to the weekend country house parties where the finest wines were served and the most entertaining orgies happened. The ludicrous but exhilarating ceremonies. The incantations, the spell-making, the strange intoxicants, the mescal and the mushrooms. The oils. The leather play and the rope play. The silk and the whips. The magick.

Somehow – and Hardit never explained exactly how – he'd got hold of a set of keys to a new world. Not a better one, necessarily, but definitely one with different laws, where the games were played to different rules. When she expressed her appreciation for this education he told her that she should have met him before the war.

'We could have gone to Frida's place, the Cave of the Golden Calf. There were things seen there that would make your hair curl and no mistake. Things you would never forget.'

'Frida?'

'The woman formerly known as Mrs Strindberg, once wife of the noted playwright and a truly splendid hostess. Queen of the Exquisite and the Execrated. Provider of a home for the beautiful despised. Forced by London's puritan authorities and narrow-minded populace to flee to America.'

'I'm sorry I missed her.'

She'd liked fucking Hardit from the first time they'd done it, but more than this she liked listening to him, and how many poets could you say that about, really?

And, finally, after many weeks of nagging, he'd done a translation of 'Jangnamah France' for her. Beautiful calligraphy in bright green ink. She'd got it framed, hung it on her wall.

The very best thing about Hardit was that he never promised her anything, certainly not fidelity. Similarly, he didn't buy her anything – not even a port and lemon – and, finally, he didn't want anything from her. She never knew when he would pop up. ('Expect me when you least expect me,' was what he said.) And she never knew what they would do, where they would go or what they'd get up to when he did appear.

She had no word for their relationship, though if she had ever been forced to name it, she might have called it love.

3

She finds her mother in the kitchen making tea and making more noise with caddy, kettle, teapot and milk jug than she needs to. She's also sniffing. It's an allergy or it's a signal of distress. As far as she knows her mother doesn't have any allergies. Oh, Mother, thinks Babs. All this quiet melodrama. All this neurosis. You'll give yourself a tumour.

'Why did you come to my room, Mother? What did you want?'

It turns out that Maurice has left all his pills behind, both the ones for the shakes and the ones for the pain.

Babs tells her mother that she thinks Maurice left them behind on purpose, that he's trying to cut down.

'They make him so sick, Mother. He says he can't think clearly when he takes them. He doesn't want to get reliant on them.'

'I just…'

She stops there but Babs knows what she's going to say. The tremors disturb people as much as his face does and her mother can't stand the idea of the children pointing, the women whispering, the visible shudders. Sometimes too, Maurice cries out with the pain and that brings him more unwelcome attention.

'And the shaking is so much worse when he drinks.'

Honestly mother, Babs wants to say. Maurice is a big boy now. He can cope. She has said this to her mother in the past and Lady Margaret always nods and agrees, and then ends up weeping, disgusted with herself, wailing that she's a bad person and then Babs feels awful. Best to head all that off.

'I know where he is,' Babs says. 'I'll take them to him.'

There's some more predictable push and pull.

'I can't ask you.'

'No, it'll be fine, it's no trouble.'

'I'm just being silly because you're right, he won't want them. He'll just be annoyed.'

'No, I'll go.'

'You don't have to.'

'I know I don't have to.'

'But it's late.'

'Not too late.'

'I worry that you won't be safe. I was sick with worry when you didn't come back last night'.

'Mother, I'm twenty-three years old.'

'Inconsiderate is inconsiderate at any age.'

'Oh, Mother.'

And so on.

This all takes some time, but it's a tug-of-war Babs wins, as she always does. Though it's a strange kind of winning, given that Babs would rather stay in and Lady Margaret really, really wants her boy to get his pills, whatever the boy himself thinks.

'You're a good girl,' Margaret says at last, and states her intention to go to bed. After all it's nearly ten, and she's exhausted with the effort of getting through another day.

'It's all right, Mother.'

Lady Margaret pauses on the way out of the kitchen. 'You are going to get changed, aren't you dear?'

'Of course.'

Until that moment she was, but as her mother dematerialises from the kitchen, she thinks, Bloody hell. You know what? I won't change. Why should I? I'll go out like this. It'll be an adventure.

And as she steps out of the door, she sees the Eric von Stroheim mask hanging by its leather strap from a hook in the hallway right next to the second-best umbrella. She takes it, looks at it and places it in her knapsack, along with the bottles of pills, her nightdress, a change of underwear and a toothbrush. Well, you never know.

4

Babs has never wanted to be a man, but she has often not wanted to be a woman. No surprise that women want to take time out now and again. The way you are scrutinised all the time. The way every man, however ill-favoured, however wizened, however dirty, will assess you to see if you'd make a wife or a lover, to see if you'd pass the obscure test by which he measures these things. Because it seems to Babs that every man does have such a test. Doesn't matter about their station in life. Tramps, beggars, priests, they all have a test.

Boys too. She is well used to being given the once-over by louts not yet old enough to shave. Would be nice to escape this meat-market appraisal once in a while. Now, out in the streets in her brother's Fusiliers jacket, with the tattered flags of sunset light signalling the dark to come and do its bit, it is Babs who gets to do the scrutinising.

She makes a decision to look at women the way a man does, with a sly intensity. And, gee whizz, the power of it. It tickles her to see the way they blush and turn away. It's true that some – one or two – return her glance frankly, and some clearly notice that she's not actually a soldier, nor even a man. A few just laugh, but for the most part women step out of her way, avoid her glance, don't look beyond the outfit. It is exhilarating.

Once or twice she hears groups of women calling after her, telling her in no uncertain terms that they love a man in uniform, but they're always at a safe distance when they do it. They're making offers but it's a game, something they're doing to amuse one another. They don't want to be taken up on them.

She tries wearing the Stroheim mask for a while, but all that happens then is that the women look away more quickly, while the men give solemn nods. Both sexes become pitying. They seem to wear blank masks of their own. No women call out lewd remarks while she's masked up. No man looks at her with challenge in his eyes. She takes it off.

Pity is a gift no one wants. It's also one you can't return.

The children give her some hope. The children who see her masked face are gleeful, elated; but the hilarity of children is rarely enough to sustain anyone for long.

She doesn't have a destination in mind, she just knows she's not going to meet her brother. The world is her oyster, she can go anywhere except the Marquis of Granby, the Porcupine or the Fitzroy Tavern, the nancy pubs where she thinks Maurice and Robert Clark might be.

She just walks. It's calming, meditative. Good for the soul, although after a while the damp gets a little too intrusive, its fingers creeping under her uniform in its perpetual quest for human skin. Damp, in this town, is just another petty criminal. It's a small-time vandal, a groper, a nuisance you have to live with, that you must always have a plan to escape. She gets on the first bus that's passing and heads for the West End.

If you can read someone's autobiography in the way they walk, then you can read an entire city's in the way its people ride public transport. The girls still wearing their summer dresses as autumn moves in, fidgeting with their bags and purses, fiddling with their hair. The men with their dead eyes and their hands that grip the back of the seat in front of them too tightly.

London's autobiography tells us that it wants to go out. But that it also wants to stay in. London has been sick for a long time and now it wants to forget all that and celebrate. London has put on cheap bright clothes and is up for anything. Yet at the same time London is tired, thinks it started socialising too soon. Is depressed. Wonders about its poor life choices. About what brought it here. London needs a cuppa and an early night. Truth is London doesn't know what it wants. Doesn't even know who it is any more. London is confused. London is angry and grieving. And afraid of its own shadow. London is out of its mind.

At this moment Babs is London too. She also doesn't know what she wants, doesn't know who she is. Isn't she also all of us when we move alone in a city? Cities turn us into phantoms, ghosts in our own lives, insubstantial and discon-nected, untethered from life.

She shifts in her seat. The chafe of the army breeches on her thighs is both uncomfortable and delicious. The weight of the gun on her hip likewise.

TEN

Animal Dances

THE CRITERION, EVENING

1

T HE Criterion. London's brightest rendezvous. Next month the Italian Roof Garden will open with its pergolas and its painted cypresses stark against white terraces. There will be fountains at each end of the room and images of snow-capped mountains. Above it all will be a roof of blue gauze to make you think of a vividly starlit Ligurian sky. All of this a lovely illusion, a beautiful make-believe space, where you can drink and dance as though you were in the heart of the Med while still cocooned against the spiteful London weather.

Music will come from Art Hickman's Orchestra. The best music. American music. Did you know, each member of Hickman's band can play four instruments! Colondon, a former violinist at the imperial Russian court, will play for you during dinner. Everyone who is anyone will come here to see and be seen. Ethel Levey, Violet Loraine, Ellis Jeffreys, Nelson Keys, Maurice Mouvet and Leonora Hughes, Phyllis Dare, Lily Elsie and Peggy Marsh, they'll all be here. And those no ones lucky enough to be admitted will also come to stare, to get a glimpse of the pantheon, to catch any glitter that falls from the wings of the gods.

Like I say, that's next month, but tonight is still pretty good. There might not be a roof garden yet, but there's dancing from seven till ten in the ballroom, with its high glistering ceiling. People from the arts like it. Ethel Levey might not be there yet, but there are stars. Those on the way up and those on the way down, they meet and mingle here.

There are the exhibition dancers too. Adele Astaire has been paid to dance the tango here, together with her kid brother Fred. Cynthia and Cyril Horrocks have danced here. If you chuck Cynthia a few quid, she'll dance with you, and if you can't afford the likes of Cynthia, well, there are plenty of other good-looking dolls who'll take a turn around the floor with you for a shilling or two.

You can also get a very decent dinner. Slap-up nosh.

'Flipping 'eck,' says Ginny.

'Heck,' says Victor. 'Flipping *heck*. Can't have sloppiness of pronunciation here. No dropped aitches. Not in these august surroundings.'

'Are you joking me?' says the girl.

'Yeah, I am actually. Come on, let's get a drink.'

Arthur John Peter Michael Maundy Gregory is the first in his group to notice Victor and the girl, and he immediately starts laughing in that big way he has.

'Good lord, Victor,' he says as he waves them over. 'What happened?'

175

'I fell face first into a policeman's truncheon.'

'Oh, that's splendid.' He claps his hands. 'Fell face first into a truncheon. I like that. Very careless of you, Victor.'

'Wasn't it?'

Arthur Maundy Gregory is a middle-aged swell, another monocled plutocrat with a luxuriant actor's drawl, beautifully turned out in classic male couture. He'd be an impressive figure if it didn't look like subsidence was affecting his face, cheeks and jowls slithering towards a flabby neck like a slow-motion mudslide. This is more than the ordinary vandalism done by time, it's evidence, Victor thinks, of the ill-health brought on by corruption and the habits of deceit.

'I'm surprised you got past the doorman looking like that,' says another of the party. 'Standards must be slipping.'

This speaker is Horatio Bottomley, Independent MP for Hackney South, newspaper proprietor and connoisseur of pretty working-class girls. He is addressing Victor, but his eyes are on Ginny.

No doubt about it, Victor is a bit of a mess. One eye is closing and his cheek is swelling. He is missing the top two buttons of his blood-spotted shirt. However, he has washed his face in the gents and combed his hair, and actually looks a great deal better than he did when he first arrived here.

Truth is the doorman hadn't even blinked as he waved him through. They all know Victor here and it will take a lot more than a bashed face and a torn shirt to get him turned away. Especially when it's young Pete Egan on the door. He might be wrong, but Victor has always felt that there was a little bit of a twinkle between him and Pete. Pretty pouty Pete had definitely looked more askance at Ginny than he did at Victor.

Glasses are filled while Victor explains how he had contrived to get into a contretemps with the boys in blue. No one around the table is outraged, or even surprised. Policemen hiring themselves out to beat up members of the public? Big deal. Tell us something we don't know.

Horatio Bottomley asks if anyone attempted to intervene.

'Only my friend Ginny here.'

'Yes,' drawls Maundy Gregory. 'Women are braver than men on the whole. More prepared to stand up to authority.'

Victor agrees with this. It's a belief Victor's had since his involvement in the suffragist struggle, since he met Christabel Pankhurst all those years ago.

Horatio Bottomley says that it is different in Russia. There, workers of both sexes instinctively help a comrade against the forces of the state. Russian workers don't ever need to know details – if they see a peasant in a struggle with a policeman, then they immediately go to the aid of the peasant. Or they did before the revolution, anyway.

'In England by contrast the ordinary man is much more likely to urge the police to get properly stuck in – go on, my son, give it some welly – than to attempt a rescue. One thing you learn as a leader of the English working class is that they can't be relied upon.'

'Yes, Horatio, such a sad state of affairs. Still, never mind, eh?'

Maundy Gregory makes a performance out of picking up his monocle and peering hard at the face of Victor's companion.

'Victor, where are your manners? Introduce us properly. Who is this charming thing? Aside from being the absolute heroine of your tale.' He doesn't wait for an answer, turns to the girl herself. 'My dear, have we met before? I feel sure we must have. I generally get to meet most of the serious beauties in London in the end.'

'Arthur,' warns Victor.

'Oh, you're one of those,' says Ginny.

'One of those what?' Maundy Gregory seems amused.

'One of those men who think women are reet mugs. You think sling us a bit of old flannel and we'll do owt you want.'

The muscular Bolton of her voice is more prominent than ever.

Maundy Gregory laughs, 'A feisty one! Just Victor's type.' His voice grows serious. 'I may not have met you before, Miss…'

'Virginia, Virginia Harris.'

'I may not have met you before, Miss Virginia Harris, but I have met a lot of girls like you. You remind me very much of Ruth, actually. I mean Mrs Grayson. What do you think, Victor? Does Virginia here remind you of Ruth?'

'I suppose, a little.' He doesn't mention that almost all young women remind him a little of Ruth these days. That he sees her everywhere he looks.

'A little?' Maundy Gregory does a wide-eyed, open-mouthed face. 'She's the absolute spit, surely you can see that, Victor.'

Victor shrugs.

'Do I look like her?' says Ginny. Between the Café Roma and the Criterion, her whole manner has undergone a transformation. She is clearly emboldened by the thought that she was Victor's saviour from police brutality. She is also liberated by quitting John Nightingale's service. No longer a babysitter and a scrubber of floors, she is free now. Free to look men in the eye, to speak up, to ask questions. Her eyes shine.

Victor shrugs again.

'You're better-looking, if anything,' says Maundy Gregory. 'Better deportment anyway. Ruth was always prone to slouching. I told her off about it so many times.'

Bottomley has a question: 'Where did Victor find you?'

'Miss Harris used to work with the Nightingales. Looked after Elaine.'

Bottomley nods, seems to be making a mental note, while Maundy Gregory does his exaggerated surprised expression again. The one where the eyebrows arch way up into his hairline. It's one he deploys a great deal. 'Old Nightingale hired the doppelganger of his daughter to look after his granddaughter? Very interesting.'

'Not really,' says Victor. He feels an urgent need to change the subject. 'Miss Harris is a footballer.'

'Of course she is. Well, I tell you what she should be doing. Phiz like that, posture like that, she should be acting. Like Ruth did. Tell me, my dear, can you sing?'

'I can carry a tune, I suppose.'

'I knew it!' says Maundy Gregory.

The band strikes up. They are no Art Hickman's Orchestra obviously, but nevertheless, they are spirited and loose. The song is a fast rag.

'Ooh I like this one,' says Ginny, and with elaborate courtesy Bottomley asks her if she would allow him to have the absolute exquisite pleasure of a dance ('Nothing too energetic, mind. No tango or anything like that') and while they trot the fox on the dance floor, Maundy Gregory introduces the other man at the table.

Leopold Saxe is a thin cove dressed in tomorrow's colours. Thirtyish, he has the look of a traveller from an extravagant future, maybe a world imagined by H.G. Wells. Clean-shaven, face baby-smooth in fact, slicked-back hair, wide Oxford bags, lime-green jacket, gaudy necktie of pale pink dots on a scarlet background. He's either making a statement or he's foreign. His manner is fidgety, his head twitches, birdlike, while his eyes are as hard and as implacable as glass. Maundy Gregory explains that this Leopold is making a fortune selling gramophone records.

'Sheet music too. There's still money there, but twenty years from now only a few Luddites will be buying that,' says this Leopold. 'People will have huge collections of records instead. Why bother to learn to play the piano when you can have the best musicians in the world performing for you in your own drawing room at a time of your choosing? People will judge each other on those collections too, the way they judge you on your books now.'

He speaks fast, as though any moment someone will interrupt, tell him he's talking rot.

It all sounds unlikely to Victor, though he does remember the comfort the gramophone player brought to the officers in the trenches. Those comic operettas the public schoolboys seemed to love. The poor bloody infantry weren't so keen, they preferred their own singing of their own songs. Obscene reworkings of music hall numbers.

The men make conversation for a while – the weather, the state of European politics – and it's clear that Leopold is not foreign, so his clothing must be a statement. They talk about what is big in music right now and Leopold tells them that while waltzes are popular, it's really still all about boogie-woogie and ragtime – and the animal dances that go with them. Sure enough, on the dance floor, Horatio Bottomley is gamely trying to keep up while Ginny Harris leads him through some strange contortions involving clawing at the air with your fingers while lumbering forward and back, occasionally circling your partner.

'The Grizzly Bear,' says Leopold.

Victor thinks how it seems both ridiculous and somehow cheerless. 'I can't see the appeal of these American imports,' he says. 'We need our own dances.'

'Clog-dances, no doubt,' says Maundy Gregory, and sniggers to himself. 'Oh, Victor, don't take offence. Just a joke. Honestly, you grow more sensitive every week. Anyway, I think the young people need their fun, especially after all they've been through since 1914.'

'This young peoples' fun might actually kill poor Horatio,' says Victor. And it's true that their friend's face is now the colour of the London sky after a Zeppelin raid, a curious mixture of slate-grey and rose-pink, and they can see the sheen of sweat on his brow from where they sit.

'Ah yes, the things old men put themselves through in a doomed chase after the nubile. The unspeakable in pursuit of the unattainable.'

When Leopold excuses himself to use the gents, Maundy Gregory explains his presence at the Criterion.

'What do you know about the Comrades of the Great War?'

'A veterans' organisation. Or at least pretending to be. They're a front for the Anti-Socialist Union are they not? A Tory alternative to the NFDSS.'

'I don't know the ins and outs,' says Maundy Gregory, a little testily. But I know that Leo wants a spokesman for the Comrades and thinks you could be the man. They'll pay decently.'

'And how did he hear about me?'

Maundy Gregory waves a theatrically airy hand. 'Oh, I've been dealing with him on some other matters, and have got to know him quite well. He mentioned his work for Comrades and the need for an able person to put their case, to get new members, to spread the word about their services. To place positive stories in the press.'

'A propagandist.'

'That's a rather sinister word for what he wants. Anyway, I suggested that you might be his man, suggested he come along and meet you here tonight. See if he likes the cut of your jib. I also believe that he may know your friend the good doctress, Ethel Vaughan-Sawyer.' He waits a few heartbeats, twists his monocle chain as if it were a string of rosary beads, settles his face into an expression that is severely pedagogical. 'Look, I have to say, my dear Victor, that this is an audition and one that you might be failing. Oh look, our Horatio has finally thrown in the towel.'

It's true. Horatio Bottomley is removing himself – slowly, regretfully, painfully – from the dance floor. He looks less like a grizzly bear and more like a wounded penguin. Perhaps he has pulled something? Old men need to be careful when taking part in sport. Meanwhile, Ginny Harris remains radiantly vivacious, readying herself to do the Duck Waddle or the Kangaroo Hop with one of the eager young men whose attention she has caught. Victor can see three of them homing in on her now like ants marching towards a pool of honey. The girl's in for a busy night. Lucky that a combination of football training and housework have kept her fit.

2

Victor doesn't know too much about the Comrades of the Great War but he does know about the NFDSS. The National Federation of Discharged Sailors and Soldiers campaigns for better conditions for war veterans. Not for hand-outs – their slogan is 'Justice before Charity' – but for what they've earned with their blood. They call for the nationalisation of industry and agriculture. Even put up candidates for election. Why would Victor Grayson of all people promote their rivals?

The way the establishment have sought to own the war is sickening. They've claimed it as a victory for the status quo when winning the war should have meant change. People deserve better than the same old gruel grudgingly ladled out by the scions of the same old landed families. Hands softened in blood patting the heads of the people who make them rich.

The people, the working people, deserve more than these memorials that the ruling class are putting up everywhere. A statue of a fine-figured young man, scanning the horizon, looking towards a glorious future. Not too many statues of men crouching, hands over their ears, shitting themselves in blasted hellscapes while the mustard gas rolls in. Comrades of the Great War was founded by the bloody Earl of bloody Derby for Chrissake. It's true Victor needs a job, but he doesn't need any old job. He doesn't need that job.

When this Leopold returns from the lav, Victor will make a point of snubbing him, of disagreeing with him about the future importance of recorded music. Will, in fact, make a point of disagreeing with him about everything. He is looking forward to it.

'Victor, will you dance with me?'

Ginny is back at their table, eyes sparkling in her flushed face. Her teeth gleam. God, she's beautiful.

'I can't.'

'Why not?'

Yes, why not? It's a good question. In fact, it is almost always the only question that ever needs to be asked about anything. At least in this case there are obvious answers: because you look too much like my late wife. Because dancing with you will remind me of all I lost, all I threw away. Because I need another drink.

He says none of this.

'Because I have important business to discuss with this gentleman,' and he gestures towards Leopold Saxe.

'Don't worry, my dear, I'll dance with you.' Maundy Gregory rises and extends his hand. 'Be gentle with me though, won't you?'

So while Maundy Gregory dances the Chicken Scratch with Ginny Harris and while Horatio Bottomley sulks at the bar, Victor Grayson uses curt sentences to tell Leopold Saxe that he won't be a salesman for Comrades of the Great War.

'Of course you won't,' says Leopold Saxe. 'I'd be disgusted if you did.' And he tells him the real reason he wanted to meet.

Ginny and Maundy Gregory move on to the Hesitation Waltz, while Horatio Bottomley deals with a young writer who would love to write for *John Bull* magazine – he has samples of his work with him too, just wants a chance – and Leopold tells Victor about his meetings with Maundy Gregory to discuss the possibility of buying a peerage. About how Maundy Gregory has been clear it will cost Saxe more than the average because he wants to sit in the Lords rather than just receive a CBE or an Order of the Garter or some other similar bauble. Maundy Gregory has also told him that there will be a further premium because of his relative youth. And yet another escalation of the fee because he doesn't appear to have done anything of conspicuous service for the nation, and still another because of his Germanic-sounding name.

'As far as Arthur Maundy Gregory is concerned my full name is Leopold Saxe-Coburg. Which is nearly as Hunnish a name as that of our own royal household, the

Windsors, the family known until three years ago as the Saxe-Coburg-Gothas.'

'And you don't actually want a peerage?'

'No, Mr Grayson, I do not want a damn peerage, what I want is the whole corrupt system blown up, obliterated.'

'You're not a music entrepreneur either, I take it.'

'I like music and I believe what I say about the revolution the phonograph is ushering in, but I'm a painter and decorator by trade. I haven't got two ha'pennies to rub together.'

Ginny and Maundy Gregory move on to the Squirrel, Horatio Bottomley is cornered by one of his Hackney constituents wanting to discuss the lack of public toilets in the borough, and Leopold tells Victor about the beautiful simplicity of the patent Kelley Turner Dictograph. The KTD.

This is how the KTD works: a man speaks with another man in one room and the words are picked up by a hidden device – the famous dictograph – and transmitted to a receiver in a different room, where they are instantly turned into grooves cut into an actual physical record. Ten inches of shellac giving you something you can play on an ordinary gramophone.

'Sound is as clear as a bell too.'

They break off the conversation as Maundy Gregory returns, saying that Ginny Harris has worn him out.

'Girl's got rhythm,' he says. 'No doubt about that.' The men watch for a few moments as Ginny and a new partner – tightly curled blonde hair, toothbrush moustache – scuttle from side to side across the dance floor.

'The Crab,' murmurs Leopold.

'I'm pleased you two seem to be hitting it off,' says Maundy Gregory, and he smiles indulgently at them both and explains that he must visit the necessarium, and that he will then circulate in the room and leave them here to chat.

'Important to make my friends feel loved,' he says. 'Important too that my enemies know I have an eye on them. Also, good that you both have time to get to know each other. I do think your liaison could be mutually beneficial.'

Ginny Harris does the Bunny Hug, the Monkey Glide and the Buzz (you make like a bee) with a succession of fops, Maundy Gregory circulates, Horatio Bottomley continues his interrogations of waitresses and Leopold explains in patient detail all that was said about his putative peerage – and who it was said by – and how the conversations were all recorded via the medium of this Turner's dictograph.

In fevered whispers he tells Victor that he actually has the recordings with him right now, including the one made of the meeting attended by none other than David Lloyd George himself – 'That's a particularly interesting listen.'

What he and his friends would really like is to engage a skilled writer, one with a name and a track record in the press, one with correct political credentials, one who could bring the material to public attention, while keeping the records themselves safe of course.

'Friends of mine tried to give you them a few days ago, but it seems your place is under surveillance.'

'And who are your friends? I mean, who do you work for?' asks Victor.

'Does it matter?' says Leopold.

Victor thinks, Maybe that's right, maybe it doesn't matter. Russia? France? America? Japan? Germany? What's the difference really? It's even possible that this Leopold represents the British socialists, and perhaps in doing this Victor will be doing a good thing. But if not, so what? So bloody what?

'Will I get paid?' he says, and Leopold just smiles – of course he'll get paid – and hands over a package that Victor has seen before. It is the one he left behind at Ethel's.

'Three discs,' says Leopold. 'Three bombs really. Ready for someone to light the fuse. You'll be like a modern-day Guy Fawkes.'

Victor takes the parcel just as Maundy Gregory and Horatio Bottomley return to the table.

'Giving your product away, Leopold?' says Bottomley. 'Not the act of a prudent businessman.'

'Loss leaders, Horatio. Just trying to convince Mr Grayson here that the future of music is recordings played in the comfort of your own house rather than so-called real people bashing away at bits of wood and wire.'

'Well, yes,' says Maundy Gregory, 'real people are all very good of course, but they're not reliable, are they? Almost never there when you need them.' Something else occurs to him. His eyebrows do their exaggerated leap. He frowns.

'You know, Leopold, I've often wondered why a modern music mogul doesn't ever seem to want to dance.'

Leopold smiles. 'No one in the music business can dance, Arthur.'

Ginny Harris is sitting down with the men at last. She has
been a bunny, a squirrel, a monkey, a bee, a crab, a chicken,
a kangaroo and many more creatures besides; feels like she's
done a dancing interpretation of every living thing that hunts
or grazes, climbs or swims, flies or crawls. She has been every
animal there is and now she is beat. Her eyes still sparkle
but now they also seem unfocused and Victor wonders if it
is just excitement – Music! London! Freedom! – or if one of
the young bucks she's been cavorting with has slipped her
something. Maundy Gregory and Horatio Bottomley are
either side of her, leaning into her space. Leopold, job done,
seems restless and distracted, while Victor is eager to get
home and to start writing, but for both Leopold and Victor
to rush off now would look odd, would invite awkward questions. Would arouse suspicions, create unease, a sense that
something was off.

Victor fills the time before he can safely leave the Criterion
by imagining a new future for himself. A firm career plan.
First, he must listen to this material on these discs. He'll
begin with the Lloyd George recording. It'll be the work of
moments to decide if it's really the prime minister speaking.
He has a distinctive voice, after all, and a very particular way
of ordering his words. It would be very hard to find an actor
to impersonate him. If it's really him, then it'll be a matter of
transcribing the words. A boring task, but a necessary one.

Next, he writes an article – no, a series of articles – each
one a damning exposé of the brazen venality of the honours

system, naming all involved, quoting them, condemning them with their own words. These pieces must be published, and not just in the left-wing press, but in the mainstream papers. *The Times*, the *Daily Telegraph*, the *Daily Express*, the *Daily Sketch*, the *Morning Advertiser*, maybe even the *Manchester Guardian*, though there's a paper that particularly hates getting its hands dirty.

They'll all be reluctant, of course, they'll hate having to publish something so incendiary, something that will dump so many of their friends right in the manure, but how can they resist it? It's a story that will sell newspapers by the absolute ton. In a cut-throat market, that's what counts. That's what being a thoroughly modern press baron means: finding the absolute best moment to sell out your friends.

It occurs to him that maybe he'll be safer moving abroad to write these pieces. He could lose himself on the continent, spend the winter in Capri maybe, that's the place where the proper socialists go, isn't it? Or New York. Where Ruth and he spent a kind of honeymoon. They were happy then, met some good people. American capitalists are bigger, brighter, flashier and trashier than their British peers, and so are their socialists.

It is Horatio Bottomley who notices her first. He can detect an incoming comely girl the way a Telemobiloscope can detect a friendly warship in fog. He doesn't have to see them; he can sense them. And when he does see them it's like an injection of adrenalin given straight to the heart. He comes alive.

'Well, looky here,' he says.

Victor is startled out of his reverie. 'Hilda!'

'Hello, Victor.'

'Well, I shall remove myself from the equation,' says Bottomley. 'Allow you to sit down. I have to say, Vicky boy, that you are demonstrating a new level of charm. Where has this heightened sexual magnetism come from all of a sudden?'

Horatio Bottomley never likes to be second best in a competition for the ladies and here he is, just making his resentment obvious.

Maundy Gregory laughs. 'Take no notice my love, our dear friend Horatio is having a bad day, come and join us.'

'I'm only popping in,' says Hilda. 'Not really my sort of place. I just needed a word with Victor.'

'Must be urgent,' says Maundy Gregory, eyebrows taking flight again. If there's something to know, he likes to know it.

'Might be. A little while ago a very excited young man banged on my door desperate to see you, Victor. I knew you were here, obviously, and I thought you might have good reasons for avoiding him, but also that you might need to know what he wanted. I made him write a note and here I am.'

From her handbag she produces a cream envelope, surprisingly unbent and uncreased despite its hurried journey across from Bury Place. 'Voilà!' she says.

As he takes the envelope, as he opens it, as he pulls out the notepaper, as he reads, Victor is aware of all eyes on him. It's like being on stage but with a hostile audience. No, it's more like being a prisoner, or a patient. Every tiny movement he makes now will be analysed, judged, dissected. He's really

191

sick of all this. Sick of Maundy Gregory, sick of Horatio, of Leopold and his fanatic's stare, sick even of Ginny, sick too of this restless music, sick of the smell of perfumed skin and new money, sick of the cheap, cloying wine, wishes he was far away from here.

The note is a brief one and in green ink. At least he has a reason to be elsewhere now. He replaces the note in the envelope – green ink! – and the envelope in his inside pocket. Victor rises.

'Well?' says Maundy Gregory.

'I must love you and leave you,' says Victor. He finds he is swaying slightly. His spine has gone soft. The act of standing takes some concentration. That's all right. Swaying's all right. It's controllable. He shuts his eyes for a moment. It's quite nice to oscillate gently, to feel the noise of the Criterion recede a little. He opens his eyes. Endeavours to inject vitality into his posture. 'The matter really is quite urgent and needs attending to.'

'You're going?' Ginny Harris sounds quite unnecessarily distraught. There's a wet hiccup in her voice.

'You're welcome to accompany me. I need to make a phone call and there may be a meeting after that, but after my business is concluded I can offer you a place to stay if you need it.'

'But I, but we, but…' she starts fiercely, but almost immediately runs out of words. She subsides. Deflates.

Maundy Gregory's interjection is swift and smooth. 'Miss Harris and I have contract details to discuss, but we can always wait until tomorrow to finalise things if you think she should go with you, Victor.'

'I want it sorted now.' Her bottom lip is out, her eyes flash. And then fade. 'If that's all right.'

'Quite all right my dear. Victor, no need to worry about your friend. We'll look after her. Plenty of room at my place.' To the girl he says, 'Or we could even get you a hotel room if that would make you more comfortable.'

Contract details? This is one of Maundy Gregory's classic moves. The I-can-put-you-on-the-stage gambit. It's not that he has any sexual interest in the girls he lures in this way himself, but he likes to introduce them to people who do. To launch them into his circle like an inventor with a new product. He did the same with Ruth, but luckily Ruth had both character and real proven talent. Plus, her family had resources. She also had Victor. Maundy Gregory's patent on Ruth Nightingale expired very quickly.

Maybe Ginny will be all right too. She's a Bolton lass and girls don't come much tougher than that. And the route offered by the likes of Bottomley and Maundy Gregory is at least a well-trodden path to a kind of freedom for girls of her class. She has spirit too. Spunk. Perhaps that will be enough to save her.

Victor nods and moves from the table. He has only gone a yard or two when he is called back.

'Don't forget this,' says Leopold, his voice sharp. Almost panicky. He holds the packet of records.

'No, don't ever forget the precious gift of music,' says Maundy Gregory, as he passes it over.

Well-oiled as he is, still Victor feels a chill hand squeeze his heart at the idea that he could have left this evidence here for anyone to find. Victor is certain that Maundy Gregory will have picked up the little yelp of concern in Leopold's voice. He has an ear attuned to nervousness. It's one of his more useful professional skills.

'Perhaps you and Miss Porter can do the Grizzly Bear when you get back to Bury Place,' says Horatio Bottomley. 'Or the Beast with Two Backs.'

'Is that a real dance?' says Ginny Harris, and the men laugh.

4

The gyrations are over, the gas jets are turned up, the world of the Criterion moves from warm, exciting gloom to chill, disappointing light. The promise of music is replaced by the dream-busting clatter of waiters and waitresses collecting plates and glasses. The talk, so vibrant, so gilded by hints of sly and dirty romance just moments ago, is dying now. The whole place seems about to suffer a dull, nagging headache. Has become old and crotchety.

Leopold has gone and Criterion staff are despatched to fetch coats and hats. Queuing for the cloakroom is for lesser mortals, not for the likes of Arthur John Peter Michael Maundy Gregory or Horatio Bottomley, or any of their guests.

Bottomley is keen to discuss the finer details of Ginny Harris's contract as a budding theatrical performer.

'Of course, we're going to have to change your name,' he says.

'Maybe your nationality too. How do you fancy becoming Hungarian? Or Russian? Yes, you could be a lost Romanov forced to take up singing and dancing following the foul murder of your relatives in the Bolshevik terror.' Maundy Gregory is doing his best to join in with this game, but his heart isn't really in it. He's just going through the motions.

'Just as long as you don't take me for a mug.'

'Of course not, dear, we'd never do that. We're English gentlemen.'

He's distracted. His mind is on Victor and Leopold. Leopold and Victor. Something about their whispered conversation bothers him. Was he wise to introduce them? These days he finds himself wondering more and more about the point of Victor, and what, really, does he know about this Leopold Saxe? Sometimes he wishes he was less of a fun-loving, freewheeling, happy-go-lucky artistic person, and more of a dry, bureaucratic type. What the Americans have started calling a details guy.

He interrupts some story with which Bottomley is attempting to amuse Ginny Harris, the Bolton-housekeeper duckling who is soon to transform into Her Imperial Majesty Princess Leonora Romanov, fallen-royalty swan. Their latest lucky find.

'Horatio, do you think we need to do something about Victor?'

Horatio Bottomley gives it some thought, strokes his moustache. 'He does seem more than usually wild of eye these days, it's true.'

'My thinking exactly.'

Nothing else needs to be said. Not right now, anyway.

ELEVEN

A Chamber Piece

CHEQUERS, EVENING

1

DAVID Lloyd George is in Frances Stevenson's mean little room and he is telling her that it is over between them. Whatever they had is gone. After what he's been told, it's quite clear they can't continue. Not as lovers, not as colleagues.

He'd arrived back at Chequers from a long, long walk, tired but also refreshed, invigorated, ready to quickly bathe and change – perhaps a bite to eat, perhaps read a chapter of his latest shilling shocker – and then head to the attics ready to assault his lover's dear body with fierce kisses. Every bit of it. Every inch of it caressed with lips and tongue.

He'd been prevented from doing this by a visit to his room from his daughter, Megan, and yes, she had left him in no doubt what she thought about his plans to buy Frances a house, but that hadn't been the main thing. The main thing, the upsetting thing, the catastrophic thing, was what she had told him about Frances and that weasel, that snake, Basil Thomson.

'You played snooker with him.'

'I did.'

'You walked around the gardens with him. Practically hand in hand, Megan says.'

'Nonsense.'

'You didn't walk around the gardens with him?'

'I did, but not hand in hand. Nothing like that. It was all above board. All completely professional. Strictly work. Work on your behalf.'

'Hah!'

She can see from his prim pout that he is thinking about the secluded corners of those gardens. The shaded places, the arbours and bowers. The bushes and long grasses that could screen lovers from casual onlookers, that could provide a romantic setting for a fumble as the late summer light faded. She can see that a whole play is unfolding on the stage-set of his mind. The sneaking hands. The kisses given and received. The stroking and the rubbing. The rummaging.

He is projecting, of course. He is extrapolating from his own behaviour. How many kisses has David Lloyd George stolen on hikes with his staff? How many bodices and corsets has he loosened after claiming that political problems are best resolved through walking and talking with a young advisor in the fields?

He's not the only one, of course. They're all at it.

She understands the urge. High-powered men leading high-pressure lives, they need this kind of outlet. Men, rich men anyway, men with power, only think rationally in the two hours or so after orgasm. Henry the Eighth, Julius Caesar,

Hannibal. Genghis Khan. All the popes. This is a story as old as time.

They can't help themselves.

'You played bloody croquet with him.'

It's galling though, this possessiveness, this double standard. It makes him look very unattractive. Anger has reddened David's face and his hair is more than usually springy. If he'd looked like a sparrow in the early hours – cheeky, perky – when she was feeling fondly inclined, well, now, seen through the lens of this distrust, he looks like a furious squirrel, one who suspects that his secret nut store has been raided.

Not dignified. Not manly.

'Megan reminded me of some of your other liaisons too,' he says now. His voice somehow both pompous and shrill.

'That was nice of her. You know she'll do anything she can to hurt me? Even if it hurts you too. And what other liaisons?'

'"What other liaisons," says she! What about Berthelot?'

He pronounces it – deliberately no doubt – as 'Berty Lott'.

'Him? Oh, please.'

'I've seen him. Creeping around. Looking down his froggy nose at everything. Why is he here anyway? Who invited him?'

'You did, David. As part of the French legation. To talk about the situation in Mesopotamia. The siege at Samawah.'

2

And she's cast back to San Remo in April. Another of the peace conferences. The victors meeting up in sundry golden resorts to divide up the possessions of the losers. Ah, the beach at San Remo. The exuberant, cheerily youthful sea. The scintillating red-tiled roofs of the houses, the butter-cream walls, the narrow blossom-scented streets. Oranges, lemons and pomegranates. The way the breeze caressed her skin and hair. Smell of salt spray. Paradise.

Frances was there as Lloyd George finalised the United Kingdom taking possession of Germany's African territories, as well as the Mandates of both Palestine and Mesopotamia from the Ottomans. David had struck a great deal, one that tasted even sweeter because of how it annoyed the French. Happy days. And even happier nights. The jolliest of jollies. If the people, those suckers exhausted by the war and crippled by fear of influenza, could have seen how their leaders disported themselves – how they did like to be beside the seaside – they might have taken offence. The success of the Russian revolution might have been repeated in England, France and Italy – even in America!

San Remo also saw a dinner for Megan's eighteenth birthday. Frances seated next to Monsieur Philippe Berthelot, trusted advisor to the French prime minister. Handsome. Dark. Confident. Old-world manners with a beguiling hint of arrogance. Fifty-three years old. Almost as old as David, but better preserved. Something of a matinee idol air about him. Married obviously, but that couldn't be helped. Everyone's married.

Philippe Berthelot had been everywhere and had done everything and could express himself with sensual extravagance in English as well as French. Philippe Berthelot was the subject of several guilty dreams in San Remo and his haughty face sometimes swims into her mind at unexpected moments even now, can appear unbidden when David lays his hands on her.

They have met once or twice since that San Remo idyll – here at Chequers and also at Downing Street – but there has been no impropriety. They've never even been alone together. Watchful eyes everywhere. So many people, not just Megan, who would love to unseat Frances as principal companion to the prime minister. J.T. Davies, he would love it – bloody love it – if David ditched her. Any excuse and he'd be worming himself into her place.

And if they were ever alone, Philippe and herself? If she could be completely certain they wouldn't be discovered? If she had, for instance, been alone and unchaperoned in the games room when he had appeared earlier? If he'd made an advance? Well, perhaps she wouldn't have discouraged him. Perhaps there would have been a brief liaison. Some serious coquetry anyway. Hard to resist a good-looking man who, in a letter sent just after that first meeting, describes your eyes as *soft and luminous*. A man who writes that your mouth is *exquisite*. A good-looking, accomplished man who pays proper attention to what you're saying. Who appreciates your subtle and successful arbitrations of delicate discussions.

Because all of that was clear from the letters too. The way he referred back to little details from their conversation – *Your knowledge of Persian arts and literature… your sympathy for Arabic people... your love of writing... your sombre dress of midnight blue...*

And it's hard to resist a man who buys thoughtful little gifts and, crucially, also remembers to send them. The delicate Norman cross that goes so well with her favourite black dress. The book of Breton poetry.

And on the more recent Downing Street visit, where they could hardly exchange more than two words together? Berthelot had proved then that he is one of those rare men who knows that a silence needn't be awkward but can be full of tender communication and sympathetic feeling. One of those even rarer men whose hands stay where you can see them, but who lets you know in a thousand little ways that if the time ever did come to use them then he would know what to do. Buttons and zips won't hold him up too long, just long enough to build anticipation. To create a necessary detour, a small delay on the road to pleasure. To stoke a fire.

So, yes, maybe if they are ever alone, she will do more than just play snooker with Philippe Berthelot. It's a nice thing to daydream about anyway.

As long as he keeps off the topic of the Jews.

It's a blind spot with him. In both letters and conversation, he can get quite boring about them. He's not alone in this, mind. So many French people – especially in the government – are completely nuts when it comes to the Jews, worse even than the Germans.

3

'You know what I'm going to do? I'm going to send a message to Shortt and get Thomson replaced, get him sent back to inspecting prison toilets. That's what he was doing before, wasn't it? Maybe I'll even arrange to have him sent back to the South Sea islands. With any luck they'll do to him what they did to Captain Cook.'

He might do it too. David Lloyd George has an amber gleam in his eye, and she knows that look. It signals the impulsivity that makes him do things however destructive they are, however opposed to his own interests. At least he seems to have forgotten about Philippe.

'David, you know what I was doing with Sir Basil? The work I was doing?'

'I'm really not interested.'

'I was saving your skin, David. I was ensuring that any investigation into what Grayson might be planning was definitively nipped in the bud.'

'Oh really?'

'Yes, really. And if you want my advice, my political advice as your private secretary, I will say that firing the head of counter-intelligence would be a mistake.'

'Ha! Sticking up for him now.'

'I'm sticking up for *you*, you silly man—'

David interrupts, has things to say. Furious things. His talk now is not so much a river in flood as a sea in a proper storm. Words whipping at her in cold torrents. In angry waves. There is thunder. Lightning. All the *Sturm und Drang* he can muster. But there's something unreal about it too. Something inauthentic. Oh, he's trying to enjoy this rage. Trying to love this tempest in his blood. The hoarse roaring carnival of it. The way it provokes his heart to stamp and shout.

Like father, like daughter, Frances thinks. David is exulting in his own fury so immensely that there's no sense in trying to interrupt too early. She needs to wait for a break in this storm and seize her moment then.

She doesn't listen to the actual words, what would be the point of that? The music of them is enough. There's volume here, all brass and drums, but she's a seasoned watcher of these performances and the longer it goes on the more convinced she is that this performance is actually a livid chamber piece trying to punch up enough to become a symphony. It's a melodrama of hurt that is undernourished somehow.

Weak.

Eventually he comes to a halt, eventually she gets to say, look you idiot man, you blind fool, there's a good chance that this Victor Grayson you're so worried about doesn't know anything about the political fund, but it's a certainty that Basil Thomson knows everything. He may even know things about it that you don't know. It's your spy chief that holds your balls in his hands. It's him you need to keep sweet. Not some old pre-war socialist whose name people hardly remember.

She doesn't actually use these words. You can't call David a fool to his face, but the sense of them is there, buried in the shadows of her measured sentences, and he hears them.

Responds with another little performance. Another little opera. This one is fiercer, there's more heat in it. His voice booms, rumbles like a coming earthquake. She worries that one of her servant neighbours in these attic rooms will burst in, seeking to save her.

Time to wait again. The hurricane will pass. It always does, in the end, if you wait long enough. David Lloyd George always blows himself out.

It takes a while, but at last she gets to repeat – several times – that being nice to this man Thomson – this deeply unappealing man, she should say – was all in the cause of making sure Lloyd George's leadership could continue without unnecessary pain. God knows there is enough to worry about without adding complications. She tells him that it's what he employs her for. To do this work. To ask a man about his school days, to let him win at snooker.

'I think the continuance of your premiership is worth a game of croquet, don't you?'

She says it softly. Her voice as calm as his was agitated, as cool as his was hot. Tries to keep a smile in it. If his rant was all trumpets, hers is all flutes. He responds with another intestinal growl of words, but she tunes out again. Lets her mind wander. He'll get to the right place in his own time. He always does.

Already she can see that he's losing propulsion. There'll be some further muttering, some more sulky discourse, but in the end he'll dwindle into a kind of capitulation. It's all such a ridiculous show too, because she also knows that – as jealous as he is – if it was vital to his career, he'd allow anything.

Sometimes Frances thinks that if David believed it was politically expedient, he'd actually encourage her to toss off the odd ambassador or jiggle the bollocks of a junior minister. A smooch in the garden would be nothing. A bagatelle.

The career comes first for David. Always has. Always will. Sometimes she wonders if it's one of the things she loves most about him. His ruthlessness, the morality that's flexible enough to accommodate almost anything. He's emotional, yes, sensitive, yes, but also brutal when it counts. You have got to love that in a man.

'David.' Her voice seems to startle him. 'It's late. Can you help me out of my dress?'

She's timed it perfectly. He can't hold back. The parliamentarian in him, already fading, vanishes in a moment. Now he is a man of instinct. A servant of his desires.

As he fumbles with buttons on the back of her dress, he kisses her neck. He grows more hurried and less dextrous as each layer is revealed. After her dress is away and thrown to the floor, he pulls off her princess slip, hauls down her drawers like a man taking down a flag, a man surrendering. He fiddles anxiously with the clips to her garter belt, kneels to roll her stockings down her legs with deep reverence, as though he were a man at prayer. She puts a hand on his shoulder to steady herself while she raises each leg in turn, and he murmurs to himself. A devout country vicar reciting psalms.

He trembles as he unhooks her corset. His breathing alters. So easy to distract a man like this. She smiles to herself.

Closes her eyes.

And, yes, she does wonder – though only for a moment – how Basil Thomson would perform these same tasks. Would he treat her like a policeman handling evidence, with care, mentally labelling every part of her? Or would he reveal a true self that is all passion and flame?

She doesn't dwell on him, though. The thought of Thomson's headmasterly frown is replaced by images of Berthelot's dark head, his eyes all dark French heat.

'Oh God, my love, my angel. I'm so sorry.'

David is fully hers again now. Now it's safe to use the words she has wanted to say ever since he began this scene. She'll soften them, though, wrap them up in sardonic tenderness for him.

'Sometimes you're a booby, David. A beautiful, beautiful idiot.'

'It's because I need you so much.'

'I know, I know.' She strokes his head.

David rises from his knees with a half-suppressed grunt. Passionate intensity isn't easy at fifty-seven. Hard on the joints. Murder on the knees. She smiles and they hold one another's gaze. She hugs him. She unbuttons him. She reaches into his fly, takes out Mr Pidyn. Dear old eager Mr Pidyn.

'Is this member ready to be dishonourable?' she says.

He says nothing. She repeats the question. Nothing more will happen until she gets an answer. She squeezes.

'Oh yes. So ready, my darling girl.'

'Finally.'

They move to the bed, lie down together, her naked, him fully clothed but with her hand holding him. She holds him the way a good groom holds the reins of a pony. Kindly but firmly, letting him know who's boss.

They kiss. Lose themselves in that for a long, still moment.

'David?'

'Yes, my girl.'

'Tell me my eyes are luminous.'

He does it, his voice is breathy. Yearning is choking him now.

'Tell me again and then tell me my lips are soft and that my mouth is exquisite.'

'They are. It is.'

'Tell me, then' – a thought strikes her – 'tell me in Welsh.'

'*Mae dy lygaid yn oleu. Mae'ch gwefusau'n feddal a'ch ceg yn goeth.*'

'Say it again.'

'*Mae dy lygaid yn oleu*' – a very deliberate pause. She squeezes gently. David gasps – '*Mae'ch gwefusau'n feddal a'ch ceg yn goeth.*'

Well, it's not French, but it will have to do. It's not sophisticated, but there's an otherworldly charm there. Welsh, she thinks, is not a sexual language, there's too much damp mist in it for that, but it has the allure of ancient legends. It speaks of the shepherding of mythical beasts. She takes him in her mouth.

And suddenly, without wishing it, she's thinking of babies. Hits her like a train. How she wants, needs, a child. And David owes her that.

It's not possible now, but if he wasn't prime minister? If he should somehow fall from grace?

4

Here's a question: how do you help your lover cope with the termination of your pregnancy? That's something they don't tell you in the magazines. You won't find that kind of practical, useful advice in *The Lady* or even in *Woman's Life.*

If we ever do live in a world where it's possible to publish such a piece, then Frances could write it. She has things to say on the subject. Serious things.

Firstly, she would write, *never, ever let them dwell on it, that's the ticket. A man's recovery period will just be prolonged if you indulge them in serious talk of health, never mind morality. Best to keep any pain – physical or emotional – to yourself if you can, or, if you really have to express your feelings, do so only to close female friends. To your lover you should be breezy, unbothered. That's the best way to help him through it.* That's Frances's experience, anyway.

Two years ago, almost exactly. Five days at home cramping and bleeding and in a sweat of fear. She was, she knew, luckier than most in her position. She had good, safe pills from an impeccable source. She had the doctor who provided them (a Liberal Party loyalist) on hand. His only fee had been his insistence that she listen to his lecture, a weary little talk about Being Careful.

She had an efficient and discreet maid, plus a few trusted friends to bring her newspapers. Friends who knew better than to shake their heads at her or pull long faces.

She also had the love and support of David, although that was necessarily at a distance. The distraction of the war. The fear of scandal. His natural squeamishness. She couldn't expect him to be by her side for days at a time, that would be unreasonable. Nevertheless, he came on the last day, when the period of greatest danger to her life was past.

He brought a casserole prepared by Megan (who knew only that her former teacher had some kind of mysterious complaint, and who wanted to practise those domestic science skills she had recently learned at school). Oh, David was so worried. Poor thing. He was stricken when he saw her, lost for words. His eyes full of tears. Then he was all apologies. Cursed himself.

Listening to all that had been irritating, frankly.

She had worked hard at lifting his mood. Had somehow found the strength to distract him. Had willed herself to rally, to enquire after how he had been coping without her advice.

She did a good job.

Pretty soon he was back to more or less his old self, back to his heavy-handed jocularity. His florid teasing.

She led him to conversations where he was most comfortable. Political gossip. Party intrigue.

Yes, she did sterling work in taking his mind off things. She can be proud of herself. It is well known that men are really too delicate for anything connected with the body and all its juices and leaks, its mucus and mess, and certainly way too fastidious for the business of ending unwanted pregnancies, and this male helplessness can undermine the whole process. Better to keep them away altogether if you can, and only let them approach if you have to. And definitely wait until the worst is over.

5

In the rafters now there are the usual scurryings and scuttlings. Somewhere in the house, someone laughs. Or sobs. House like this, it's so hard to tell. And here, entwined on this hard and narrow servant's bed, David apologises for his lack of trust in her, his lack of faith. He becomes almost tearful as he says he knows how much she does for him and if it wasn't for his family he would…

'Hush, my love.'

She kisses him, sits up and turns her face away, keeps her eyes fixed on the little table underneath the window with its still life of bottles and jars. The paint and the powders, the armour a modern woman needs to take on the world. She makes a decision. She won't tell him about her need for a child. Not tonight. She doesn't want to see that panic in his eyes. She can face most things, but not that. Not tonight at any rate. It will have to be faced soon. But it can wait another night.

Right now, she's going to lie back and think of the changes she's going to make to Chequers. She'll prove Megan right. She's going to be lady of the manor. Queen. David owes her that too. She can't rule at Downing Street, and she can't even go to Wales, never mind Criccieth, but she will become the Queen of Chequers.

Her head fills with plans, with ideas for furnishings. Thomson is right, the place is antiquated, it's like a boys' school. Needs shaking up. Needs light, colour, some European influences. It's never going to be Versailles, but the place could make a bit more effort, could shine a little more brightly.

Frances is confident that she can help Chequers with that.

TWELVE

Bad Angel

THE WEST END, NIGHT

1

WHEN Babs alights from her omnibus in Piccadilly Circus she has no sense of why she does so. No thoughts in her head at all. She just knows she can't stay on board for even one more stop. She is compelled by a simple need to be up and moving, rather than sitting. She needs to feel the damp, vaguely fungal, air of London on her face, to feel her feet on the solid, metalled streets. A person can only cope with the stop-start jolt of a bus for so long, only tolerate that tang of petrol in your mouth for a little while. Plus, when you're on a London bus at night, the electric chiaroscuro of the world beyond the window looks beguiling, beckons you towards it, dares you to get off and immerse yourself in it. London at night can be a minx when she wants to be.

As soon as she's on the pavement, she spies the swaying silhouetted figure of Victor Grayson taking his leave of the Criterion. He does it with a quick embrace of a young woman in a well-cut coat and, after she has moved off with a wave into the Saturday night crowds, there is a more intense clinch with the uniformed doorman.

In this second, lengthier cuddle the squeezing seems both harder and more exploratory. Hands move from shoulders to waist to buttocks. Then Grayson is away, pulling up the collar of his army greatcoat against the drizzle. Watching this, she gets it, suddenly knows why she is where she is.

If there is one thing her reading of Crowley has taught her it's that there are no accidents, no coincidences. We are worked on by forces we conjure up ourselves, our footsteps driven by magick created inside us. Whatever happens to us is what we have chosen. Wherever we find ourselves is the result of following the compass of our own desires.

Listen, whatever you want to do, your unconscious will help you. Will guide you. Wherever your ordinary daytime work-aday mind is afraid to go, your unconscious will push you towards it. Your unconscious, let's call her your lovely, beautiful Bad Angel, your Angel of Life, is unimpressed by your ordinary self with all its timidity, its beige acquiescence to the material world. Your conscious self vacillates, weighs up the pros and the cons. Gets lost in conflicting advice. Is paralysed by the sticky quicksand of Thought. But the Bad Angel knows. The Bad Angel acts.

The Bad Angel brings you and your brother's old service revolver to the place where you can see the traitor to the working class. Where you can gaze upon the man who is emblematic of all the turncoats who urged the workers to put away their dreams of utopia, to stop trying to build Jerusalem, and to instead feed themselves into the meat mincers of the Western Front simply to preserve the satanic mills of the ruling class.

Now she comprehends why she chose to get off the bus at this exact spot. This is what it's all been for. This is why she put on the uniform and got the gun. This is the magick that she has been brewing in her guts.

Her heart races, she can feel the blood in her body fizzing, popping, bubbling. Her mind, though, her mind is tranquil, calm.

She follows him now. She sees him check a piece of paper. It seems to take him a while to get the information he needs from it. When he begins to walk, he moves slowly, carefully, like an old man. That's who drunks are: people who have voluntarily made themselves old, who have given themselves dementia. And she had sexual intercourse – of a kind – with this man only this morning!

She feels no shame. Just a kind of angry wonder. She almost laughs out loud. Maybe it was somehow all part of the plan. Maybe she just has to trust the process.

It's an effort for Babs to go slowly enough to make following Grayson look natural. She has to pause in front of shop windows as if she is entranced by the products on show there. The hats. The umbrellas. The pipes. The women's dresses – though she moves quickly when she realises how odd that might seem to passers-by.

Whatever is on display there, really, she is taking the chance to check her reflection. This is no hardship. Each time she does it she enjoys again the sight of herself as a man, as a soldier. She looks – it has to be said – great. Properly great. Like an elfin Valentino, in fact. Maybe it's the way she seems to take up more space in this martial jacket, these hard-wearing army trousers. The confidence a uniform – more or less any uniform – gives you. Maybe it's that green and khaki are her colours. Maybe it's the peaked hat, the titfer that is both silly and serious, comical but not to be messed with.

Standing in front of the Swan & Edgar department store, she has to remind herself not to make feminine gestures. She can't, for instance, adjust the angle of this hat, however weird it feels to have her hair bunched up beneath it. That's what a woman would do, not an officer from a regiment of the line. Not even one who has been to a major public school.

As she ambles and meanders, looking, she hopes, like a carefree – maybe tipsy? – soldier home on leave, she becomes aware all over again of the impact she has on other people. She's no longer scrutinising the women – she has to keep her eyes on Grayson – but she is more alive to the way she herself is eyed up by both sexes. The further she gets from the centre of things, the bolder everyone she passes becomes.

A man asks her for a light. He is stocky and exhales the smells of tobacco and fish. She laughs inwardly as she shakes her head. She knows what he wants. She knows that look in a man's eye. Does he know she's a woman dressed up? Probably, she thinks. He either doesn't care, or it's what he prefers.

The man looks her up and down. Steps into her space. Squints at her.

'Never met a soldier what didn't smoke,' he says.

What does she do now?

Nothing. She doesn't have to do anything. The man shrugs, smiles, walks on.

She walks behind Grayson for about an hour, she guesses, following the oily river east. All the time trying to gather the nerve to run up to him, to grab him by the arm, make him spin round and face her, but problem is she doesn't really have a plan for what comes next. She knows he has to pay for what he's done, but what form will that payment take? The heat in her blood has cooled now, she could turn back, but she knows that if she did she'd be dogged with a sense of having failed at some important task, even if the exact form that task should take isn't clear to her.

She is sure that Grayson must notice he's being followed, but no, apparently not. Behind her the nervous noises of the West End – the petulant horns of the taxis, the chatter and hum of the revellers leaving the theatres and the restaurants, the dirty thrum of the car engines – are replaced by mutinous whispers of rain on increasingly deserted streets.

Such people as you do see now are huddled in doorways. Hollow-cheeked children, slumped drunks. Slim youths in thin jackets with hungry, opportunist eyes.

As she passes a group outside a pub – one still brazenly serving despite the hour – someone shouts, 'Atten-shun!' and the group laugh.

She passes a couple of vagrants pushing their belongings in perambulators. One of them stops, straightens up and salutes with a mocking parade-ground vigour.

'Sah!'

His companion in vagabondage gurgles happily. 'We was in the Grenadiers,' he says. He belches.

A few yards further on a teenage streetwalker, narrow-shouldered in a grubby red dress, face all challenge and sharp points, asks if the officer would like to go somewhere for a kiss and a cuddle. Maybe something more. She knows a place, very clean. The girl's voice lacks conviction though her eyes glint with a mixture of fear and defiance. It's a mix that some people – some men – might really go for. Babs shakes her head and the girl seems relieved. She nods.

'Please yourself,' she says. 'I knew you was a fairy soon as I saw you.'

'I'm not a… I'm not a fairy. I'm a girl. A woman.'

The kid is unfazed. More relaxed, she looks at Babs hard for a long second. Laughs, claps her tiny hands together. They're rough and chapped, faintly indigo with cold.

'Yeah, I see that now. I'll still do it with you. Cost you a bit more though, like.'

She sounds apologetic.

'You're all right.'

'You got any brass? As a gift, like. I'm starving. Haven't eaten today.'

And maybe not yesterday either, thinks Babs. She hunts around in the pockets of her uniform. She has exactly three pence in coins and a five-pound note.

The girl chuckles. 'I don't mind a note,' she says. 'As long as you don't expect no change.'

Babs thinks she likes this girl. Would she have had this same happy, resilient spirit if she'd been forced to live like her, to make her way like this? Would she still be laughing? Almost certainly not.

'How old are you?'

'Twenty-three,' says the girl.

'Really?'

'Of course not really. You're a bit thick, aren't you? I'm fourteen. Or I will be soon. Anyway, thanks for the scratch.'

As the girl hurries off, she calls back over her shoulder, 'Don't worry, miss. I won't tell no one you're a tom!'

Babs hadn't thought of that. It plays out in her head. A whole film. One with a murder in it. One her brother might like. The girl tells a brother, a father, a pimp – who may be the same person as one of the others – and they hunt for her, chase her down. *The sport we could have with a tom*, she imagines them saying. *A rich tom at that. Will round off the night in fine style.* Or words to that effect.

Inspired, she pulls her brother's pistol from its holster. If she waves that in the faces of anyone that comes after her, well, it might give them pause. Babs has never understood the appeal of weapons before, so she is surprised by how comforting it feels. How snug. The sensual curve of the handle. The reassuring heft of it.

But now there's a moment of consternation, of confusion. She's lost Grayson! Can't see him anywhere. Dawdling like he is, he's still got ahead of her. The jolly banter with the juvenile tail has held her up too long. Ah, well, maybe it's for the best.

2

And Grayson? What is he doing? What is he thinking? He doesn't seem to see the people bunched in the passages between the houses, he doesn't seem to feel the mizzle, or notice the fried-fish, piss and smoke stench. He doesn't fear the city's shadowed holes and corners. He pays the children, the women and the cripples he passes as little mind as he pays the scrawny cats that flit from doorway to doorway. He also ignores the drunks who laugh too loudly outside the public houses. His body heading doggedly, stubbornly – if unsteadily – through the fog.

Grayson is known for his long solitary walks, and he knows London so well by now that he can find almost anywhere in the city without the need for any thinking whatsoever. If all else fails, when the last paper to consider employing him has closed, he could always become a hackney cab driver. He feels sure he already has the Knowledge. His feet have already learned it. It's in his bones.

Untethered by any need to think, his body weaves through the East End's ammoniated dark, snaking between the feeble puddles of ghost-light provided by the intermittent gas lamps. Not enough to see by, just glimmering flakes of silver to aim for. A narrow thread of phosphorescence pulling him gently towards his destination.

Oiled like this your inebriate can slide across the city, feeling invincible. Not so much on the pavements, as above them. Like Jesus gliding on the water, he can go anywhere. Who is going to stop him?

Without his consciousness to guide him, Victor is free to cross continents in his mind, to wander over the entire world without obstacles and to mix epochs while he does it. He is physically in London but he is also roving soggily between many other places. Right this second, for example, he is in New York, walking between the skyscrapers with his new wife on a trip paid for by soft-hearted British socialists.

3

Was that when he was happiest? The period after that total collapse in February 1913, when he was prescribed a long rest by his doctor? His friends had formed a committee of leading leftists to raise monies to send him on a long trip. A kind of honeymoon. Sweet of them. He had joked about the lengths his so-called comrades would go to in order to rid themselves of him, but he was also touched.

He was, of course, pleased to receive the money – £106 16s. 10d. coming from supporters all over the country – but just as heartening was the fact that so many people wanted to help him, that was the best medicine, that put colour in his cheeks. Lead back in his pencil.

Within eighteen months almost none of these friends and supporters were still talking to him. They had almost all abandoned him. That's the simple price exacted by debt, and the things we do to escape the weight of it.

All Debt wants is all you have, your material possessions, sure, but also your dignity, your self-respect, your principles.

These things quickly become unaffordable luxuries when you slide into Debt's chill embrace.

Ruth and he had been in Theobald Street then. Living in one room, sleeping on the floor, a sugar box used as a table. Victor was too ill to undertake speaking engagements and too exhausted to write. Desperate times. The epitome of modern metropolitan living in the very epicentre of the empire it emphatically wasn't. As soon as the money came through they left the relentless grind of the London winter and went to Italy.

Five weeks there and they were off again. Driven away by the sirocco that made Victor's illness worse, they undertook the long sea voyage to New York. With the donated money they rented a bungalow in Long Island just fifty yards from the Atlantic. Four months there and they moved to a small flat in Manhattan – £106 16s. 10d. went a long way in those months before the war.

So, let's ask again: was it in New York that Victor Grayson was happiest?

No, frankly.

He found the city raw and crude, too hastily constructed to be properly habitable. The same painful twang, throb and thrust of industrial London but with none of its mitigating history. As he told Ethel Vaughan-Sawyer, the buildings were all atrocious and had not even any pretence to architecture.

The real trouble with Victor's American experience was not anything to do with the architecture. Of course it wasn't. It was instead the problem that afflicts everybody who chooses a geographical solution to their troubles; wherever you go, you are condemned to taking yourself with you. You can't wriggle out of that.

They had whiskey in New York too – unlike now – and if you had no money for coal, furniture or firewood, then the flats there could be as cold and as austere as any in Theobald Street. And if you are the type of person who considers beds, chairs and tables to be luxuries, while also thinking that grog is an essential, then your circumstances are likely to be bleak.

Friends in England continued to be generous – they sent more cash when the initial gratuity ran out – but they couldn't be expected to fund Grayson's sabbatical forever. Neither Victor's charm nor pity for his bride could make that happen.

So finally the couple did what all outgunned insurgents have to do in the end – they surrendered. They returned to England to prepare for Elaine's birth, to attend to various court cases and to live off the charity, not of socialist friends, but instead of one very specific capitalist: to wit, one John Nightingale, banker.

And yet, as Victor moves through London now, it's not the misery of New York he remembers, not the terrible buildings or the cold or the way sickness came to claim him again, instead it's the exhilaration he had felt when Ruth announced she was expecting. The way he'd felt a joyous kick to his heart.

You know, don't you, that the prospect of fatherhood does amazing things to the eyes? Makes you see everything in sharp outlines, brings a special light to even the most mundane objects. And the object made most vivid to Victor wasn't mundane. Ruth. God, she was beautiful that day. Seemed like that day was the first one in months when he had seen her properly.

She was pale, so pale that she was almost blue. She was nervous, she was shy. She was way too thin. Several times she had to flutter out to the bathroom to puke. She stank of vomit and sweat, and he loved her more then than he ever had.

And now, as his body negotiates the slippery streets – the potentially lethal combination of rain and dog shit – he begins to weep the way only a drunk can weep. The self-pity, the overwhelming sense of loss, the prayer to a God you don't believe in for one more chance. Just because you've stopped believing doesn't mean you stop asking for help. *If you let me put things right this time, oh Lord, if you let me get away with this, then I'll change. Lord, if you help me get through this, then I'll go to see my daughter again, as soon as I can, and I'll make up for my abandonment of her, my cruel rejection of her. You wait, Lord, if you do this thing for me, I'll be the best man, the best father, the best socialist there has ever been. I'll even live back up North if I have to.*

This is Victor Grayson's last prayer and it is his most fervent, his most desperate search for God.

4

Behind Victor, Babs listens. An insomniac seagull skreiches its anger and frustration. Water splooshes against barges in a fatigued rhythm. *Shush kiss*, the river goes, *shush kiss*. There's also a strange groaning that could be anything. Something or someone in distress, or the growl of some infernal engine that never stops running. An implacable hum. Could be the sound of the city itself. Could be the exhausted moaning made when you distil the sweated dreams of eight million Londoners.

Footsteps. Leather soles slapping against wet and broken pavement. Two forward, two back. Two forward, one back. The drunk's waltz. No animal dance, this. This is something completely, desolately human. She listens a moment more, then hurries towards the sound, marvelling as she does so at how easy it is to move dressed like this. How free it feels. How fast you can go.

Victor Grayson has paused outside the door of a particularly mean-looking terrace house in a particularly mean-looking street, one where the pavement is flayed and cracked. Although it is one with an incongruously expensive motor car outside. Don't see many vehicles like this around here.

It's not yet midnight but there is scarcely a light in any of the windows. The people have hunkered down and out of sight. There's little comfort here for anyone. Grayson is checking the address on his scrap of paper, squinting at it through the tired rain and his bombed vision. Clearly it is important to get this right, just won't do to knock on the wrong door at this time of night.

Which is when he sees Babs.

She's been prowling after Victor for a small eternity without his seeming to have the slightest suspicion that there is someone behind him, and yet something makes him glance around now. There is a stretched moment. He's drunk, it's raining, there's a good fifty yards between them, plus she's dressed as a Fusiliers officer. Impossible for him to recognise her, surely?

As he takes a few steps towards her, she fights an impulse to turn and flee, but she has got things to say, questions to ask. She has a reason for trailing him here, even if she hasn't quite worked out what it is yet.

She also has a gun in her hand.

Victor Grayson strides forward. He seems to have sobered up suddenly. He moves briskly, purposefully, in a way he hasn't the entire way here. Babs feels fixed in place. Pinned. She can't think of anything to say, anything to do. Her throat is full, frozen. Her hands come up as if to ward him off.

Again, let's not forget that she has that pistol in one of those hands. A 1915 service issue .38 Webley revolver, the standard sidearm given to all British army officers since 1887.

'Who the hell—' he begins. Then he laughs and, more gently, 'But I know thee lass, you're...'

He stops, something shimmers across his face. Some confusion, some fear, some blurring in the memory. Maybe it's *not* that girl from this morning? That girl with the cheerful fingers, the playful tongue? That's the thing about developing the drunk's nightly senility. You can't trust anything you see, anything you feel. You're never certain about the true nature of things. Your world is populated by everyone you've ever met, all together, all the time. Now, for example, could it be that it's actually Ruth in front of him? Ruth wearing his army uniform. She would do that sometimes. One of their games. Just for laughs.

Everything's a costume, he finds himself thinking. Everything we do is just acting. Everything is dressing up. Preacher, politician, soldier. Father, husband, lover. We put on the outfit, learn the lines, stand in our appointed places at the appointed moments. Told when to move, when to breathe. All our movements blocked out in advance somehow. Even your attempts to fight against what's been set up for you – trade union activist, working-class scholar, parliamentarian, wilful degenerate – they too feel like roles given out by some hidden director. Nothing much to do with him, with his essence.

The gun takes action then, goes rogue, leaps in her hand, then leaps *from* her hand, and is gone, is spinning through the air, hitting the ground before she hears the noise of the shots.

Later she will swear she never pulled the trigger, that her finger never went near it. The gun just did what a gun does, what it needed to do. Later still, she will wonder if the gun did what Victor Grayson wanted it to. Or maybe it was a pact between the three of them. Maybe Victor and Babs had brought the gun to life. Maybe Babs, Victor and the gun were all in it together, had created the magick together.

In the houses the gas jets are being turned up, oil lamps and candles are spitting into life. Doors are banging open, shadows are stumbling out into the street, and from the terraced house that Victor had been approaching, a man is running towards the little tableau – the little monument if you like – made by the slight figure in uniform and the fallen man in the greatcoat.

THIRTEEN

A Rum Do

1

I T is late but Chequers is not yet asleep. There's been a little
gathering organised. Edward Shortt, Sir Basil Thomson,
J.T. Davies and various other, more junior, civil servants
and backroom Johnnies are submitting to the efforts of the
French delegation to recreate the *jolie* spirit of the first peace
conferences. The decent wine has taken effect and the party
atmosphere, somewhat forced at the beginning, seems genuine
now. The good brandy has come out – not that the French
will admit that it's better than they're used to – and there are
snacks. Cheese and cream crackers (Crumpsall's not Jacob's.
Unpatriotic to serve Jacob's given that company's Irish ori-
gins). There are also the last of the pinwheel cookies left over
from that working luncheon. They're going down very well.

The gas jets are dimmed to a soft woody light, something
a bit more conducive to conversation. And, of course, it may
also have been the intervention of the baby that contributed
most to lifting the mood.

The guests are attended by blandly smiling, perfectly unobtrusive female servants. One of the more bohemian British officials has brought down a gramophone, although no one is dancing yet. That will come later when the serious men have retired to their quarters, leaving the space for the younger folk. For now, the music is merely tinny background noise, a thin accompaniment to the sonorous squabbling of Aristide Briand, Philippe Berthelot, Edward Shortt and their deputies.

It seems none of these learned diplomats – several of whom had held senior posts in 1914 – can agree how the whole damned thing got started. This is discourse all of them have had many, many times. In parliaments, in front of inquiries, at banquets, in nightclubs, around the dinner table with their wives, in bed with their mistresses, always the same plaintive refrain: how the blazes did we allow ourselves to get dragged into that infernal mess? Aren't we meant to be the brightest, best, most civilised people on earth? Aren't we the most advanced society there has ever been? The wisest generation? The one with access to all the books of philosophy that have ever been written? The generation who have sloughed off the chains of superstition and the mind-forged manacles of religion?

Was it a kind of collective madness? Was it the calls from Honour, from Duty – those gruesomely seductive twins whose wishes must always be fulfilled, whatever the cost, whose voices always seem impossible to ignore?

There is some consensus that both the Austrians and the Serbs were at fault and that if someone had knocked their heads together early enough, then all the bloodshed, all the *grief*, could have been avoided.

'That should have been the kaiser's job,' says someone. J.T. Davies probably, the voice is milky enough for it to be him.

'The kaiser couldn't find his own arse in the dark with both hands,' says someone else.

A third someone opines that when it came down to it the whole thing was the fault of the Jews. There is much nodding at this from the French side. 'Come on now,' says an English voice. 'That's not entirely fair.'

Sir Basil Thomson isn't paying much attention to who is saying exactly what to whom. Words are just words and most talk is simply about the speaker impressing his personality on the room. A good detective is not distracted by patter, he looks for other, more important, signals. He is that tiresome audience member at a music hall magic show, the one who refuses to be impressed, who won't be hypnotised, the one who must look to see how the trick is done, who has to spot the sleight of hand. The man immune to things that are point-lessly impressive, and whose only satisfaction comes from uncovering the truth, however disappointing.

The skilled policeman looks hard at the background details, at facial expressions, at what is communicated through body language, through nods and winks. To be effec-tive the head of C Division, like a prison governor, must be fluent in the language of the blink, the dialects of the twitch and the fidget. All the various accents of the body.

Sir Basil Thomson also knows that much of the talk of the men is just designed to attract and hold the attention of the women. This male noise is as ubiquitous as birdsong and has much the same purpose. Here I am, these men are saying. Notice me. Love me.

Sad really.

Not counting the servants gliding silently from group to group with their bottles and their plates of cheese, there are just two females in the room. Two females and one baby.

Those females are Megan Lloyd George, still a child if you were to ask Sir Basil, but even he might admit that tonight at least she is doing a good impression of a fully grown woman. She holds her glass with some poise. Seems to be holding her own in conversation. Laughs at the right moments and not too loudly.

There are some giveaways, however. Her face is flushed, her eyes glistening, her hands often moving to her hair, seemingly to pat and smooth, but actually, Sir Basil suspects, to do the opposite, to ruffle and tousle and tease. To make her look a little wilder, a little more like the wanton creature she'd like to be. Why, Sir Basil wonders, do so many young women from respectable homes want to look like they've been dragged up from the gutter these days?

The other female is Irene Baker and the baby is hers – adorable young Francis Baker, nine months old and very prettily asleep.

Young Francis hadn't been asleep when Irene had first come into the room with him clutched to her bosom. He hadn't been adorable either. He'd been bawling, furious. Yelling at top volume with that blood-curdling sense of betrayal that's only ever forgivable in babies. Immediately, a handsome young diplomat had detached himself from the tangle of floppy-haired clerks grouped around the Lloyd George girl. He had rushed over to mother and child. Philip Baker.

'You sort him,' Irene Baker had said, thrusting the squirming bundle of raucous purple sorrow towards her husband. 'And yes.'

'What?' said Philip Baker, confused.

'Yes, I've fed him. Yes, I've burped him, Yes, I've played with him, sung to him, cuddled him, given him an extra blanket. Yes, I've done every bloody thing I can think of and now you have to do something, because the next thing I try will be throwing him out the bloody window.'

'Right,' said Baker. 'I'll take him.' He spun away towards the doors, banged out into the corridor. Everyone stared after him. It'll be an interesting challenge: Olympic medallist and League of Nations negotiator versus angry baby.

Conversation had been effectively stilled by this little interruption and now that the baby had gone, the trite trill and skip of the music was suddenly very audible.

'Drink?' This was one of the servant girls who was holding out a flute of fizzy something.

'What a good idea,' said Irene. She drained her glass in a couple of swallows, handed it back to the serving girl and took another. 'You watch, he'll come back in and the bloody child will be sound asleep. Does it just to spite me.' She was frazzled but she was smiling now. Relief was smoothing out her face and the colour was returning to it.

*

And that is exactly what had happened. The Olympic silver medallist had indeed managed to coax his son into slumber.

'A talented man,' said Megan Lloyd George to Irene Baker.

'Yes, it can be infuriating. I'd love to find something that Philip can't do. You know he's going to take my name? Going to change his own by deed poll. I was Irene Noel before we got married and as soon as the paperwork is done we're going to become the Noel-Bakers.'

'But that's marvellous!' said Megan. 'What a tremendous thing to do.' A pause, then, 'I wonder where I can find a man like that?'

'I suggest working in hospitals, it's where I found Philip anyway,' Irene said as she took baby Francis – now fully adorable and silent – from her husband. 'Thank you, Philip,' she smiled. 'This young lady was just wondering where she can find a man like you.'

A lesser man might have blushed, but Philip just grinned, a quick flash of perfect teeth.

'Not many like me around.'

'For which I think maybe we should all be grateful.' Irene's smile was wider now.

Genuine young love. Sickening, isn't it?

Sir Basil Thomson was on the edge of their little group, but no one was paying him any attention. Megan in particular was very pointedly not noticing his presence. He didn't mind. That was the way he liked it.

Sir Basil knew Philip Baker was able, knew it better than his wife. Knew it better than anyone. It's why, despite the fact that Baker had been a conchie, despite the fact that he'd also been an academic – both groups Sir Basil generally despised – he had hired him. Philip Baker was on the C Division payroll. Of course he was. Couldn't let a man like that – an Olympic silver medallist! – waste all his time in a talking shop like the League of Nations.

He'd also been recommended by a man Sir Basil trusted, another ambulanceman – a man who had seen Baker work under fire and been impressed with his calm demeanour, his grace under hard metal falling from the sky. He'd been recommended by Hardit Joshi. These days it is Joshi who often acts as his recruiter-in-chief.

Babies, Sir Basil is thinking. Babies could be valuable additions to the wild service. Useful weapons. Ones designed to be part of the distinctive armoury of women. What a brilliant way to create an expedient disturbance. Who knows what could be planted or removed – what messages passed – while a roomful of high-status diplomats is distracted by the perfect disorientation device that is a baby in full cry.

Anyone glancing over now would see an anonymous man in an old-fashioned suit, slightly paunchy, a closed-off face, stern in the way middle-aged men so often are. Inside he's smiling, however. He's had a good thought. A kind of epiphany: Indians, conchies, women, babies. Once you begin to open your mind to new possibilities, you find they flow towards you from every direction.

Sir Basil has noticed that Loverboy – the young advisor who was hogging the solitary Chequers phone earlier – is in the room, is flitting between groups, a little like the servant girls but without any of their anonymous grace. Sir Basil notices that he avoids Megan and Irene, or, rather, makes them his last resort after all the groups of men seem unwilling to make a little space for him. What makes him so shy? Is it loyalty to that moll back in London? Is it just that he's a little frightened of women? Or the opposite, that he's dismissive of them? Is it the baby that puts him off?

When Loverboy does finally get to the two women, they stop talking and spend a few minutes politely pretending to listen to him. It's a thing that women do. Something occurs to Sir Basil and he wanders over to the group, timing his arrival nicely to interrupt whatever anecdote or observation Loverboy is attempting to inflict on his audience.

'Mrs Baker,' Sir Basil Thomson says, 'young Francis looks like he might be quite a weight.'

'Yes, he is rather.'

'Perhaps we can help with that.'

'We?'

'The government. The civil service. My colleague here,' he gestures towards Loverboy, 'will, I know, be very glad to look after the child.'

Loverboy looks stricken for an instant, but rallies. 'Why yes, I suppose I could—'

'Good, good, if you go and take young Francis to one of the armchairs by the window, then Mrs Baker can make the most of this reception. There are some interesting people here.'

Irene Baker seems briefly uncertain, then makes up her mind to agree.

'Why yes, thank you. That'll be nice actually. Just for ten minutes or so,' she attempts to reassure Loverboy now. 'I'll be nearby of course, but, yes, a chance to see my talented husband in action is a rare thing.'

'Take as long as you like. Enjoy yourself. Your son is in the hands of professionals after all, is he not?' He turns a watery smile towards Loverboy, who picks up his cue.

'Yes, absolutely. Super,' says Loverboy. 'I love babies.'

'Good lad,' says Sir Basil.

The boy takes the baby – gingerly, and very, very carefully – and heads over to the brown leather armchairs by the room's big windows, trying to ignore the pitying looks from his fellow advisors. It's funny, Sir Basil thinks, how it is the smallest acts of revenge that give the most pleasure, and he watches as Megan Lloyd George and Irene Baker waft over to where Irene's husband is making the French prime minister laugh, and doing it in the premier's own language too.

The night moves on. Sashays and sways. The light seems strangely orange now. Drink is spilled. There are crumbs of vol-au-vents on the carpet. Men become quarrelsome or affectionate depending on their basic nature. Some attempt jokes, others take offence at these jokes. Some begin to take more of an interest in the servant girls, who respond to sallies from the men with quick, nervous smiles.

Though it's not really his place, Sir Basil Thomson tells the girls they can all knock off if they like. Their relief is obvious, their gratitude likewise. They've been on their feet for hours and the last thing they need is to be fending off the advances of pissed-up civil servants, even if some of them are French.

Mrs Baker says goodnight. This takes time. Everyone needs

to cluck over the baby. There is, after all, no one in this world more sentimental than an ambitious politician.

'If only they took a few babies into the debating chambers of the League of Nations, might make everyone a little more reasonable, eh?' This is Premier Briand and everyone around him agrees noisily. Yes, yes, babies at the negotiating tables, natural bringers of bonhomie. Look at that angel face, that smile, those pudgy little hands grabbing for his mother's hair, how could anyone not feel better-disposed towards his fellow man once they've seen that?

On the edge of the group, Sir Basil smiles again. So slow, these politicians. He is, as ever, way ahead of them.

'It's a rum do, isn't it?'

'What is, Minister?'

Edward Shortt has been on good form, he has made sure he's exchanged pleasantries with everyone, including the girls serving drinks and the policeman guarding the entrance to the room. He has even made the effort to be civil to the French diplomats.

'David not being here. This was such an opportunity to get things sorted out before the meeting.'

Sir Basil knows what he's saying. Nothing is ever really decided in an official sit-down meeting. Everything important is sorted beforehand in whispered conversations at drinks parties like this, or over games of snooker or cards. You're more likely to solve some knotty problem of world affairs while standing next to a politician at an adjoining urinal than you are at an official meeting.

'You know where he is, of course?'

Yes, yes, he knows all right. Sir Basil will have the transcript in the morning. It will be a disgusting read. He feels a hot flicker in his stomach at the thought of it. An electric twitch in his groin.

'Such a waste.'

For a second, Sir Basil thinks the Home Secretary is referring again to the missed chance for informal diplomacy, two prime ministers meeting over drinks and cream crackers, but a moment later it becomes obvious that this isn't the waste the Minister is talking about at all.

'That poor girl,' Shortt says. 'Throwing her life away on a man like that.'

The music is turned up. There is loud, performative laughter. Smiles that were pasted on earlier are slipping and peeling, real faces can be glimpsed beneath the diplomatic veils. The euphoric glug of bottles being poured, the jubilant pop of another champagne cork. Nearby, a man talks with his mouth full. A repellent, wet and sloppy sound.

It occurs to Sir Basil that the Home Secretary is wrong about the effect of the prime-ministerial absence. It is probably good that Frances Stevenson has kept her lover away from this little San Remo reunion. David Lloyd George is not at his best in this setting. Ends up declaiming and speechifying when he should be listening and then flattering. He can also be a little boring, frankly. The chances of the Mesopotamia problem being solved in the British favour are probably higher without him here.

Tomorrow, after a night with Frances, our prime minister will be clear-headed, full of a sense of his own virility. The

French delegation on the other hand may not be quite as brashly dogmatic or as fiercely pedantic as they usually are. Hungover men don't linger on detail, they just want the meetings to be over. They will often agree to anything.

Speaking of the French delegation: look, there's Philippe Berthelot, that irritatingly suave, impossibly serious advisor to Premier Briand, dancing cheek to cheek with Megan Lloyd George. Maybe we could encourage something there, thinks Sir Basil. It is perhaps worth thinking about.

A moist cough. A bovine and apologetic plod is standing just behind him.

'Yes?' Sir Basil says, a little sharper than he means to be. He can't help it, these uniform types get on his nerves, they just do. The copper seems unperturbed.

'Mrs Lloyd George is here, sir. Car just pulling up outside.'

2

It's the sort of situation that could easily become a crisis. But it is also the sort of problem that Sir Basil knows how to solve. First, Philip Baker is despatched to take Mrs Lloyd George to one of the better drawing rooms, to make sure she has tea and pinwheel cookies, and to make an appropriate fuss of her. The perfect job for a skilled expert in League of Nations diplomacy. He's already soothed the daughter, let's see how he gets on with the mother.

Next, he gets the kid he'll forever think of as Loverboy to run up to the attics and to discreetly, but really bloody urgently, make the prime minister aware that his wife is downstairs, and that maybe he should put some trousers on. Some pyjamas at the very least, and then get back to his own room and make it look like he's been spending the evening reading: government papers or his ridiculous western novel, it doesn't matter, just make it look like he's been having the quietest of nights in ahead of talking to the French about Mesopotamia tomorrow.

Once he's sent these men off to do these errands, he moves to where Philippe Berthelot and Megan Lloyd George are almost, but not quite, entwined. They haven't exactly crossed the line from respectable flirting to scandalous petting, but they are definitely butting up against it.

A quick word with the Frenchman and he is off. It's a dignified retreat as these things go. Sir Basil is impressed by how he takes time to bow towards his dance partner, how he takes the trouble to kiss her on both cheeks. How he makes sure he's made a pretty little speech about how enchanted he is to have met her, how he hopes they will meet again.

He doesn't appear rushed at all. His striding towards the door seems purposeful rather than hurried, and yet the whole manoeuvre takes less than a minute.

They say a withdrawal under fire is the most difficult of all military operations, and yet Philippe Berthelot has proved it can be done with some grace and aplomb.

Megan Lloyd George is a different – and very much less dignified – matter. The eyes that had glittered earlier are now fogged. All her limbs are loose, floppy. Without the sturdy Berthelot to lean on she sways alarmingly. All her bones are spongy. She is also truculent, resistant when it is suggested she might like to go and join her mother. This resistance is all the more vexing given that Sir Basil is fairly sure that she'd been the one who summoned her mother in the first place.

He could imagine the call: *Father's flaunting his mistress. Fawning all over her. And she's loving it. Lapping it up. It's humiliating. She's rubbing our noses in it, Ma. You need to do something about it.* Something along those lines. All delivered with a blabbermouth copper well within earshot, which means there will be hints and innuendo in the papers within days unless he has someone lean on some editors. He sighs. It all takes so much *time*.

In the end the plod comes to life and they practically carry her out. Baker might have handled her better, but he can't be in two places at once and the copper does it efficiently enough, no doubt employing the techniques he learned during the struggles with the suffragettes.

In Sir Basil's considered opinion it is actually helpful that Megan has got herself into this state. Dealing with their daughter's waywardness could be a bonding experience for husband and wife, a chance to get to know each other again. At the very least it's going to be something for them to focus on that isn't David and Frances. Perhaps, you never know, it'll even make the prime minister think a little about how his actions affect his family.

Sir Basil Thomson has no intention of having a conversation with Mrs Margaret Lloyd George himself. Not tonight. He has met her once or twice in the past and she's altogether too formidable. Too forthright. Sir Basil Thomson knows about interrogation and knows enough about Mrs Lloyd George to know you don't want to be quizzed by her if you can avoid it. She's an absolute force. There are few men who could withstand an inquisition led by her. In a different world she'd have been an asset to the service, actually.

3

A knock on the door, soft, hesitant, easily ignored by the bodies moving together on the bed. Then a second knock, louder, less ignorable, then a cough, and a prime-ministerial climax is emphatically thwarted by an advisor bringing urgent and unwelcome news.

Of course, a private secretarial climax has also been choked off. But, thinks Frances, who cares about that? All right for David to grumble and growl and swear and wrap himself in a blanket and waddle to the door to give which- ever idiot servant this is what for, but she, she has to lie in frustrated silence, trying to keep herself simmering. David will despatch the hapless coitus-interrupter with some choice words and he'll be back in bed and Mr Pidyn will be hot and straining and ready to go again in seconds. Frances is not like that, her irritation runs deeper, her passion can be chilled for days by this kind of malarkey. Once she's off the boil it can take ages to bring her back.

The conversation at the door.

'What? What is it? Young man, you'd better have a damned good reason for coming up here at this hour.'

'It's your wife, sir.'

The change in tone. A high note of sudden concern. 'Is she all right? Hurt? Is she ill?'

No, the young advisor says, it's worse than that. She's here. At Chequers. And asking where you are. Sir.

Well, that's that then, thinks Frances, and she lies back and surreptitiously but quickly, efficiently, brings herself off beneath the covers. Meanwhile her lover undertakes a panicked search for socks, pants, trousers, shirt, while he tries to comb his wild hair into something less obviously carnal than its current wrenched and disordered state.

As her own heart rate returns to its equilibrium, Frances helps him gather his things. She calms him. Reminds him that he just needs to state, over and over again if necessary, that he is the bloody prime minister. That a bloody prime minister's work is never done. There are always documents to read, papers to sign, officials to discuss policy with. She tells him that he just needs to smother Margaret's complaints with extreme and boisterous affection.

'You just repeat that you are delighted to see her, thrilled, that you wish you had more time to give her, only the French delegation, the situation in Ireland, in India, in Mesopotamia, etc., etc. She knows how it is. What you have to remember, David, is that Margaret doesn't expect you to be faithful, perhaps she doesn't even want you to be faithful, she just wants to know that you aren't about to leave her, aren't about to give up politics for love, that you aren't about to set up home with your much younger mistress' – she brushes away the signs of dandruff (a physical response to the anxieties of leadership, she's always thought) from the shoulders of his jacket – 'and have babies with her. And you aren't, are you?'

He says nothing. A silence that is as unsurprising as it is very, very eloquent.

'Well, there you are then.' Her voice is sharp, businesslike, but flecked with warmth too. 'So. Button up your breeches, rinse the taste of me from your mouth, check there are no stray hairs between your teeth, and go and kiss your wife.'

FOURTEEN

Curtains

1

I T takes less than three seconds for Hardit to see that there's no hope for Victor, and then he's off approaching those ghostly figures from the other houses in the street, the ones converging on the scene like famished cats approaching a dustbin spillage.

'Nothing to see! Police matter! Back inside your homes, please. And don't touch the fucking car! You two! Here!'

He beckons over two men, one fiftyish, the other maybe twenty years younger, but both similarly dishevelled. Rag-and-bone-man trousers. Donkey jackets. Father and son.

'You need to get this man into the house.' He indicates the terrace he has come from. 'Be gentle now.'

He raises his voice again, turns once more to the people in the street. They have retreated a little, but they seem generally disinclined to return to their houses. This is entertainment. Some of the women have children clinging to

244

their skirts, staring with saucer-shaped eyes. A baby starts to howl.

'Come on, off you go. You can read all about it later in the *Evening News*. Less exciting than you think. Chop chop!'

To Babs he whispers, 'You get in the house too.'

The men have placed Victor on a stained couch and depart, each clutching a one-pound note and each with instructions to go home and to tell no one about what has happened here. Neither man gives any sign that he has recognised Victor Grayson. They would have done once. Babs meanwhile subsides, stupefied, into an armchair opposite. The house smells of men, she thinks. Smells of boredom, loneliness and sweat. The whole room permeated by fusty dreams of violence.

Victor seems to be coming round. He's gasping, gurgling, guttering.

'He's going to be all right, isn't he?'

'No,' says Hardit. He is curt, brusque.

'It's bad, eh?' This is Victor from the couch. His eyes are closed, his breathing shallow and fast but his voice is firm.

'Yes,' says Hardit. 'Massive tissue disruption. Three quarters of an inch all round the wound path. Severe blood loss. Curtains, I'm afraid, matey.'

There's a sigh from the wounded man on the couch. It's like a tyre deflating.

'You're absolutely sure, I suppose?'

'I was a medic in the war. I know what I'm talking about. Saw this a thousand times. I'm sorry.'

'I thought you were a soldier, a Tommy.'

'I never said that. Just said I was at Passchendaele. And I was. Drove an ambulance. Bandaged men up, tied tourniquets. Collected body parts and put them onto stretchers, or into sacks, depending on their condition.'

2

One day Hardit Joshi will write down his war experiences. Why not? Everyone else is doing it, so why can't he?

It began in Suffolk. An exceptionally sunny day in that glorious summer of 1914, and he was polishing one of the many vehicles belonging to his employer, Ranjit Singh, the man the British were pleased to call His Highness the Maharajah of Barwani. The gleam of it. The heat coming off the chrome and the steel. The crunch of hot gravel. The sticky black sweat of the tyres.

'Hardit! Hardit!'

'Sir?'

Hardit was always somewhat amused when he talked with the maharajah. His voice always contained a sliver of sunlight. In those days he saw himself as a kind of Jeeves to the maharajah's Wooster. He'd got hold of some of the first Wodehouse stories in the early days of the war and had immediately spotted the resemblance. His employer was not a total idiot, but he was a man of sudden enthusiasms, brief but overwhelming passions. Maybe he wasn't like Wooster, more like Toad in *The Wind in the Willows*. Like many boys who'd been to a good Indian school, Hardit had developed a taste for English literature. He even retained a soft spot for Kipling.

Maybe his boss was like both characters. Bertie Toad, that was the maharajah. Perhaps that was unfair, but then, how fair was it that he, Hardit, was polishing the man's car for a few shillings a week and sleeping in a modest crib in the attic of this vulgarly huge English mansion, while His Royal fucking Highness got to indulge every whim, from polo to politics, without any fear of failure.

It wasn't that HRH didn't fail, by the way – he failed plenty – he just had no fear of it. Wealth is more than a very, very strong safety net. It also works as a vaccination against learning.

It wasn't even that Hardit wanted so very much from life for himself. Some peace in which to read and write, that would do, that and the chance, every now and again, to heat the blood of these cool English folk he had somehow landed among.

The maharajah's latest enthusiasm back then was the newly declared war in Europe, and that morning he had decided to support the empire by purchasing a fleet of Rolls-Royces to act as ambulances.

'And you, Hardit, are going to be the driver of one of those ambulances. Not only that, you're going to be my team leader, my captain. My top man in France! Is that not terrific!'

Terrific.

Yes. Hardit was meant to be overjoyed by this promotion, and it was clear that refusal was unthinkable, would be pointless, best to say yes now and wait for his employer's passion to abate.

'Well, all right, I mean, I'd rather be a flying ace, but I can assure you, I'll give it my utmost.'

Aeroplanes? He saw the idea flicker across HRH's guileless face, but then his master's forehead puckered, his impeccably waxed moustache quivered, and he responded, no, no, no, ambulances are more necessary than flying machines. Maybe later.

And so it was that Hardit found himself in the abattoir of the Western Front. His Sikh squad worked alongside a Quaker detachment, both units ecumenically picking up the off-cuts from all the butchery, some of that meat still pulsing with life. One of those scorched pieces of hewn flesh was an intelligence officer, a C Division man who, it turned out, was looking out for recruits to infiltrate seditionist groups in India.

'It's taken me nearly three years, but I think I've finally got my commanding officer to agree that it might be a good idea to recruit actual Indians for this job,' he had said. 'And you seem bright and you obviously want to get away from here. And perhaps when you get back to England, we might have a drink?'

Those English officers, incorrigible. Even on the brink of death they were propelled by their pricks.

Hardit did get back to England, courtesy of a very timely bout of appendicitis, although that C Division officer didn't. Poor sod died of his wounds on the way home. Hardit would have been happy to have a drink with the man too. He wasn't really his type, being portly, pockmarked and thoroughly public school, but before he slipped off this mortal coil, before the bell had finally tolled for him, that officer had provided an introduction – in green ink – to Sir Basil Thomson, who had in his turn sent a telegram to Ranjit Singh. The maharajah had been impressed and pleased for Hardit, had given him his second-best car as a leaving present, which was decent of him.

It is Hardit Joshi's belief that it always behoves a gentleman to show gratitude when he can, so he works hard for Sir Basil, and is confident that he has made himself indispensable, and so his word carries some weight. Didn't he get Sir Basil to hire his friend from no man's land? Baker the Quaker has done well since Hardit's recommendation got him a cushy number with the intelligence service. In England that's how a man makes progress. Someone puts in a word for a friend and that friend puts in a word for someone else. There are worse systems.

3

A still moment in Palmerston Street. Then Victor Grayson gasps, hisses. Sucks his teeth. Stifles a groan. Babs finds that the ringing in her ears has grown less but now she's aware of a cannonade of pain in her arm. An ongoing reverberation from elbow to wrist. The recoil of the revolver, she supposes.

'But curtains... You're sure?' Victor says. His breathing is noticeably even shallower, even faster now. The notes in his voice appear like tiny birds in a circus magic show. They twitch their wings and they're away.

'I've told you, yes.'

'How long?'

249

'Few hours. Maybe a couple of days. Won't be pretty. You know how it is.'

Victor does know. He remembers icy hours in the trenches spent listening to men screaming for their mothers, begging for someone to finish them off. Sometimes this wailing could last for a whole day and a whole night. Our own snipers trying to perform a last service for their comrades by ending their suffering. He knows how hard it is for a man to die. How much effort it takes.

'You can't get me to a hospital?'

'Won't help. And in any case we can't take you, I'm afraid. Too awkward.'

Victor coughs, spits, turns his head and chokes out a thick black gobbet of blood and gore.

His eyes open for a second. He tries to smile. 'Pointless to ask for morphine I suppose?'

'Sorry,' says Hardit.

'Well, you know what you have to do then, don't you lad?'

'Yes. But not here.'

'Fair enough. You've got booze though?'

'We've got booze.'

'OK. We best get on with it then.'

'Yes.'

And Babs sees that Hardit is crying. Silent tears navigating their way down his cheeks.

Victor's eyes are still closed but he can sense Hardit's distress.

'Come on, soft lad, don't take on so. Get me a drink.'

Hardit tells Babs that the whisky is in the kitchen, and can she go and find it, please?

'Whereabouts is it?'

He is tetchy. 'I don't know, it's in there somewhere. Just look for it, will you?'

Because of his tone – he's never spoken to her like this before – she opens every cupboard, every drawer, the smell of damp belching into the room every time she does so. No whisky. She checks everywhere again, assaulted by the toadstool whiff of mould again. She's nervous of going back into the parlour empty-handed, but also maybe it's a good way of putting off seeing Victor blowing and wheezing as the life wriggles out of him.

Only Grayson isn't blowing and wheezing. Not any more.

On her haunches, her muscles straining with the effort, she pauses in her rooting-around in the cupboard under the sink – nothing here but candles, various types of polish and rags – and listens hard. No sound at all from the other room. She stands and hurries back through to where she left Hardit and his patient.

Victor is lying face down on the couch now, Hardit is behind him with a knee in his back and pulling hard on a scarf looped around the wounded man's neck. He rises as Babs enters the room.

'Couldn't find the whisky,' she says.

'No,' Hardit says.

'What are you doing?' she says, her voice clogged, hardly audible even to herself. She repeats herself, making an effort to be louder, stronger. Biting out the words. 'What are you doing?'

'Done now. And you know what I was doing. Finishing what you started. And doing it clean. Next time you kill a man try and do it like this. Garotte. Quick and clinical. Painless. Shooting, my dear Babs, is for amateurs.'

He shows her the vibrant sun-yellow silk scarf he's used to throttle Victor. 'This is called a *rumāl*. Very simple, you loop over the neck and pull tight while applying pressure to the back with a knee or a foot. You see the knot at the centre? This is to help crush the larynx. Makes the whole process faster, while also preventing the target from crying out for help.' No longer tetchy, he has the manner of the authoritative teacher. The kind you always do your homework for. 'You're not going to faint or throw up are you?'

'No. No.'

'Good. The technique has a noble tradition. Been used in India since the sixteenth century, though I actually learned it from the French in the war. They call it *la loupe*. Chin up, girl. Worst is over now. We're on the home straight. Can you drive?'

'Yes.'

She remembers how she had submitted to the army's one-day driving course, then the fun of whizzing around the Kent countryside in an army Sunbeam, delivering messages, orders, vital supplies (though one time it was to supply emergency madeira for a regimental dinner, and another time it was to answer a desperate need for quail's eggs for some young subaltern's twenty-first birthday lunch). 'I thought you said you weren't going to do it here.'

'I also said we had drink. It was best he didn't know exactly when it was coming, let him think he had a little time. To let him think there was still something to look forward to even if it was only a shot of cheap whisky. He closed his eyes; I flipped him over. *Et voilà*. Bob's your uncle. Do you think I'm cold?'

'Well...'

'Well, I'm not. What I am is professional. Doing things you hate but that you know have to be done and doing them as soon as you can. That's the mark of a professional person. Not even that, it's the mark of being an adult. The trouble is, we live in a world of children now. Most people can't handle doing what needs to be done. This is especially true of English people, I find.' He stops, looks at her hard, but with a tender light in his brown-gold eyes. 'We should probably do explanations. You probably have questions.'

'Can we do questions and answers later?'

'Fine with me.'

Babs is impressed by the way Hardit can haul Victor's weight over one shoulder and get him outside to that opulent saloon while she just hovers around ineffectually, opening doors for him and whimpering.

While Hardit gets Victor to the car he has to shoo away a dozen giggling children and their fathers. Hardit tells them firmly that there's nothing to see here, which is clearly a lie. The people round here may have seen men mortally wounded by gunshots before, they may even have seen men that have been strangled, but they won't have seen them placed in the back of a luxury vehicle. A 1913 red-and-silver Vauxhall Prince Henry Tourer no less. The car commands respect, and Babs and Hardit get esteem too, simply by virtue of their association with it. Babs is sure it is only the power conferred by the car that keeps them from being manhandled by the denizens of Palmerston Street. An Indian man and a young woman giving orders to rough working men – well, that's taking a chance. You need an extra-special permit for that. The Prince Henry Tourer in all its chrome pomp is that permit.

'Remember you're driving.'

Shit. Yes. She had been about to get into the passenger seat.

'Where are we going?'

'I'm not entirely sure yet. Just follow my directions.'

She is reminded again of that WAAC vehicle course. The lugubrious female instructor, sixtyish with sad grey eyes. A governess in a previous life. The sense that she wished there had been a major war years earlier, that she was more than a little jealous of the fun Babs was going to have. Of the doors that would open for her now that the men were out of the way. What that instructor had wanted from the war was that it would do away with all the men. It wasn't that she wanted them all dead, she just wanted them to never come home. Maybe the war would take them to some huge and perma-nent trench where they could live together where all little boys belonged, in the mud with the rats and the slugs.

'Is this a test?' Babs says now.

'I suppose it is, sort of.'

A test. Right. And what will she get for passing it? she wonders.

The car stammers into gear, and they're about to move off when one of the smallest of the children gathered around the motor approaches and taps Hardit on the arm.

'Here. The geezer. He dropped this.'

He hands over the package which Victor Grayson has carried with him from the Criterion.

'Thanks, chum,' says Hardit. 'Much obliged.'

As they lurch away Hardit tears away a corner of the brown paper packaging.

'Gramophone records,' he says. 'And a notebook.'

'Stop here, I won't be long. Keep the engine running.'

She looks around, doesn't recognise exactly where she is. She has been concentrating so hard on not stalling, not bumping into anything, not losing control, not letting herself think about the stiffening body in the back seat, that she hasn't really taken in any signposts. It is noticeably more suburban than the tight mesh of streets that is the East End. The houses have gardens, the iron railings around them have fancy filigree. There are hedges.

There's also one of the new telephone boxes on the other side of the road. It stands guardsman-like outside a large modern pub. She guesses that within a year or two they will be everywhere, every couple of yards there will be one of these spaces. A place out of the rain, a kind of shed where men can indulge their hobbies and interests. A place to drink, urinate and fornicate. Maybe, sometimes, those men might even make a telephone call. Yes, she can imagine it: a swig from a bottle, a grope of a tart, a burning piss, and then a satisfying few minutes spent shouting down the line at their wives, their children or their mothers. All without getting wet. Tuppence well spent. A bargain. Progress, she thinks, it's a marvellous thing. Of course women will use these kiosks too. They'll use them to find out where their men are.

4

It has taken a while for the bruised policeman to fetch Basil Thomson from his little cubbyhole, the humid bunker where he has been reading the day's transcripts, including the latest – extremely entertaining – account of the conversation that very recently took place between the prime minister and his redoubtable wife.

'Well, sir, the Victor Grayson problem is solved,' says Hardit Joshi. He doesn't bother saying it in Tongan. It's late and he's too tired for that kind of nonsense.

'The Dawson letter did the trick? I thought that might make him think about what he was doing.'

'Didn't need the letter. We won't ever need the letter.'

In a few brief sentences Hardit explains about Babs, about the gun, about how he plans to take care of things now.

Sir Basil Thomson sighs, exasperated. Why is nothing ever simple? Why is nothing ever straightforward?

He knows that, actually, this is the whole reason people have jobs. If there are no problems, then there is no need to employ people to resolve them, and the whole economy of the empire would collapse. Nevertheless, these kinds of mishaps are always irritating, however much fixing them might be necessary to the maintenance of a healthy financial system.

He sighs. Nothing is ever simple. Nothing is ever straight-forward.

'So, we have a new problem now,' says Hardit.

'What to do with the woman?'

'Exactly.'

'She's the one you've been going on about.'

'Yes.'

It's a while before Sir Basil Thomson speaks again. It costs Hardit fourpence just to wait on the line in this foul-smelling box. It's only been here three weeks and yet already it whiffs intensely of London. A ripe mix of smells – beer, tobacco, urine, rage and sorrow.

Sir Basil Thomson has spent the time thinking about what Frances Stevenson said about the future utility of female soldiers. She was persuasive, he thinks. He can imagine a monstrous regiment of women using their natural feminine duplicity in the service of their king and country. All those seductive wiles. He thinks of the dancer Mata Hari flirting with her French guards as she awaited execution. He thinks too of the servants moving invisibly between the groups of politicians earlier this evening. Thinks about Mrs Baker and her baby, effortlessly seizing the attention of a roomful of power. Thinks about Frances and all the women around the world in her position. If we assume, as we must, that every leader has his mistress, then that is a lot of potential blackmailers and assassins for a nation to call on if they need to.

'What does she look like?' he says now.

'Pretty, boyish.'

Boyish. Of course. Aren't they all these days? The sign of a civilisation in decline. What, he wonders, happened to all the womanly women? The voluptuous ones. He thinks again of Miss Stevenson: there's a woman who curves in exactly the places that she should.

'Could your, er, friend pass unnoticed in a crowd?'

Hardit thinks about this. 'I should think so, if she had to. My, er, friend could also very much stand out if she needed to.'

'How old?'

Hardit resists the urge to sigh. He's told his boss all this before, although he always suspected Sir Basil wasn't really taking it in, that his mind was on something else.

'Twentyish.'

'Intelligent?'

'I'd say so. Quick-witted anyway. She's read a lot of books.'

'Well, that can't be helped.'

'No.'

'Athletic?'

Hardit thinks of her long legs, the artless confidence of her stride, he thinks of her lean and muscled arms, her broad shoulders, pale and freckled. Thinks of the vigorous way she translates imagination into action. All that happy torque and force in the bedroom.

'Definitely athletic. Maybe you should see her for yourself?'

Sir Basil makes a decision. 'No need for that. I trust you. No, you get your way. We'll take her into the service. I think that's the best thing. She starts at the bottom, though. Female clerical officer grade. Usual civil service terms and conditions. If she gets married she has to resign. Make sure she understands all that. Promotion will depend strictly on merit, and she'll have to pass all our fitness tests and suchlike. What do you think?'

'I think that's an elegant solution, sir.' A thought occurs to him. 'What if she doesn't want to join us?'

'I think if you explain how limited her other options are then she'll agree to this proposal. If she is, like you say, unusually clear-thinking for a woman.'

It is very obvious what Sir Basil means by this. It's this or it's nothing. This or she disappears. This or oblivion. On balance it is a fair offer. An exciting new job with some autonomy and a decent salary. Chance for promotion. A pension. What modern woman could ask for more than that?

'Anything else?'

'Only that Victor Grayson was carrying a package when he arrived at the Palmerston Street flop – which will need liquidating by the way. Appears to be gramophone records. Plain labels. Do you want to have a listen before we get rid?'

'You know me, Hardit. I listen to everything.'

'There's also a notebook. The famous memoir I think.'

'My Search After God?'

'That's the one.'

Back amid the imperial upholstery of the saloon, Hardit does the explanations, keeps it as short as he can. C Division, his role in it as a factotum, a point man, an assassin without portfolio, a man who can do dirty jobs cleanly. And no, Hardit is not his real name.

'Vacancy for you if you want it,' he says.

'Do I want it?'

'You most definitely want it. If you don't take it then you're a murderess and it's prison or worse, and think about how your dear old mama will feel about that. The disgrace and everything. Take the job and tonight's shenanigans just represent your first assignment. Can't lie, though, it could be dangerous.'

'How dangerous?'

'Main danger is you'll be bored out of your mind. It's like all jobs now. There's paperwork. There's filing. Although there are also compensations.'

'Such as?'

'The usual ones. Money, security. Occasional excitement.'

'Excitement like tonight?'

'Not like tonight. Tonight, my dear, has not been exciting. Not for me anyway. Tonight was simply damage limitation. A sweeping-up job. Best forgotten.'

He's lost her, though, she's somewhere else in her mind, away with the faeries.

'Weird, isn't it?'

'What is?'

'How murderess is less than murderer. How poetess is less than poet. Actress is less than actor.'

He thinks about this. 'But then again,' he says, 'lioness is more than lion.'

'Is it? Yes, yes I suppose it is.'

They head east. Hardit knows a place where the river deals with messes. Where it will make a properly weighted body vanish. Where it will help with the forgetting. The river is reliable in that way. Treated right it can be a good servant.

*

The sky is blue-black and wet. The drizzle covers them like a thin and dirty sheet. Like a grubby shroud. London lies exhausted all around them. Exhausted but restless. A giant twitching to the beat of desperate dreams.

They drop the body from a narrow wooden jetty, its ancient boards crumbling, the remains of a forgotten crossing. A place well known to highwaymen and footpads a hundred years and more in the past, but a relic now. A pointless projection into the Thames just at the point where it starts to gather pace, the place where the river begins to sense the proximity of the city and grows excited, eager to get there, only to slow to a sluggish, disappointed crawl a mile later when it meets the stinking, silty reality.

Victor Grayson's days of making an impact are over and his body hardly makes a sound as it rolls into the water. The soft suck as the current pulls him under is like a kiss. You could almost convince yourself that he is acquiescent, that he wants to go, that he has simply offered himself up, slipping into that muttering darkness with gratitude in his heart. Just another body dissolving in the greedy river, merging into it without resistance, without protest, enfolded for a moment in the demulcent embrace of the Thames, and then gone. No grave, no marker, no place of pilgrimage for any followers. As if he'd never been. The river accepting him placidly, as its due.

They watch the burnished surface for a few silent moments. I feel nothing, thinks Babs. Nothing at all.

'Well, that's that,' says Hardit at last.

'Yes, that's that,' says Babs. She thinks for a moment. 'What's next?'

He takes a while to reply.

'I don't know about you,' says Hardit, eventually. 'But I'd like a hot drink. Then a bath. Then bed. Sound all right?'

'Yes. It sounds all right.'

A drink. Then a bath. Then bed. It is, she thinks, the best most of us can ever hope for.

FIFTEEN

An Astute Observation

1

I N a grand town house in Abbey Road, a young woman
gropes for consciousness already knowing that everything
has changed. Anticipation and dread wrestle like lovers
in this bed with its faint traces of perfume and whisky.
Yesterday, she was a servant; today she is a singer, a dancer,
embryonic music hall royalty. She rolls her new name like
a gobstopper in her wide mouth. Leonora. She's also naked,
as pale as a fish in a moonlit pond, and not sure where she
is. Not even certain that everything that happened wasn't
all some mad dream. Her stomach fizzes. Every part of
her aches.

2

In Marylebone, a woman allows her daughter to pour her a
small absinthe. Just a touch of the Green Fairy. It's early for
strong liquor, but she didn't sleep so well. She was worried

about her friend, Victor. He looked so lost yesterday. Fierce and lost. A dangerously vicious cocktail of emotions.

3

In Palmers Green a man with a carbonised face sits in the flickering warmth of a darkened cinema. He half watches the fluttering images, half listens to the clanging piano, the chatter in the stalls, the muted laughter. The kids twitting each other, their parents restless in these cramped seats. He ignores for the moment the hand on his leg, the hand that is advancing slowly north from his knee to his upper thigh. Will this sort of thing still happen when they get the Palmadium? He tries to concentrate on the film. *Yankee Doodle in Berlin.* A piece of nonsense. Bothwell Browne as an American aviator behind enemy lines, disguising himself as a woman to make a mockery of the German High Command. A shame his sister isn't here. She'd like it.

4

A girl on a train, six years old. She's going home. The air in here is smoky, her scalp itches and she's too hot. Her mother and her sister are dead, and she has a terrible conviction that she will never see her father again. The carriage smells of soot and cigarettes. She's hungry, she needs the toilet and she misses her nanny. On the seat opposite a man sprawls, legs spread, claiming as much space for himself as he can. *The Times* is spread across his knees, though part of the newspaper has already slipped to the floor. He'll be annoyed when he wakes up. He's dribbling, his mouth slack. He has the grey face of an old shark. He dreams of dead children.

5

In his immaculate office, a man looks up from his Remington mid-sentence. Something has disrupted his flow. An insistent pigeon? A church bell? A clock striking the quarter-hour? A rifle shot? He listens for a moment. Nothing now. He continues to stare through his gleaming office window at the trees outside. They have a drab and muddy look, not dead but not too alive either. Yesterday he learned they are called wild service trees. Great name for an indifferent thing.

Thinking of the girl who told him that, he smiles. He closes his eyes, the better to conjure the image of her blue eyes, her hair curling around a supple neck. The way her breasts rise and fall under a plain dress.

This won't do. The whole fate of the empire depends on his not getting distracted from his task list, relies on his staying on top of things.

6

A man and his lover listen to gramophone records in a bedroom in a second-division stately home. The room is chilly, indifferently furnished, smells of muddy boots, old sweat, recent sex and ambition. The man has the bright marble eyes of a bird. It's his voice coming from the phonograph horn and it is rich, powerful, deep. Musical. Welsh. His words captured forever, making promises he won't keep. It is remarkable how his voice remains ageless, even as his body grows weary. He rises from his chair with a curse – *Mae hi wedi cachi arna*. He lifts the needle from the disc. Yanks the record off the turntable with rough fingers, hurls the brittle black plate of it at the wall. It doesn't break, doesn't shatter as it was meant to.

'Oh, David,' breathes his lover. Men, she thinks. Sometimes it's hard to keep your patience with them. Still, at least his wife and daughter have gone home. That's something. She sinks back onto the pillows. Tries to enjoy the sudden quiet, the Sunday languor. The minute his family had departed, he'd brought her a cup of tea and the papers. Nice to be served by him for a change.

The news from Ireland is depressing. The papers are full of last night's explosion in Cork, the arrest of Countess Markievicz MP, the fact of armoured cars on the streets of Belfast, but Frances Stevenson finds that she doesn't want to discuss any of that. There's another story that has caught her eye. She points it out to David.

'"Woman Kills Rattlesnake",' he reads. It cheers him up. He laughs.

'She'd mistaken it for a necktie. Turned out to be four feet long, but she didn't panic. Bashed its head against the floor until it died.'

'The modern woman,' says her lover. 'She's a tigress. An Amazon. Not to be trifled with.'

'An astute observation, Prime Minister. Although…'

She pauses, waits, her eyes dance. His anger has passed, the thunder and bluster evaporating as fast as it had appeared. She finds she likes him again. Desires him again. She even likes what she heard on the record. He was jovial, witty. Selling his baubles like they were hot roast chestnuts at a Christmas market. Her mercurial old showman. Irresistible. When he does leave politics he might make a great salesman.

'Although what?' he says.

'Although sometimes even Amazons quite like to be trifled with.'

'Do they, my Puss?'

Yes, she thinks. Yes, they do. Now, just bloody well get on with it.

And, unknown to the prime minister David Lloyd George and his mistress Frances Stevenson, crouched in a narrow gap behind one of the room's stud walls, a man from C Division of the Metropolitan Police winces. He cringes. He writes everything down. These people, he thinks, these bloody people.

EPILOGUE

'WELL, Basil, we should probably talk about your book.'
About bloody time.

His agent, Albert Curtis Brown, his publisher, Nelson
Doubleday, and Sir Basil Thomson himself, former assistant
commissioner of the Metropolitan Police and head of CID,
have been in Marcel Boulestin's fancy new place for two
hours and have talked about everything except their reason
for meeting. War memorials, rugby football, English public
schools. Doubleday and Curtis Brown are both American and
therefore obsessed with the British class system, they find it
endlessly fascinating.

The men have also chewed over the juiciest details of the
latest divorce (her fourth!) of the actress Peggy Hopkins Joyce,
and they have discussed various fashionable isms. Spiritualism,
Bolshevism, fascism and feminism, obviously, but also more
interesting ones such as nudism, voyeurism and sadism. Curtis
Brown and Doubleday have revealed some mildly titillating
details about the erotic lives of their most popular authors –
those young lady writers, what are they like? – and Sir Basil

has reprised some of the better tales from his time working in Fiji and Tonga. The story of the Fabulous Mbalolo is always one that bears repeating, always goes down well.

While chatting in this pleasantly unproductive way, they have also managed to get through soused herring, artichoke salad, a truly magnificent tête de veau, cèpes à la Bordelaise, plus a brace of braised quail, their skins satisfyingly crisp and salty. Sir Basil has even sampled Boulestin's famous oeufs en gelée. Now they are on to desserts, which for Basil is splendid caramel-topped profiteroles filled with the thickest whorls of best Jersey cream. All of it washed down with some fine Château Cheval.

'I love it.' Doubleday clears his throat. Does it theatrically. 'It is without doubt your best work so far.'

His smile is wide, showing all his big white American teeth. He is thirty-six and a handsome man. A wrestler's physique, movie-star cheekbones, something of the college football ace in the set of the shoulders. Sad eyes. He went to a military boarding school for a while in his youth and the effects still linger.

'I don't know about that,' says Sir Basil. He's brusque. Sharp. He's a typical British writer in that he hates criticism but is somehow also just as uncomfortable with praise.

'I do. It's great, really great. Better than *Lady* even. It's terrifying in its way, and it sheds a fierce light on mysteries our leaders would prefer to be kept in darkness. Not only that, but I admire the way it's written. Such pace, such brio, such audacity. Vivid, wry, ribald, and short too, which we always like in a book. Bravo. *Chapeau* doffed.'

He raises his glass, silently toasts Sir Basil across the laden table. Bathes him again in the warm light of his American grin. Then he takes a breath, runs a hand through his abundant hair, rearranges his features into a more solemn mask. Here it comes, thinks Sir Basil. Here it bloody well comes.

'I can't publish it, obviously,' says Doubleday.

This is, as every writer knows, the very worst kind of rejection. Someone saying that they hate your work, even telling you that it makes them ill, that they feel infected by it – and in the past that has happened to Sir Basil – that is not a bad rejection. That just means that the book is not for them, that they are the wrong reader. But if the people who love it won't publish it, well, what are you supposed to do then? How are you meant to feel?

He keeps his face bland, covering his hurt with another chomp at his profiteroles, but Curtis Brown, an old friend as well as his agent, notes his distress and is quick to intervene on his behalf.

'Forgive me for saying so, Nelson, but that is preposterous.'

Tubby, balding, pink in the face, the sixty-year-old Curtis Brown is not a handsome man in the way that Doubleday is, but he is an intelligent and vigorous one. Powerfully persuasive too. He has Personality. He is also hard-headed. Not one to back down in an argument. He is, let's not forget, the agent for both Kenneth Grahame and A.A. Milne, and no one is more demanding of agency ruthlessness than the writer of warm-hearted fables for younger readers. When it comes to contract negotiations, Winnie-the-Pooh and Mole are represented by a real Rottweiler.

'Shall we have a liqueur?' says Doubleday. 'I often think a lunch without a liqueur to finish is hardly worth having. You might as well have had a boiled egg.'

Which is how Sir Basil finds himself sipping at an unwanted and sickly Cointreau as Nelson Doubleday explains his reasoning.

The events described in Sir Basil's book are too recent, he says, most of the protagonists are still alive, some still in the most senior positions in government. If this book gets into the shops there will be lawsuits, ruinously expensive ones, and they won't simply be costly, they'll be undignified. It's not just public figures either, who might just rise above the potential libels, no, there are private individuals named here. Some of them with pockets deep enough to go to court. To take just one example: the doctor Ethel Vaughan-Sawyer has a case for defamation, as have the other ordinary civilians mentioned in the manuscript. And then there's the Maharajah of Barwani. There's a man with endless resources and he's well connected too, a Knight Commander of the Indian empire no less. You don't want to get into a fight with him. And what about the Noel-Bakers? The hint at a possible relationship between the brilliant economist Philip Noel-Baker and the prime minister's teenage daughter? That could cause no end of trouble.

'But mostly I'm worried that you can't make the meat of the story stand up,' he says. 'You admit that you were not present for most of the conversations and events you describe here. It's all been reconstructed – brilliantly of course – using your imagination. It's pure conjecture. We don't even know for sure that Victor Grayson is dead, never mind that he was murdered by the PM.'

What can Sir Basil say to all this? He's a novelist, not a journalist. He might have hoped that a publisher would know the difference.

'I was there for the most crucial parts of this story and I have spoken to people who were present at other important moments,' Sir Basil says. 'And I haven't invented anything that couldn't be true. And there's no denying that Victor Grayson has disappeared.'

'But, as I say, no proof he's dead.' Doubleday flashes those teeth again and there's a brief silence at their table. 'He might have simply decided to lie low, to lead a private life. He might have decided to emigrate. There are a million possibilities.'

'Yes,' sighs Sir Basil. 'Maybe he's running a tearoom in Margate.'

He could say more, but decides not to. What's the point? Instead he looks around the restaurant at the members of the London literary elite who like to gather here. Look at them all, high on their own fame, on their own wit, laughing, eating, gossiping, declaiming, stuffing those smug, self-righteous faces. Lady Ottoline Morrell is in with her paramour Bertrand Russell, author of *Why Men Fight*, as well as her one-time protégé, the damp-eyed Mrs Virginia Woolf, authoress of *The Voyage Out*. Her face is readable even if her books aren't, and that face tells us that she's morbidly unhappy again.

Arthur Conan Doyle is here, as are Herbert Wells and the appalling suffragist Mary St Clair, among numerous other equally noisy, equally opiniated, but less accomplished sorts.

'This is a new form, Nelson,' says Curtis Brown eventually. His chin juts, his eyes are hotly pugilistic. 'It's an experiment in memoir. The first important book in an entirely original genre, you can think of it as a non-fiction novel, if you like. It's a whole new thing.'

Doubleday laughs. 'Good try, Albert, but what this is really is an experiment in revenge, it's a way of hitting back at the man who dismissed Sir Basil here from a job he loved.' A sip of Cointreau. 'And I haven't even mentioned the explicit sexual content which, I have to say, Basil, makes dear old David H. Lawrence look like Edith Nesbit.' He grows serious, his voice drops to a near whisper. 'Besides, if what is written here is correct, then it will be too damn dangerous to publish. Physically, I mean.' He signals to the waiter for another round of drinks.

In conclusion, he tells Sir Basil and Albert Curtis Brown that – with great and genuine regret – he must pass on this wonderful book. He doesn't meet the author's eye as he says this. The weasel.

Sir Basil has the paranoid feeling that his fellow writers have overheard his humiliation. It seems unlikely, the place is full of clamour, and the other diners are mostly of the type that much prefers talking to listening; nevertheless, he finds himself wondering if his defeat here will be written up later in half a dozen spiteful diaries? The place is a favourite watering hole of leftists after all, and modernist ones at that. People who reflexively hate the police, even while those bobbies that they despise so much are keeping them safe in their comfortable North London townhouses.

He could make one final effort to defend his book. He could say that the things that seem most improbable, well, they're the things that he knows for a fact actually happened. And let's not forget that Victor Grayson's disappearance was most convenient for Lloyd George, who, as we all now know, was selling honours to the highest bidder. Frances Stevenson, lovely girl that she is, is also a kind of provincial Lady Macbeth. The power behind the throne. Not that Lady Macbeth would have allowed herself to get knocked up by her lover the way Frances was knocked up by David Lloyd George. Twice.

He could say all this, but he can see that it would be futile, demeaning even.

'There are other publishers, Nelson.' His agent still fighting the good fight.

'And I think they'll pass for the same reasons.' Another pause to receive drinks, to take another sip, to savour it, to converse with the waiter about the splendid menu. 'I have an alternative plan, however.'

'Do tell,' says Curtis Brown, dryly.

The alternative plan is to commission a series of new books from Sir Basil instead of this one. The first will cover his childhood as the son of an archbishop, taking in his time at Eton, his accomplishments in rowing, etcetera, while the second half of that volume would take in his time in the colonial service in the South Pacific.

'The Fabulous Mbalolo.'

'Exactly.'

The next volume in the series would focus very much more on his time running prisons in Liverpool, London and Dartmoor, before a final volume that will cover his time in the intelligence service.

'In a discreet way, I suppose,' says Curtis Brown. 'Nothing that will frighten the horses.'

'Well, certainly nothing that will land us in jail or dumped in a ditch with a .38 bullet in the back of our brains,' Doubleday laughs. 'A fun look at some of the spies you captured and the cunning tricks you used to accomplish it, that sort of thing. The arrest of Mata Hari for example. Something a bit *Boy's Own*, anyway. Something that makes the nation and its governing class look at least a little bit noble.'

He means no affairs. No mistresses. No abortions. No cash-for-honours scandals. No mysterious deaths of troublemakers and rabble-rousers. None of these things, even though they all happened and can be defended as being true. Mostly true, at any rate.

'I don't think so, Nelson,' says Sir Basil. He makes it very clear that his integrity is not for sale. Not at any price.

And then Nelson Doubleday names the figure he is willing to advance for the world rights.

A prolonged quiet. Sir Basil wonders if the coteries of Fabians, Fenians and feminists on the surrounding tables have overheard that sum. He very much hopes they have. He sneaks a glance at the Woolf woman: her mouth seems even more downturned and crooked than usual. Yes, she bloody heard all right.

It is his agent who breaks the silence.

'I think the next round is champagne,' he says. He raises an arm and snaps his fingers. 'Garçon!'

'We even have a title for the new book,' says Doubleday. 'It's up to you of course, you're the writer and it's your book not ours, but we were thinking *Scenes of Change*. Any good?'

No good at all, Sir Basil thinks. A truly terrible title.

'I like it,' says Curtis Brown. 'Has a ring to it.'

'A couple of conditions,' says Doubleday. 'We'll need all the material relating to this book' – he taps his forefinger on the stack of pages next to him – 'not just this manuscript but any notes you have at home. We can't risk any pirated material leaking out and undermining the campaign for *Scenes of Change*.'

'Yes, of course,' says Curtis Brown. 'Very sensible.'

'And I want to assure you both that we will pull all the stops out for this series. Special editions for the circulating libraries, advertisements in all the major publications, reviews too, of course, not to mention the speaking tours here and abroad. We'll make Basil Thomson a brand, one as well known and as popular as Pears soap. It's an exciting project, one the whole Doubleday family is very much behind.'

'Good to know.'

The champagne arrives and it is excellent. Cold and crisp, with all the correct citrusy notes. And very, very expensive.

Just as there are many ways to kill a man, there are many ways to kill a book. Of all these ways, the best and easiest is with money. As Sir Basil always used to say to new recruits to the Met: 'Before you despatch someone, see if you can buy him first. It's far less messy in the long run.'

This is the way Sir Basil Thomson allows his book to be put to sleep. Or almost. Because he keeps his copy of the original manuscript. The one he typed himself, using a green ribbon in his trusty Remington. The one unique copy of his novel, in green ink.

In this world, with the way things are now, it's a fool who doesn't get himself insured.

ACKNOWLEDGEMENTS

Thanks are due to my editor, Mark Richards, and all at Swift; to my agent Euan Thorneycroft and Jessica Lee at A.M. Heath; to the hawk-eyed and forensic team of Gesche Ipsen and Alex Billington for copy-editing and typesetting; to Dr Jim English for his close and careful reading of an early draft; and especially to Caron, who, once again, had to share her home with the cast of a book for way too long. There have been better behaved guests.